GIRL

ALSO BY BLAKE NELSON

BOY

GIRL

BLAKE NELSON

SIMON PULSE

NEW YORK   LONDON   TORONTO   SYDNEY   NEW DELHI

SIMON PULSE
An imprint of Simon & Schuster Children's Publishing Division
1230 Avenue of the Americas, New York, New York 10020
This Simon Pulse paperback edition June 2017
Text copyright © 1994 by Blake Nelson
Cover design and illustration by Regina Flath copyright © 2017 by Simon & Schuster, Inc.
All rights reserved, including the right of reproduction in whole or in part in any form.
SIMON PULSE and colophon are registered trademarks of Simon & Schuster, Inc.
For information about special discounts for bulk purchases, please contact Simon & Schuster Special Sales at 1-866-506-1949 or business@simonandschuster.com.
The Simon & Schuster Speakers Bureau can bring authors to your live event. For more information or to book an event contact the Simon & Schuster Speakers Bureau at 1-866-248-3049 or visit our website at www.simonspeakers.com.
Interior designed by Steve Scott
The text of this book was set in Palatino.
Manufactured in the United States of America
10 9 8 7 6 5 4 3 2 1
Library of Congress Control Number 2016958368
ISBN 978-1-4814-9498-4 (pbk)
ISBN 978-1-4391-2054-5 (eBook)

"She meant you no harm . . ."
—Red Hot Chili Peppers

PART ONE

1

IT WAS OCTOBER OF MY SOPHOMORE YEAR AND IT WAS raining and I was sitting in my room with my geometry homework watching it get dark outside. Downstairs my mom was fixing dinner and I could hear the news on TV and my dad would be home from his dentist office soon. And I was drawing in my notebook and leaning on my elbow and then the phone rang. I sat up. I listened and my mom yelled, "Andrea! Telephone!" I ran into the hall and picked it up and it was my friend Cybil. I asked her what she was doing but she wouldn't answer so I yelled, "I got it!" As soon as my mom hung up Cybil started crying. I asked her what happened and where was she? She said she was at a pay phone at Sunset Mall. She'd been there all day and she couldn't go to school because she'd shaved her head. I asked her why she did that but she was crying so much I couldn't understand her. I told her to come over if she wanted and she sniffled and said she would. Then I hung up and went back to my room and I could smell the food cooking downstairs and then the garage door opener turned on which meant my dad was home.

Cybil was not my best friend. Darcy McFarlane was. Cybil was sort of my loner friend I guess. She was odd and not really in any cliques. I mean she wasn't unpopular, she just wasn't anything. She was good at sports and was on the soccer team and she was friends with some jock girls. And sometimes she hung out with Marjorie Peterson, who smoked cigarettes. But mostly she just drifted around and she would come talk to you sometimes but never try to get in with your other friends or anything like that. And it was weird because I didn't know why she would shave her head. It wasn't like she was into extreme fashions. Or maybe she was. The truth was I didn't really know what Cybil was into. But it looked like I was going to find out.

I watched out my window. Then I saw her coming down the street. She wore an oversized raincoat and a stocking cap that was so far down on her head she looked like a mole. Then I thought my parents might freak out so I opened my window and waved for her to go around to the garage door. She did and I met her there and snuck her up the stairs. She looked terrible. Her eyes were all red and swollen and her raincoat was soaked through to the skin. I got her into my room and shut the door. She looked at me once and then down at the floor and then she pulled off the stocking cap and her skull was just like . . . just really weird and bare and like a shadow. Then she started crying and I sat with her on the bed. I asked her why she did it and she mumbled something about Todd Sparrow and she thought it would be cool and she didn't know why. And I was like, "Who's Todd Sparrow?"

But she didn't know that either, he was just some guy downtown, some guy she met. I got toilet paper from the bathroom. I sat with her while she blew her nose. I stared at her head. I felt sorry for her but in a way it was her own fault. She did it. And then I touched the stubble and it was like a million little dots and it felt like sandpaper except weird because the skin was soft like a baby.

2 THAT NIGHT ALL I COULD THINK ABOUT WAS CYBIL walking into school and everybody staring at her and how horrible it would be. The next day was Saturday and I went to her house and we looked through her attic where her mom had a bunch of hats and old wigs and costume stuff from the sixties. None of it really looked right but we found a black wig that was sort of normal and we brushed it and fiddled with it but it still looked like the sixties. Cybil tried putting on a scarf and sunglasses which might have passed downtown but not at Hillside High School. Especially not on sophomore hall where people teased you over anything. So then I called Darcy and she was like, "Cybil did *what*?" And she came running over to help but mostly she just wanted to look. And then it was getting late and nothing was working and we were getting desperate so Cybil called Marjorie.

Marjorie loved Cybil's shaved head. She kept touching it. She didn't care about wigs or hats or thinking up disguises.

5

She wanted to know who Todd Sparrow was and how did they meet and where was he now? Cybil couldn't really describe him except that she met him at Metro Mall downtown and he was in a band and he was a free spirit with the purest soul of anyone she ever met. And of course Marjorie was trying to be so cool and telling us about some weird people *she* knew at Metro Mall. Like these punk girls who took LSD and their skinhead boyfriends.

Then on Sunday the four of us rode the bus downtown to look for Todd Sparrow. Cybil wore her stocking cap but Marjorie kept bugging her to take it off so she did and people were totally staring. And then Marjorie took us to London Dungeon which had all these punk clothes and miniskirts and hippie sunglasses. And Marjorie kept trying to get Cybil to look at stuff, trying to get her away from me and Darcy. And then the saleswoman came over and she had a nose ring and Marjorie was trying to impress her and acting so tough and it was just embarrassing.

Then we went to Metro Mall. We were really nervous and looking around for Todd and every time we saw someone we all looked at Cybil but it was never him. So then we went for pizza across the street and he wasn't there either. Then we went to Scamp's for frozen yogurt and then to Poor Boy Records to see if Todd's band had a tape but the guy behind the counter had never heard of Todd Sparrow. So we looked at records and Marjorie claimed to know some people in a band but they were from England and I swear, she was the biggest liar and I didn't know why Cybil was friends with her. And all this time it was like Cybil had forgotten she didn't have hair. Especially in the record store where they were too cool to even notice. And after that we walked back to the bus stop and Marjorie tried to impress Cybil by waving to some punk girls. But they didn't know Marjorie and one of them flipped us off. We didn't care though because some boys on skateboards were following us and yelling to Cybil and when they tried to catch up we just ran!

That night Cybil came over to my house but this time she didn't have the stocking cap and she came to the front door and my mother almost fainted. She thought Cybil had been in a car accident. I told her that was the style now and my mother said, "You look like you've been in a car accident." And then she called my dad over and he put on his glasses and looked and my mom said, "She looks like she's been in a car accident." It was extremely embarrassing but Cybil didn't care. She had on black skateboarder shoes and a huge T-shirt and she was obviously getting ready to face Hillside with her new look.

At school the next morning I was so nervous for Cybil I thought I was going to be sick. After first period Darcy came to my locker and nobody had seen Cybil yet but after second period the word was out. "Cybil shaved her head!" "Cybil's a skinhead!" "Cybil's a Nazi!" Me and Darcy stood by my locker and tried to tell people what really happened. She did it for love. She did it for Todd Sparrow. But nobody had heard of Todd Sparrow and they didn't want to know the truth. "Cybil's a Moonie!" "Cybil's a Buddhist!" After third period we finally saw Cybil. She was walking down the hall with Marjorie and everyone was watching her and boys were touching her head and she was blushing and slapping their hands away. When she got to where Darcy and I were standing we couldn't even talk to her. Marjorie stood right in the way and it looked like they were going to walk right past. But then Cybil saw us and pushed by Marjorie and told us that Richard Kirn had talked to her all through biology and he wanted to start a band and he wanted her to be the singer! Marjorie pushed in and said that Richard Kirn was a dork and a science nerd and that everyone made fun of him at junior high. But Cybil and I had both said how cute he was and how nice. And Cybil wasn't listening to Marjorie at all and I thought how Cybil had survived shaving her head and how great it would be if she went out with Richard Kirn.

Cybil had survived but something happened to Marjorie. She was gone from school on Wednesday and Thursday and then on Friday she had a black eye. Everyone was whispering about it. Rebecca Farnhurst said that her brother accidentally hit her with a badminton racket. And then Cybil quit the soccer team, which freaked out Mr. Angelo since she was one of the best players. Then she had her first band practice with Richard and they got Greg Halverson to play drums and then Greg shaved *his* head and everyone talked about it but only for a little while because he was weird and no one was really friends with him. And Cybil and Richard started hanging out and thinking up lyrics and figuring out the philosophy of their band. And Darcy and I even went to a practice in Richard's basement but it didn't sound that great. Richard wasn't very good at guitar and Greg played drums so loud you could barely hear Cybil sing.

After a couple weeks Cybil's hair grew back. The only problem was it was too short in front and it stuck up everywhere and it made her look like a chimpanzee. She didn't care though because she was having a crush on Richard. Or she thought she was. She wasn't sure. Because sometimes he seemed so nice and other times he would criticize her singing and it wasn't like *he* was so great on guitar. And it was too confusing to be in a band with a boy you liked but it was still exciting and every day Cybil would tell me and Darcy what happened at practice and we would discuss it and try to figure out what he was thinking. And then Greg got a crush on Darcy and that was awkward because he didn't have any friends. But since he was the drummer of Cybil's band we tried to be nice to him and Darcy talked to him sometimes in the hall.

Cybil and Richard had a million different names for their band but when they finally played their name was Bed Head. It was at a special matinee show at a bar downtown. And it was scary because Darcy and I had to lie to our parents and take the bus and walk through this bad neighborhood. And the first person we saw was Marjorie but she was with a punk girl and they wouldn't talk to us. And the audience was mostly downtown people and street types and there was a skinhead sleeping in a corner with his head on his knees. And really, there were more people in the bands than in the audience. They were all running around in confusion and everyone was arguing about where they could put their stuff and who was going first and who was going last and who was "headlining."

Bed Head went first. No one paid attention. Cybil had her skateboarder shoes and her big T-shirt and she kept looking back at Greg, trying to figure out when to sing. And Richard was doing this weird hopping thing while he played his guitar, I guess he was trying to be weird or cool or something. Cybil just stood there. You could see her trembling. She was so scared she could hardly sing. They played about fifteen minutes and when it was over she was so upset she wouldn't talk to us. And then Richard freaked out because he thought someone stole his favorite sweater but it had just fallen down behind the stage.

Cybil was depressed for weeks after that. It was worse than when she shaved her head because she wouldn't cry, she would just be really cold and not talk to you. She started sneaking off campus at lunch and skipping last period study hall. Some days I wouldn't see her at all. And it was so weird because it seemed like she was right on the brink of becoming popular at school.

I mean, not like truly popular but like everybody was into her shaved head and talking about her but then she totally gave up. But I knew she still talked to Richard on the phone every night so maybe it was a blessing in disguise and she and Richard would fall in love. And then one day Darcy read some of Cybil's song lyrics in her notebook and she thought Cybil was suicidal and she was going to tell Mrs. Schroeder but I told her not to. And then I got in an argument with Darcy because she wanted to have a normal sophomore year and Cybil was getting too weird and Darcy didn't like going to bars. And I said how it *was* really weird and Darcy said she still liked Cybil even though she didn't understand her. And I said me too and we talked for three hours about Cybil and if there was really such a person as Todd Sparrow or if shaving her head was just a cry for help like we learned in suicide awareness.

And then over Christmas vacation Cybil had sex with Richard. She was the first of my friends to have sex. And it was so weird because I always thought when it happened we would talk about it a lot more but Cybil was being so distant we were afraid to ask her. And then Darcy decided to go out with Greg since he was bugging her all the time. They went to a movie and then for pizza and the next day Darcy said he was totally insane. He thought everyone at school talked about him and he thought he was going to be famous and he was building a recording studio in his basement and he thought all these bands would want to come there to record their albums.

And then Mark Pierce asked me out. He was a senior and on the basketball team and he seemed nice. So I went and we saw a movie and had frozen yogurt at Scamp's and it was pretty fun. And then there was a Christmas party at Julie Cavanaugh's and she let some guys jam in the basement and also Cybil's band except now their name was Thriftstore Apocalypse. They were great even though most of the people didn't even understand. Like Rebecca Farnhurst and her friends were all dressed up and trying to act weird and "alternative," as if the whole thing was just a joke. And that night I went in Mark Pierce's car and we made out but it was awkward because I didn't really like him that much.

Then in January Darcy got her license and we started going downtown to the city library to study and we met these two boys Derek and Jonathan, who smoked and were into underground bands. And one day we were all sitting outside on the steps and this street guy came over and asked if we had a cigarette. Jonathan gave him one and he stood over us and lit it and you could tell he was on some trip. Like he was going to try to trick us or something. Then he squatted down and started talking to us and that's when I saw how incredible he was. His voice was sort of raspy and soft but he had the clearest, brightest blue eyes I had ever seen. And the sides of his head were shaved and he had beads in his hair and little bells. And he was talking to Jonathan about the band on Jonathan's T-shirt and then he looked at me and Darcy and asked us what kind of music we liked. I was too stunned to talk and Darcy said, "Lots of different kinds." But her voice was shaking and he could tell we were scared of him. So he thanked Jonathan for the cigarette and stood up and started walking away. And I looked at Darcy and she looked at me and then she yelled out, "What's your name?" He was wearing a black overcoat and moccasins with no socks and he looked like a dream and he turned toward us and smiled and he was Todd Sparrow.

3 AFTER I SAW TODD SPARROW SOMETHING DEEP INSIDE me began to change. It was not a big change and I didn't shave my head and I didn't really think any differently about my life or Hillside or anything like that. But one glimpse of Todd and you immediately realized how limited you were and all the things you *could* do if you could just break out of your normal existence and stop worrying about what everyone thought. That's probably what happened to Cybil, she felt that freedom and she didn't know what to do with it but she had to do something. So she shaved her head. That was my theory. Cybil wouldn't really discuss it. And we were having frozen yogurt at Sunset Mall one day and I was jabbering about Todd and life beyond the boundaries and Cybil said, "Wait until you get out there. Then you can see how great it is." Which seemed sort of pretentious. But of course she had spent a whole day with him and shaved her head and what had I done? Not much. So I just ate my yogurt.

Meanwhile back at school Greg was getting scarier by the second. After he went out with Darcy she made the mistake of telling everyone about their date and all the things he said. And besides that he was in the chimpanzee phase of his hair growth and he looked pretty ridiculous. And then me and Darcy were standing by my locker and he came over and he was all agitated and trying to say something and finally he spit it out, "Thanks a lot for spreading all those rumors about me!" And then Darcy freaked out and yelled at me because I told her to be nice to him. But it was her own fault because she told everyone how weird he was.

But the real reason for tension between me and Darcy was Mark Pierce. He kept asking me out. And he was a senior and popular and a jock and I guess people were surprised that he liked me. And it was an awkward situation because if you're not that popular, people don't want you to suddenly start going out with popular people because it screws up the social order. And Darcy and I never had dates freshman year and now I was getting some and she was stuck with horrible Greg Halverson, who might be okay to have in your band but not as a boyfriend or even to have publicly following you around.

Dating Mark Pierce. It was so weird. He'd call me on Thursday and ask me if I wanted to do something on Friday and I'd say, "I'd love to," which was what you were supposed to say. And we'd go to a movie or for pizza and then we'd park someplace and make out which was fine except I knew he was on this schedule in his mind and pretty soon he would want sex. And I didn't really *dislike* him and I wouldn't even mind that much if he was the first one because Cybil and Richard were doing it and Rebecca Farnhurst had done it and Wendy Simpson did it with a boy from Bradley Day School when she was drunk. So Mark would be okay. And it was inevitable anyway. And it didn't seem like you were really part of things until you did it because that's what everything was *about*, like jokes and TV, and even the ends of extension cords were either male or female and when you plugged them together, what was that? But then I also remembered when Tracy Schwartz did it in junior high and how terrible that turned out. And after the Tracy thing me and my best friend, Carol Mahoney, even made a pact that we would only do it for love, especially the first time. But we were just little kids then, in junior high, and this was real high school now, which was a totally different situation.

And then Thriftstore Apocalypse was going to play at this new all-ages place called Outer Limits. But Darcy was so scared of Greg she wouldn't go. And I couldn't drive. And it was the only time they played since Julie's party and I didn't want to miss it so I called Mark Pierce. The show was in the afternoon and Mark picked me up and you could tell he had trouble figuring out what to wear. He had an old sweater with holes in it that maybe he thought was alternative or grunge or something. And he was nervous and he couldn't find the place and you could tell he never went downtown. And then I saw the Outer Limits sign and I was like, "Turn! Turn!" but he couldn't because he went too far. So we went around the block but he couldn't get back because it was a left turn only. And he was getting so pissed and I felt bad for him and I thought I should have just taken the bus.

When we finally got there Mark paid for me and we went in and another band was playing. There weren't that many people but Cybil was standing by the side and she waved to me and I ran over. And she started telling me about the singer onstage whose name was Nick and their band was called Pax, which meant "peace" in Latin and wasn't that cool? But I was like, what about Richard? She just shrugged. And I didn't want to be a drag so I watched Nick sing and I couldn't see Richard anywhere. And poor Mark Pierce was standing in the middle of the floor looking like a suburban jock in a holey sweater. And Cybil said, "What's Mark Pierce doing here?" And I said, "He brought me." And we both looked at him and you could tell how out of place he felt. And Cybil was just in love with this Nick person and swaying back and forth with his music and I watched Nick but he didn't seem that cute to me. He looked weird and sort of deranged.

Poor Mark Pierce. I stood with him while Thriftstore Apocalypse played. And I wanted to dance but he didn't want to but then some other girls did and I danced with them. And then afterward Mark and I sat on the curb outside and these two girls sat next to us and they were checking out Mark and then they lit cigarettes and started gossiping. They had cool retro dresses and I had on my favorite Gap skirt which wasn't very cool I guess. And then Mark said he didn't think any of the bands were any good. He said he didn't mind if they wanted to be artsy but if they couldn't play their instruments why did they think they could go onstage? He said his friend Scott Haskell could play Scorpions solos and stuff off the radio and he wasn't even in a band. Then he said that the Outer Limits people were pretentious and the girls were stuck up and they thought they were so cool but they were obviously losers.

When the show was over Greg pulled up his station wagon and they loaded their stuff. Then he and Richard came over to us and Richard tried to say hi to Mark Pierce but Mark would only grunt at them. And then I told Richard I had one of their songs in my head and he got so excited. He was so happy. I even sang it a little, not as good as Cybil of course. He was ecstatic. He said that should be their first single. He said they were thinking of making a record and Mark Pierce scoffed and Richard tried to explain how easy it was and then Greg started talking about the studio he was going to build in his basement and everybody rolled their eyes, even Richard.

Then Cybil appeared and she wouldn't look at Richard and they all got in Greg's station wagon and drove away. I said to Mark that something was up between Richard and Cybil and he said, "Yeah, they're having sex." Then we got in Mark's car and drove around the block and got stuck in that same left turn only. Mark got so mad he just drove over the partition and floored it. I felt sorry for him then because he was doing all this for me, wearing the sweater and standing around and getting checked out by snotty girls. So then we went to Scamp's and had frozen yogurt and talked about neutral subjects like people at school and how he scored twenty-four points in a basketball game. Then he told me a long story about when he and Scott Haskell went to the beach and snuck into a blues bar and Scott asked the guy if he could jam but they wouldn't let him and so they got really drunk and made out with some sleazy beach girls.

After that we drove around and parked and made out. Then we talked and Mark said how he thought Cybil was okay and how he defended her to his friends when she shaved her head. And he thought the Outer Limits scene was all right in some ways. He was leading up to asking me for sex but I changed the subject to clothes. I complained that my Gap skirt was too boring but he said I looked really cute in it and how I was the cutest girl at the show. And then he told me how sexy I was and how I had a great body. And then he let down the seat and got on top of me and we made out more intense than ever. And it was so strange because he was Mark Pierce, senior, with a car, and very cute, who millions of girls liked. And I felt like I should like him more and I tried to but it was hard in the dark when he was just this big weight grinding into you.

At school I told Darcy she was stupid not to come to Outer Limits and Greg was no problem and anyway Mark Pierce would protect her. And then after school we went to a thrift-store in Sherwood Oaks and I looked through the dresses for something like the girls at Outer Limits had. But the dresses were all of gross material and not that cool. I found a couple that seemed okay and we went in the dressing room and I told Darcy about Mark Pierce getting on top of me and if you could have an orgasm from making out. And I was saying how easily I could have had sex with him and didn't she think it was inevitable really, and was it dishonest if you didn't like them that much? Darcy said it wasn't about being honest, it was more about if you're ready or not. And I asked how you know if you're ready and she said, "If your friends are all doing it, then you are." And she was trying on hats and I was trying on dresses and then we talked about Mark's friend Scott Haskell and if he was Darcy's type and if we should double-date. And I picked out the least ugly dress and as I put my regular clothes back on I watched myself in the mirror and imagined I was in Mark Pierce's bedroom and we had done it and he was asking me to stay but I couldn't because I had a meeting to go to or a flight to catch or something important to do.

4 ON MY SIXTEENTH BIRTHDAY IT JUST RAINED AND rained. Cybil and Darcy and me went to a movie and had frozen yogurt at Scamp's and then we went home because Cybil was bored and Darcy had homework and I was getting depressed. At home my parents had a cake and my brother, James, called from San Francisco and his stupid wife, Emily, got on and talked for about ten hours about how she was finally pregnant. And then Grandma Marr called from Phoenix and she was sending money. And everybody made such a big deal about the fact that it was "sweet sixteen" and it seemed so stupid that a girl has to be sixteen and seventeen and everybody gushes over her like this is the big high point of her life. When boys are sixteen nobody cares. They get drunk and crash their cars and get in any kind of trouble they want. They can have pimples and smell bad because nothing matters for them until they grow up and have important jobs bossing people around. But if you're a girl everybody says you're *blossoming*, you're so *beautiful*, here let's take a picture so when you're old and ugly you can look back and *remember*.

Mom took the pictures. Dad gave me a card that said he would take me to the DMV on Saturday and I could get my license. And then my mom started crying for no reason and my dad was getting all weird and not looking at me. That's another thing about sixteen, you're a woman now and everybody hates you for it and even your own dad won't give you a hug because the neighbors will think he's a pervert. The whole thing made me mad so I escaped upstairs to my room and listened to a tape Cybil gave me and brushed my hair and picked at a zit on my forehead.

On Saturday Cybil wanted to come to the DMV because she didn't have her license yet and she wanted to see what it was like. So we went and she and my dad quizzed me and I got them all right because I was so nervous I'd memorized the whole book. And then the test lady called out "Andrea Marr" and off we went. It was a hard test too because it was in Sherwood Oaks and it was all these malls and these super-complicated inter-sections with a million cars coming from every direction. In one place I had to turn left and I turned and somehow ended up in the Food Plus parking lot. It took forever to get out and everyone kept cutting me off. And when we got back to DMV, I smiled at the lady and walked over to my dad and Cybil and I swear I was dripping with sweat.

I passed. I got my license. But big deal if you don't have a car. Darcy had her sister's car and on the first day of *me* having *my* license *Darcy* drove us downtown to the library. And we were hoping to see Derek and Jonathan but they weren't there and so we went to Scamp's for frozen yogurt. This was my real birthday party. The boy behind the counter was totally cute and gave me extra because Darcy lied and said today was my birthday. And we sat by the window and talked about everything like which girls were jealous of me going out with Mark Pierce and how cute Scott Haskell was and where we should go on a double date. And then two hippie women walked by in Guatamalan pants with their butts jiggling like Jell-O and Darcy was like, "Gross!" and I was like, "Haven't they heard of underpants?" And we were giggling and making fun of everyone and saying all the things we would never do when we got old.

Mark's idea for a double date was to go to the beach and spend the night in a motel. I thought that was a little much. Mark and I had not really talked about sex and he probably thought that meant we were going to do it. I didn't really know what I thought, which probably meant I would. But what about Darcy and Scott? We couldn't go to a motel on their first date. So instead we went to a movie and then for pizza and Mark and Scott paid and Darcy asked me in the bathroom if Mark always paid for me. I said yes and Darcy said didn't I worry that he'd think I owed him and he'd want sex? I hadn't thought of that. The date wasn't going well anyway. Scott Haskell was a junior but you'd never know it by how he acted. He shot spitballs and talked back to the waitress and he was totally obnoxious. Afterward Mark said he was just nervous and he really liked Darcy. And she hadn't minded him that much and he was cute and a lot of other girls liked him so I guess she was still interested.

So we decided to go to the beach. I told my parents I was spending the night at Darcy's and she said she was spending the night with me. I'd never done that before but Darcy said it always worked. We left on Saturday during the day and Mark drove and he had a cooler full of beer. When we got there we had to go to several motels because he was too young and he didn't have credit cards but finally we found one. We went in and there were two double beds and we put our stuff down and there we were. In a motel. Scott turned on the TV. Darcy checked out the bathroom. Mark brought in the beer. Then we went for a walk on the beach and Mark looked so handsome in his raincoat and with the wind blowing his hair. And we walked arm in arm and it was so mature, like we were adults, like we were in a magazine *at the sea*. Then we walked back through the little town and went to McDonald's but Scott was sticking his straw in his nose and acting like a moron. And then it started raining and we went into the video arcade, which was sleazy but sort of fun. Me and Darcy played Mario Brothers and Mark did Kung Fu and Scott played a game where he flew a jet and shot people and he was gritting his teeth and pounding the buttons like, kill kill kill.

Back at the motel room we ordered pizza and watched TV and then Darcy wanted to take a shower so I went with her but then Mark and Scott wanted to come too so we all put on our bathing suits and got in the shower. It was a tight squeeze and then Scott turned on the cold water and Darcy started shrieking. Scott asked us if the cold water made our nipples stick up but it wasn't making mine because I was the farthest back. And Mark kept touching my butt and I could see he was getting an erection. And then Darcy saw it and then she really started shrieking and Scott sprayed Mark with water and said "Down boy! Down boy!" And the cold water was hitting Darcy and she fell out of the tub and then I tried to get out but Scott undid my bikini top and it almost came off. And the boys were still spraying each other and I tried to cover myself and then Darcy grabbed a towel and whipped Scott with it and Mark got him in a headlock and Darcy was going to pull down his pants but then the doorbell rang and it was the pizza.

We ate pizza. We drank beer. Then we went outside and the night was really still and the stars were like an explosion across the sky. So we all got dressed and got some blankets and went for another walk. It was so beautiful. And Mark was getting all cozy and putting his arm around me. And then we went up in the dunes and started making out. And Darcy and Scott were really getting into it and then they got up and went over the hill and I asked Mark what they were doing and he said, "What do you think?" I didn't know. And then Mark kissed me and put his hand between my legs and at first I wouldn't let him but then I did. And then he whispered for me to close my eyes and open my mouth because he had my birthday present. I knew he was going to do something stupid but I did it anyway and he put something in my mouth and it was a condom packet. I spit it out and I was like, "Thanks a lot!" But he said he meant it. That's what he wanted to give me for my birthday. He wanted to make love to me because he was falling in love with me and that was the best present he could think of. He said we didn't have to do it right then but sometime. Whenever I wanted. Then he started whispering how sexy I was and undoing my pants and putting his hand in and I guess it felt okay. And there was still no sign of Darcy and Scott and it was quiet and the sand was cold and the waves made a rushing sound. Then Mark undid his own pants and got his penis out. He wanted me to touch it so I did but that just made him more horny and he started begging me and I said no and he said "Back at the motel?" And I said, "I don't think so." And he said it would feel *so good* and this was the perfect place with the beach and the scenery and everything. But I didn't want to. Not with Darcy and Scott right behind us. And after a while they crawled back over the dune and Darcy was buttoning her shirt and Scott was grinning so big. But Mark was getting cranky and he wanted to go back and drink beer so that's what we did.

The next day I just wanted to get home so our parents wouldn't catch us. Mark dropped us off at Darcy's, where we could wash our clothes and get the sand out. Of course I wanted to know what she and Scott did in the dunes and she said not much but enough to leave a mess all over his jeans. I said, "Darcy, it was only your second date!" But she said she had to do it because if she didn't he would get this pain in his testicles and he wouldn't be able to walk and the baseball coach would know and then everyone would think she was a tease. And then she said I was getting too weird about boys and why was I so uptight lately? It was true. The problem was Mark Pierce. I couldn't tell if I liked him or if I should trust him or if he should be the one. And it seemed like I should decide because I was sixteen and a virgin and I couldn't put it off forever. But when I asked Darcy if I should break up with him she was like, "No way!" But that was just because she liked Scott Haskell and he and Mark were so popular it was like this big honor for us to be dating them.

5 IN THE CAFETERIA ON MONDAY DARCY AND I ARGUED about sleep. She thought it was bad to get too much because it made you tired and gave you zits. But I said it kept your skin young because it was less time being awake and dealing with stress and getting old. Then Greg walked by and we both looked away super fast and prayed he wouldn't come over. We watched him go past and he didn't have anyone to sit with and you could tell how embarrassed he was. That's how lunch was at Hillside. Totally brutal. Like if you didn't have any friends there was nowhere to hide. Fortunately Scott Haskell and Brian Babbit came over and sat with us. Then Mark Pierce came and Renee Hatfield. Renee sat right across from me which was sort of scary because she was a junior and popular and a total gossip. And Mark was talking about how he almost got in a fight at baseball practice and Renee was scoffing and then Scott grabbed Brian's orange and wouldn't give it back. And Renee was teasing Mark and then Scott tried to make a basket with Brian's orange and accidentally hit a freshman girl in the head.

And then Mr. Angelo lifted Scott up by his hair and marched him to the principal's office and as soon as they were gone Mark threw Scott's sandwich at some sophomores but they wouldn't throw anything back and everyone complained how boring the sophomores were this year.

And it was weird because from that day on it was like we were this little clique of Mark, Scott, Brian, Renee, Darcy, and me. It was nice to have someplace definite to go at lunch but it also made you feel stuck. Like you always had to sit with them no matter what. I mean, Cybil and Richard didn't even come to the cafeteria. They'd eat outside or sneak across the street to Taco Time or sometimes they would go on fasts or eat trail mix or weird vegetarian stuff that Richard would bring. And everyone thought I was Mark Pierce's girlfriend now and all the sophomore and junior boys started looking at me differently, with a new respect. And I suppose I should have felt lucky but mostly I felt restless and like I didn't want to sit in the exact same place every day listening to Mark's jock stories or Renee's gossip or watching Scott blow bubbles in his milk.

I guess I was lonely for Cybil. So one day at lunch I snuck over to Cybil's locker and went to Taco Time with her and Richard. I hadn't hung out with them in weeks and it was awkward because Richard was wearing this strange coat, it was like a woman's raincoat and he had on these black leather shoes and Cybil wore her mole hat and they looked totally bizarre. And they *were* bizarre. At Taco Time they went through this whole routine of ordering veggie burritos and one of them had to get the value meal and the other had to get a certain size pop so they could get the Scooby Doo glass. It was very complicated and they were obviously deeply entwined in each other's lives but the thing was, *they weren't in love.* I mean, it didn't seem like they were. They didn't even seem like boyfriend and girlfriend. They were like two crazy people in a park or two eccentric inventors and sometimes even the words they used were like nonsense, like their own special slang and you didn't know what they said but they understood perfectly.

We sat at a booth and Cybil ate her burrito and Richard told me all the news about their band. He asked me if there were any other songs that stuck in my head and which types of songs did I like. I said I was just a boring high school girl and who cared what I thought? But he said that was exactly the point, it was demographics and I was a perfect test market. That sounded insulting but I didn't say anything. Instead I asked Cybil what happened to Todd Sparrow. She said he was in Seattle and Richard said, "Yeah, but he's coming back." So then we talked about Todd Sparrow and his band, Color Green, and how cool they were and how Thriftstore Apocalypse should play a show with them. Richard said there was a whole youth movement coming up and it was like a revolution and all the old hate bands were fading off the scene. Punk was over. Bands like Pax and Color Green and even Thriftstore Apocalypse were taking over. Then Cybil said she wanted to change their name and Richard said, "We already discussed it." But Cybil said she thought Thriftstore Apocalypse was dumb and Richard said, "But people are starting to know it." And Cybil said, "So what, it's still stupid." And then she sipped her Coke and Richard talked to me and Cybil just stared out the window at the cars going by.

After fifth period I ran to Darcy's locker. I told her that Todd Sparrow's band was called Color Green and Thriftstore Apocalypse was going to play with them and there was a youth revolution and all the new bands were taking over and wasn't it exciting? Darcy didn't think so. She wanted to know where I was at lunch. I said I went to Taco Time with Cybil and Richard. She said Mark was making jokes about me. I said, "What kind of jokes?" She said, "Jokes about how you're a virgin." But then she said that Renee actually started it and she was making fun of Mark and it wasn't really Mark's fault. I told Darcy that I hated Renee and her stupid gossip and I didn't care about Mark or Renee or any of them. And Darcy was being so mean and just putting her books in her locker and not answering me. Then I said, "If you have sex with Scott Haskell you will always regret it because he'll just use you and he'll tell everyone." And then I walked away and I was shaking because in the last forty minutes I had realized that Cybil and Richard were too weird to be my friends and Darcy was too fake to be my friend and Mark was too much of a jerk and suddenly I was standing dangerously close to the edge of the cliff of not having any friends.

But when I saw Mark Pierce after school I did not worry about not having friends. I stomped past him and he just stood there scratching his head. And when I got home I went straight to my room and put in a punk tape Cybil gave me and turned it up full blast. Richard was right, there was a new generation and I wasn't going to let some dumb Hillside people like Mark Pierce or Renee Hatfield or even Darcy hold me down with their stupid games. And I put on my thriftstore dress but when I tried to zip it up the zipper got stuck and it ripped. And I tried to pin it but it still didn't fit right and anyway I looked all wrong with my boring hair and no makeup. So I went into my mom's room and put on some lipstick and then I looked even stupider and I pushed my hair up under a baseball cap and that looked worse. But all the time I kept watching the mirror because I was seeing something I hadn't seen before. I hadn't really grown in the last year but something was different about my body. Like I was more coordinated or more graceful or maybe *less* graceful. It was hard to describe and it was bugging me and I pulled off the baseball cap and shook out my hair and then I saw what it was, I was getting *sexy*.

At school the next day Darcy came straight to my locker and apologized. She said that her loyalty was with me because she knew that Renee was always going to put us down but that Mark really did like me and she really liked Scott Haskell and couldn't I just stay with Mark for a little while longer? "How long?" I said, "Long enough for you to have sex with Scott?" And she said *no* and that I shouldn't talk like that and didn't I know that Cindy and Dave had sex every day after school? Or that Terri Ferguson had sex with a boy from Central Catholic? And then she said it was almost summer and we were almost *juniors* and if you liked a boy you were crazy not to at least try it, and as long as you used a condom and everything, why not? I could think of some reasons why not but I didn't say them. And I couldn't believe Cindy and Dave did it because Cindy was so ugly in junior high and people used to wonder if she'd *ever* get a boyfriend and now, not only did she have one, she was having sex with him. Darcy said they went to Cindy's every day after school and did it on her brother's waterbed and Dave told all his friends and Cindy bragged at lunch and showed her diaphragm and we both said how disgusting diaphragms were and how you had to be *fitted*.

6 AND THEN AT SCHOOL ONE DAY DARCY RAN UP TO me and announced: "Saturday. Party at Brian's. We're going." But I had just talked to Cybil and I had an announcement of my own: "Sunday. Thriftstore Apocalypse. Outer Limits!" Darcy was not impressed. I said, "And guess who might be there?" She didn't want to guess so I told her, "Todd Sparrow!" And then she got all weird like would I please just come to Brian's with her, like it was the last favor she would ever ask me. And I was like, "Of course I will, Darcy, jeez." But it seemed sort of selfish that she didn't even care about Thriftstore Apocalypse.

But I was still excited about the party. And when Darcy told me it was in Weston Heights I was even more excited since that's where all the rich people lived and they always had the best parties. I wore my favorite Gap skirt with a new top from Image and red lipstick and my hair parted to one side like I saw this one girl had at Metro Mall. I looked pretty "downtown" I guess, not totally but sort of. And it was a beautiful night and warm and smelling like springtime but when we got there Scott Haskell came running down the driveway to make fun of my outfit like, "What's Andrea supposed to be?" Darcy had jeans and a boring shirt and Scott kept looking at me and then Darcy grabbed him and said, "Stop staring!" Then we went inside and it was scary because it wasn't just a Hillside party, there were people from Bradley Day School and Portland Episcopal and there were really cute guys and hippie girls and everyone was dressed up. One girl even had a cool retro dress like Outer Limits. And everyone was talking and laughing and having fun and I was sure glad I wore a skirt.

But poor Darcy. She took one look around and she was like, "Bathroom!" We ran up the stairs and found Mrs. Babbit's bathroom which was huge and luxurious and had lighted mirrors. Darcy wanted to use my lipstick and obviously she was regretting her boring outfit. So we put on lipstick and eye stuff and I made my hair part even more severe and Darcy did hers the same way and I didn't think she'd leave it but she did. Then she dug through the laundry hamper and found an old flannel shirt.

She put it on and cuffed her jeans and I guess she looked sort of grunge or something but mostly she looked like Darcy dressed in Mr. Babbit's dirty shirt.

Back at the party nobody noticed our makeover. But then in the backyard some boys came up to us and offered to get us beers. They were sort of dumb except one boy who was tall and had horn-rimmed glasses. He was watching everyone and you could tell he was *amused.* He had a cool haircut, short but with thick bangs that bunched up on top of his glasses and when his friends went to get the beer I saw he had a cool fifties jacket. But it was embarrassing too because I knew me and Darcy looked stupid. I mean, the other boys thought we were "downtown" but a real downtown person would think we were playing dress-up. Then Darcy started talking to him and she was trying to act cool and she was sort of insulting him. But he didn't care. He just kept nodding his head and smiling to himself. And then Mark Pierce came over and put his arm around me and Scott Haskell came over and he looked at Darcy and said, "So what are *you* supposed to be?" And the horn-rimmed boy said we were "hipsters" and he just laughed at all of us and it was so embarrassing.

And then more people came and everybody was getting drunk and Scott Haskell was pissing in the bushes right in front of everyone. And me and Darcy drank some beer and I kept burping. And then Mark Pierce found me and whispered to me how sexy I looked and did I want to go somewhere? I said, "Where?"

and he said there was a room upstairs. So we went upstairs and the room was way at the end of the house and it was a little kid's bedroom with bunk beds. Mark went to the desk and I felt drunk and sort of numb, like he was my husband or my father and he was going to take care of me. He turned on the desk lamp and turned it to the wall and switched off the main light. He wanted everything to be perfect. Then he led me to the bunk bed and sat me down and started kissing me and unbuttoning my shirt. And he was being really gentle and sweet except he smelled like cigars. I asked him if he'd been smoking and he said *shhhhh* and he smelled like beer too. Then he laid me down and we were really making out and then he took off his pants and I could feel his penis inside his boxer shorts. He put my hand on it and I squeezed it and he started moaning. Then he lifted me up and pulled off my Gap skirt and his face was totally concentrating. He was trying to hurry before I changed my mind. He kicked off his boxer shorts and tried to sit up but then he banged his head on the upper bunk, really hard so the whole bed shook. And he swore and held his head and I was like, "Are you okay?" He nodded that he was. Then he hobbled over to the desk and got out a condom and ripped it open. And he held his penis and tried to put the condom on it but it wasn't working right and he was grimacing and swearing to himself. Then a stream of blood ran down his cheek. At first he just brushed it away but more came and then he looked at his hand and it was all bloody and then he really started swearing. I got up and went over to him but he pushed me back toward the bed and then he looked at his hand again and he was so pissed. He was still trying to put the condom on but now the blood was getting in his face. I pulled my skirt back on and got him to sit down in a chair. I dabbed at his head with the boxer shorts but he was so angry and swearing so much it just made it bleed more. Finally I convinced him to go downstairs and I held the boxer shorts against his head while he put on his pants. When we got down the stairs Renee Hatfield said, "Looks like someone got their brains fucked out." Then Brian Babbit came over and said, "Oh, shit," and they led Mark into the kitchen and pushed me out of the way. Which was fine with me. I didn't want to look at it. And then someone drove him to the hospital for stitches and I just wanted to leave. I went looking for Darcy in the backyard but she wasn't there and Scott Haskell and another guy were pissing in the bushes and Scott was totally drunk and bragging that he fucked Cindy before she even knew Dave and what a slut Cindy was and what a stupid bitch.

I just wanted to find Darcy. I went back in the house and everyone was drunk and I went out front and there were cars parked everywhere and then I turned around and the boy with the horn-rims was coming right toward me. I turned back toward the cars and yelled "Darcy!" But there was no answer. And the boy with the horn-rims stood beside me and looked around like he was trying to help. And then he asked me if the guy with the bloody head was a friend of mine. I nodded. And we stood there and he told me his name was Kevin and he asked me where I went to school. I told him Hillside and he said he went to Learning Center downtown which was where all the weirdest people went, all the artsy types and rich kids and gay people. And then Darcy came running out of the house and she was all worried but I told her Mark was okay and everything was okay but I wanted to leave, like *now*. But she didn't want to and she was drunk and then Scott came charging toward us and he had his shirt off and Darcy squealed and ran and Scott chased her down the street. And then Kevin said he was leaving and I could get a ride with him.

Kevin had a Volvo. We got in and he got out his tapes and asked me what kind of music I liked. I said, "All different kinds." He picked something and put it in and started telling me about the band. I didn't really listen, I just let him talk and tried to rest after all the excitement. And my mind was so scattered I didn't even know where we were and then we were downtown and he asked me if I wanted to have coffee. It was eleven and I still had an hour until I had to be home so I said okay. So we went to this fancy cafe where all these really fashionable people were. The tables had bright white tablecloths and nice silverware and we had tea and I was so thirsty I drank both our waters. And when I finally started to relax I was so exhausted I felt like I'd been drugged. So I went to the bathroom and sat in a stall and I swear, my head fell into my lap and I almost fell asleep. And I was *so glad* I didn't have sex with Mark Pierce. And then I started to cry and I wanted someone to hug me like my dad or Darcy or Cybil but they were all off somewhere else. I was by myself. And I was downtown in a fancy restaurant with a boy I didn't even know. So I got up and went to the mirror and fixed myself up as best I could. And when I walked back out the room was so bright and loud and people were talking and men were staring and a waitress almost ran me over and I barely made it back to the table.

Kevin took me home. He didn't put any tapes in this time. I had to give directions and I was getting paranoid that he'd think my neighborhood was stupid because of the big Sunset Park sign at the entrance and all the suburban houses that are exactly the same with two-car garages and 2.2 kids. But when we got there someone had spray-painted SUBURBAN DEATH on the sign and we were both like, *cool!* And then I told him my friend Cybil was in a band and he got really interested and he knew someone who was in a band. And I told him about Thriftstore Apocalypse and Pax and meeting Todd Sparrow of Color Green. And he said he'd been to Outer Limits and how cool it was and I said I loved Outer Limits and Thriftstore was playing there tomorrow and he said he couldn't go but maybe he'd see me there sometime. And I was like, "That would be so fun!" And then he let me out and as he drove away I kicked myself and thought, *Why didn't I tell him my phone number?*

7

SUNDAY MORNING IN SUNSET PARK WAS LAWN MOWERS
revving and basketballs bouncing and Mom talking to
Mrs. Crenshaw in the driveway and Lizzy Rosen tanning next door with her Walkman on and Dad reading *The Sunday
Oregonian* and Rob Dickerson washing his car across the street
and just the whole suburban thing. But not me. Not this Sunday.
Thriftstore Apocalypse was playing at Outer Limits at four o'clock
and I was getting ready and listening to a punk tape Cybil gave me.
The band was called Girl Patrol and the singer was snarling her
words and sounding super tough. And I was fixing my hair and
practicing snarling and then I tried putting some black eyebrow
pencil on my lips and smearing it in with my lipstick and it turned
purple and looked sort of vampire-ish like the deathrocker girls at
Metro Mall. And then I wondered if Marjorie would come to the
show and I felt sorry for her because she had pretty much vanished
from everything and you barely ever saw her at school. She would
be good at snarling. The trouble with me was I didn't really hate
anything that much. I mean, I guess I hated Scott Haskell for being
so sexist. And I sort of hated Renee Hatfield. And of course I hated
Hillside because it was my high school and I hated all the suburban
stuff and the malls and everything even though I still shopped there.
And Sunset Park was stupid, obviously, and Mrs. Crenshaw was a
gossip and Rob Dickerson had a gross moustache but so what? I
didn't care what they did. They could do whatever they wanted.

So then I got out my thriftstore dress and fiddled with the
zipper and tried to figure out why it fit so badly and if I should

38

wear it to Outer Limits. Then Darcy called so I talked to her while I worked on it. She told me about the rest of the party and how Scott Haskell threw up in the kitchen sink and how Mark Pierce came back from the hospital and everybody cheered him and did beer bongs and then afterward Renee invited a few *select* people to her pool to go skinny-dipping. Then Darcy asked me where I went and I told her I went downtown with Kevin. She was like, "Downtown? With Kevin?" So I told her the whole story and she couldn't believe it. And she was like, "That guy with the horn-rims? Is he gay?" I said he went to Learning Center and she said, "Well, that explains it." And then she wanted to know if I was going to break up with Mark Pierce and all of a sudden I got so mad and I was like, *I* never even said I was going out with him and it was everybody else who said I was his girlfriend. And then I said how Renee Hatfield and stupid Scott Haskell were such jerks and Darcy said, "You don't mean Scott Haskell," and I said, "*Yes*, I *especially* mean Scott Haskell." And she said he wasn't that bad and I said, "You should have heard what he said about Cindy!" And she was like, "What did he say?" So I told her and she got totally defensive and said there was no way Scott did it with Cindy because he had told her every girl he had done stuff with and sworn on it and she was getting mad at me like I had made it up. And I was like, "Darcy, I'm not saying he did it, I'm saying he *said* it." But she was still being weird and blaming me and when I hung up it was such a relief. And I turned up my tape player and started bopping around to Girl Patrol and I was so glad I was going to Outer Limits and getting away from the

Hillside crowd. And my parents had already told me I could use their car since it was Sunday afternoon. And I put on my dress and looked in the mirror and practiced sneering and looking bored and I was ready!

But then I went downstairs and my mother was like, "Where did you get that dress?" And she yelled for my dad to come look at his daughter and it was totally ruining my mood. I tried to tell them it was the style and my stupid mom said, "What's the style? Wearing rags? What is this stain on the back?" And my dad said, "What happened to your lips?" and I looked in the toaster reflection and I still had the black stuff on my lips. I tried to rub it off with my finger and then my mom picked up my hair and let it drop with disgust and I said, "It's the *style*!" And my mom asked my dad if I should still get the car and my dad shrugged and said there was no law against driving a car dressed like a clown. And then my mother looked at the zipper of my dress and said it was ripping out and I thought she wasn't going to let me wear it but then she threw up her hands and let me go.

And the whole time I was getting ready it didn't even occur to me that it might be weird to go by myself. I guess I thought it would be like the other times, a couple people standing around and mostly people from the bands and I'd hang out with Cybil and Richard and I wouldn't have to worry about Mark Pierce or anybody else, like what *they* thought or if *they* were having fun. But when I drove past Outer Limits there were all these people on the sidewalk and I started getting nervous. I parked far away and spent several minutes doing my lipstick and fixing my hair and adjusting my part. But that made me more flustered and finally I just got out and took a deep breath and started walking.

I never felt so self-conscious in my life. I had to walk down Broadway right past this sports store and all these jock types were standing there and they stared at my dress and all I could do was look at the ground and keep going. And then I went around the corner to Outer Limits and I could feel the people turning to look at me and it was like someone punched me in the stomach, I could barely breathe and my heart started pounding and I didn't dare lift my head. I got to the door and went inside and immediately looked around for Cybil or Richard. *But they weren't there.* And the room was dark and cold and the floor was dirty and there was no place to sit and I just wanted to cry. But then I remembered how Cybil always sat on the stage between bands so I sat on the stage and bit my nails and fiddled with my hem. And I pretended not to look but I could see the trendy girls talking outside, probably analyzing my outfit and discussing how stupid it was and wondering why would someone come to Outer Limits dressed like a clown?

Then I was saved. Greg's station wagon pulled up on the sidewalk and drove all the trendies away. And then Cybil and Richard got out and I jumped up and ran to meet them. And I was so happy to see them I was jumping around and they looked

41

at me funny and Richard was like, "Andrea, are you okay?" And Cybil said, "Where did you get that dress?" And I said, "At a *thriftstore!*" And then I asked Greg if they needed help moving their stuff and he said sure and I grabbed this metal thing but he said that didn't go in. And then Cybil told me to calm down and she gave me something to carry and I guess I was being sort of hyper.

When the stuff was all moved we went back out to the sidewalk. The trendy girls had come back and were leaning on Greg's car and I stood with Cybil and she told me how she was flunking French and how Mrs. Renault hated her but her mom wasn't going to let her play in the band if she didn't pass. I sympathized and then I told about Brian Babbit's party and how I almost had sex with Mark Pierce. Cybil said, "You shouldn't have sex with him, you should have sex with someone you really like." But who did I really like? Cybil didn't know. So then I told her about Kevin and I said he was more like Richard, at least in how he dressed. And anyway he wasn't a typical Hillside guy like Mark or Scott Haskell, and Cybil said Scott Haskell gave her the creeps worse than any guy she knew.

Another band played first and they were terrible. They banged their guitars with drumsticks and one guy hit a shopping cart with a bat and it was just a lot of noise. Then Thriftstore Apocalypse played and they were great but people weren't into it that much. But I did notice that a lot of the trendy girls watched Cybil very closely, including one girl who seemed like the trendiest of them all. She had a short bob that was dyed a reddish rust color and she was smoking and standing by herself and all the other girls kept their distance. After Thriftstore played Cybil and Richard were in a good mood and Greg talked to me and I asked him where Marjorie was but he didn't know. And it was weird because it was only last fall that Marjorie brought us downtown and showed us everything and now we were all here by ourselves.

The next band was Pax and we all sat along the side and ate the carrots that Richard brought. Then there was some sort of commotion around the door. Everybody looked but I couldn't really see and then Nick did a headstand onstage and fell into the drums and everybody went back to looking at him. Then, a few minutes later, Richard leaned over to me and said, "Todd Sparrow is here." I said, "Where?" and I looked around but I couldn't tell which one was him and I wasn't sure I could remember what he looked like. But then I saw him. He was sitting across from us and he looked awful. He was really skinny and dirty and his hair was dyed yellow and he had skinhead boots that were old and held together with tape. But his face was the same, really angular and dark and sort of cocked downward like he was about to attack you or something. And who was he sitting with? The trendy rust-haired girl. And she was telling him something and smoking her cigarette and he was sort of nodding and not looking at her. And I looked at Cybil and Richard to see their reaction but they just sat there chomping their carrots.

When the show was over I helped Cybil and Richard carry their stuff back out. And everyone hung out and sat on the curb and Todd Sparrow was there with some other severe-looking people and I wondered if Cybil was going to talk to him. And I asked Greg if he ever heard Todd's band and he said, "No, but I've heard they're intense." And I looked over and there was another boy with really scraggly hair in his face and the most shredded jeans I had ever seen and you could tell he was with Todd, they were band partners, they were Color Green.

The next day at school I sat with Mark Pierce and the gang and I told Darcy about the show and how intense Todd Sparrow was but how Cybil wouldn't talk to him. And Darcy wondered if Cybil made out with him when she shaved her head but I said, "Wouldn't she have told us?" Darcy said, "Why? She doesn't tell us anything else." Which was true. But I said maybe it's our own fault since we still hung around with these idiots and I pointed at Mark and Scott Haskell. And Scott Haskell heard me and said, "Hey! What did she just say? What did Andrea just say?" And Darcy said that I called him an idiot and everybody laughed, fortunately. And walking back to our lockers I told Darcy we had to go to this store called HOP! that Cybil told me about because we were going to the wrong thriftstore and that's why none of the dresses fit.

8 AT HOP! THE DRESSES FIT. IT WAS DOWNTOWN
and it was the coolest place. And when we went to London Dungeon that time I was so scared of everything. But I wasn't scared now. And the boy behind the counter was super cute and super nice and there was cool music and cool posters and the clothes were fantastic. I found a cute summer dress for fifteen dollars and this funny red dress with cows on it. Darcy got a tie-dyed shirt and a skirt and some white pumps that were only six dollars. And everything was clean and the zippers worked and they had cool raincoats and I picked out a beach hat like the one Greg wore when he shaved his head. And Darcy got a Mod belt and I got a gray cardigan sweater that said "librarian" on the tag. And then Darcy said we should get bobs but the cute boy told us not to, that all the girls he knew were growing their hair out. And when we went back to the dress rack Darcy whispered to me that we shouldn't buy everything now so we could come back and talk to the cute boy some more.

Afterwards we went to Scamp's for frozen yogurt and I wore the cow dress and the cardigan and everyone was looking at us. And then Derek walked by the window and at first he was just going to wave but when he saw how cute we looked he had to come in. And Darcy was so jealous because Derek was complimenting me and looking at the funny cows on my dress and Darcy knew her tie-dyed shirt was not enough. You had to get a dress and have a whole look. Derek was going to Monte Carlo later, which was an underage dance club, and he told us how cool it was and invited us to come. But Darcy didn't want to, she wanted to go back to HOP! first and get a better outfit.

Meanwhile there was only one week of school left and I was still sitting with Mark Pierce at lunch. It was okay though because he was about to graduate so he had other things to do besides pressure me for sex. And Brian Babbit was graduating too and all the seniors were going through their last rites of high school and getting nostalgic and sentimental, which for the boys meant drinking tons of beer, taking their shirts off, falling out of pickup trucks, etc.

And then Renee Hatfield's parents went to Hawaii and she started having people over to her pool after school. At first me and Darcy weren't invited but then Mark took us and Renee was like, "Oh look, Mark brought his girls." And then some other people came over, including Jim Dietz who was senior class president and going to Yale. And he brought some senior girls and Scott Haskell made tequila sunrises and everybody sat on lounge chairs and listened to Jim and Mark tell basketball stories. And the senior girls talked and Scott talked and Renee teased Mark about how he always "scored." Darcy and I were silent of course. Then Jim left with the senior girls and Renee started arguing with Scott since Jim hadn't given her enough attention earlier. And me and Darcy drank our sunrises and luxuriated in the lounge chairs in our bikinis and T-shirts and it was pretty fun except when I stood up to go to the bathroom I was so drunk I almost fell on my face. I made it to the bathroom but everything was so strange and out of joint and I put a towel over my head and looked in the mirror and I hardly recognized myself. I went back and told Darcy how drunk I was and she said, "You're not that drunk," and immediately spilled her drink all over herself. Then she told me if I was too drunk I should go in the bathroom and throw up and I was like *yuck* but she said to do it, it worked. But I didn't want to. I went inside to the TV room and watched MTV instead. Then I stretched out on the couch and put my head on a cushion and then I fell asleep.

When I woke up I thought Darcy was pulling on my shirt and my head was all heavy on one side and when I opened my eyes Scott Haskell was straddling me. His pants were down and he was holding my shirt up and he was masturbating on me. And I was so stunned I just stared at his penis which was purple and pointed right at me. And his hand was going like crazy, milking it like a cow and he was like *shhhhhh* and I hissed at him: *"What are you doing?"* I grabbed my shirt back and tried to get up but he held me down. And the stuff started coming out and I kicked him and said, "Get off!" And the stuff got on my leg and I kicked him really hard and he fell off the couch. And it was on my leg, this gross slime, and I grabbed the towel and it was like having an insect on you, I wanted it *off*. And I stood up and wiped my leg and Scott Haskell was groaning and rolling around on the floor. And I kept finding more of it, this gross stuff, and some was on my arm and some was on my shirt and I was so pissed. And Scott was still on the floor, sneaking his pants up while he pretended to be passed out. And then he said, "I am *so* wasted," and I stepped over him and I swear, I almost stomped on his face.

I ran to the pool and it was dark now but Darcy was still sitting there reading a magazine. And Renee and Mark Pierce were getting cozy in the deep end of the pool and I told Darcy we had to leave right now. She asked why and I started to explain but just then we both heard this horrible gagging noise coming out of the bathroom window. It was Scott Haskell throwing up. *"That's* the problem," I said and Darcy listened for a second and there was another gagging noise and then a splattering sound and Darcy made a face and said, "Gross!" I said, "That's not the worst of it," and I made a motion like a guy jerking off and she looked at me and I showed her the wet spot on my shirt. And she gave me this suspicious look and I was like, "Darcy, *I was asleep!"* She listened while Scott gagged some more and I noticed that Renee and Mark Pierce had separated and were coming over toward us. They wanted to know what was going on. Especially Renee. She was like, "What's the matter, Andrea?" and she had that catty look she gets and I thought *you bitch* but I smiled and said, "Oh nothing, I just remembered I have to go home." And I grabbed Darcy and we got out of there.

Darcy drove. She was in shock. And I felt sorry for her because even though she knew how crazy Scott was she still felt like he was her boyfriend. And she said he'd been bugging her for a blowjob and she was thinking about doing it but now no way because what he did to me was so uncool. And the more I thought about it the madder I got and I said maybe I should tell everyone at school. But Darcy said not to because it would make her look stupid and me look stupid and guys would just twist it around and make it our fault. And then we stopped at 7-Eleven to get some ice cream but we didn't get out of the car because all of a sudden we both understood our situation with Mark Pierce and Scott Haskell. We were groupies. We were these little sophomore sluts who guys like Mark Pierce and Scott Haskell jerked off on. And all this time we had tried so hard to not identify ourselves with them and that was exactly what they wanted. They didn't *want* us to be their girlfriends, they were *glad* we were stupid and didn't make any demands and just hung around so they could fondle us whenever they wanted. And Mark Pierce never loved me, he didn't even *like* me, he just liked how stupid I was. And he was probably having sex with Renee Hatfield the whole time, probably right this second they were in her parents' bed doing it and laughing their heads off. And then Darcy said, "I don't feel like ice cream." And I said, "I feel sick." And Darcy started the car and drove us both home.

Three days later was graduation. I wouldn't have even gone except Darcy's brother was graduating and she didn't want to go by herself. I looked all around in case Scott Haskell was there but I didn't see him. In the gym Darcy sat with her parents and I sat with Rebecca Farnhurst, who was telling everyone

49

that Mr. Angelo said we were a bad generation and in ten years the kids would be good again. And then she started gossiping about how Cindy wanted to videotape having sex but Dave didn't want to and they were arguing about it at lunch right in front of everybody. And all I could think of was Rebecca finding out about Scott and spreading it all over school. So I just stared straight ahead and tried to ignore her. I watched the seniors line up to go onstage. Mark Pierce was in the line. And Brian Babbit. And Jim Dietz. And they were all laughing and having the greatest time. And then the line started moving and up they went, getting their diplomas and shaking hands with Mrs. Katz, our principal. And all the parents took pictures and celebrated and congratulated each other, as if a monkey couldn't graduate from Hillside. And Rebecca nudged me and pointed to Mrs. Parmeter, who was picking at something in her ear. And everybody giggled and made fun of her and also Mr. Angelo, who was sweating and dabbing his face with a napkin. And I thought about how we were just a job to them. We were like so much grass growing, or weeds maybe, they watered us and fertilized us and when it was harvest time, they chopped us down and cleared us out and started over with the next bunch.

When it was over everyone threw their graduation caps in the air. Some of them zoomed really high and others just sort of flopped up and fell right back down. And everybody cheered and hugged and I snuck outside as quick as I could. And I just wanted to leave but then I couldn't find Darcy and I was stuck in the parking lot, moving backward as the people poured out. And people were loading their cameras and hugging each other and then I saw Mark Pierce with his parents and my whole body cringed. So I hid behind some other people and watched him through the crowd. They were taking pictures: Mark with Mom, Mark with Dad, Mark with Brian Babbit, Mark with Jim Dietz, who everybody wanted in their picture, Mark with Renee Hatfield, who tried to kiss him but she just got his cheek because Mark Pierce never looked anywhere but straight into the camera.

And I was getting a headache and it seemed really muggy all of a sudden and I leaned on a car but it was hot from the sun and it burned me. And then I burped and I remembered the tequila and Scott Haskell and his horrible penis and it was so awful I almost threw up. And I felt dizzy and weird and I looked for someplace to sit down but everything was cars and barkdust and asphalt. And my neck started to tingle and stars came in my head and I had to kneel down really fast so I wouldn't fall. Then I went to a different place, a place totally away from Hillside and Darcy and everyone. It was peaceful there and nice but then I came back and I was in the gym and all these people were running around and waving air at me and sticking stuff in my face. And Mrs. Schroeder was giving me water and telling everyone to stand back. And Darcy's dad was there and he was slapping my hand and Mrs. Schroeder told him not to worry, that every year someone fainted at graduation, it was just such an exciting moment for young people.

9 **ONCE SCHOOL WAS OUT THE BIG QUESTION BECAME,** what would I do over the summer? My parents thought I should go back to Camp North Pacific. It was up in the San Juan Islands above Seattle and my mom knew someone who knew someone and they had sent me there for two summers in junior high. But I was sixteen now and I was too old to go there as a camper, even if I wanted to, which I definitely did not. So then they suggested I be a counselor but I was way too late to apply. So then they said I could go on the grounds crew or something and they were serious. In fact they were adamant. I was like, *the grounds crew*? Their argument was what else was I going to do? And they were obviously worried about me hanging out downtown and wearing weird clothes and Cybil shaving her head, though they wouldn't admit it. And I was totally caught off-guard and didn't have any arguments against them. And my mom still knew the someone who knew someone. So they won. I got signed on to the maintenance crew. I was going to wash dishes and cook and do laundry for ten weeks for almost no money. I felt like I was being sent into exile.

The first week was the worst. The people on the maintenance crew were the lowest people in the whole camp. They were from Harper's Ferry, the little town nearby, and they had accents like Canadians, like "ay?" all the time. There was an older woman named Rita and a boy about my age named Brad who looked like Scott Haskell, blond and with freckles but sort of dopey and not really as cute. The girl counselors were all girl-counselor types, rich and perky and cheerful. And the boy counselors were the same, big teeth and Izod shirts and just too perfect. And being on the maintenance crew they wouldn't even notice me anyway except some who remembered me from before and they just looked at me like *What happened to you?*

The work was super hard and at first I was so tired I could barely stay awake at night. I'd eat dinner and crawl in my bunk and that was it. But after a while I would read some, just whatever books and magazines were lying around, and then Rita started giving me better books. One was about these artists in Paris who had sex all the time. I read that one a lot but it made me horny which made me lonely which made me depressed. But then after the first couple weeks I got used to everything and it wasn't so bad. Our building was separate from the rest of the camp and we could stay up as late as we wanted and we had a little porch and steps to hang out on. And one day I passed one of the counselors with a group of screaming camper brats and I was actually glad I was on maintenance.

By July I felt pretty settled. It was getting hotter at night and we'd sit outside and Rita would smoke and Brad would read comic books and I would write letters to Darcy and Cybil. Darcy was working at The Gap at Sunset Mall. She had a sort of boyfriend named Michael who worked in the mall except she thought he was gay because he would never touch her except sometimes he would let her give him back rubs. She said it was driving her crazy and she was so horny she thought she might explode. Cybil was practicing with Richard and Greg and trying to get a job. She didn't write as much and her letters were mostly about fights with her mom or the new Girl Patrol record or some weird girl she met at the mall. Her biggest news was that she had convinced Richard to change their band name to Sins of Our Fathers. I wrote to Darcy how boring camp was and how stuck-up the counselors were and how cool Rita was and how cute Brad was, which was a slight exaggeration but she would never have to know and it made me feel better. To Cybil I mostly asked questions and tried to encourage her and tell her how much I liked her band and how sometimes their songs came into my head. And I asked her what she thought I should do next year in terms of which boys should I like and how should I dress and what did she think of boys from Learning Center? She never really answered these questions but that was okay. And sometimes I wrote song lyrics for her band, not that I would ever show her but just for fun and to see if I could do it. And sometimes I fantasized that Kevin and I were in a band together and went onstage at Outer Limits and everyone talked about us, even Todd Sparrow. But mostly I just wanted a boy to think about, and *not* a camp counselor and after a couple weeks I started thinking about Brad because he was shy and nice and he was really the only boy around.

And he must have been thinking about me because one night before bed he came and sat with me on the steps. He didn't usually smoke cigarettes but he bummed one from Rita and smoked it really fast. And when he finished it he bummed another one and smoked that one really fast. Then he whispered to me if I wanted to go into town with him that night. His plan was we'd sneak his motorcycle out of the main garage and walk it out of camp and then start it and ride into town which was about ten miles. I was pretty reluctant but he said he'd done it before and then Rita said, "And while you're there get some cigarettes." She'd heard the whole plan and by saying that I thought she was sending me a message of *go for it* so I said okay.

And it was weird because I'd convinced myself that Brad was cute but as soon as I was involved in his plan he seemed sort of dopey again and as we walked to the main garage he seemed really bony and awkward. He smelled nice though and he pulled me over to the trees and then went by himself into the garage and wheeled out his motorcycle. It made a soft whirring noise and I didn't usually like motorcycles but I liked his. And we walked it along the road and coasted it down the hill and all the time I kept looking back. But no one had seen us. We had done it. We had escaped Camp North Pacific.

Brad started his motorcycle. He revved it a couple times but quietly and not in that loud obnoxious way that I hate. He got on and I got on the back and grabbed his T-shirt but he made me put my arms around him and sit close because it was safer. So I did and he started going, slow at first and with the headlights off because the moon was out and you could see okay. And it was scary but sort of fun and then he turned on the light and speeded up and I grabbed hold and we were *flying*! And there were little pockets of cold air and warm air and everything smelled like pine trees and cinder dust and I rested my chin on Brad's shoulder and scooted forward on the seat so I was totally against him. And when we got to the main road we went super fast and that was really scary because we didn't have helmets and the pavement was old and gravely. But Brad zoomed straight ahead and I closed my eyes and put my face in his back and I figured if I died it was my parents' fault because they made me come here.

But we didn't die. We got to Harper's Ferry and the only problem was, what were we going to do there at 11:30 at night? We drove down the main street and Brad told me to watch for cops because they knew him and they'd tell Mr. Fitch at camp. And the only thing open was Lenny's Tavern anyway so we zipped through town and into this poor neighborhood with these shack houses and junk cars. We pulled into a vacant lot and parked and I asked Brad where we were going and he said we were visiting someone. And then he took my hand and we snuck through some trees and we came out in the backyard of this horrible little house. And I was getting scared and I said I wouldn't go any further until he told me whose house it was. So he did, it was his mom's.

The next thing I knew we were creeping across the lawn to one of the windows, which was flashing from a TV inside. We crouched under it and Brad smiled at me and did *shhhhh* with his finger and then straightened up enough to peek inside. Then he bent down again and his face was dark in the shadows and he froze for a second and then he squeezed my hand and led me around to the front of the house. "Mom's got company," he whispered and he pointed at the pickup in the driveway. He snuck over to it and quietly opened the passenger door. Then he waved me over and made me hold the button so the inside light wouldn't come on. I asked him whose it was but he was busy going through the glove box and looking under the seats. Then he popped the seat-back and pushed it forward and whispered "Score!" I was pretty much terrified by this point and looking around but the street was deserted and the other houses were quiet. And then Brad started handing me stuff, a half-carton of cigarettes, a big flashlight, a bottle of whiskey, and then there was a *clunk* and Brad pulled himself out from behind the seat and he had a gun. It was a real gun. It was big and black and totally scary. He opened it and pulled out one of the bullets and snapped it shut again. Then he dropped into a crouch and pointed it at the house and made a silent motion like he was shooting. And I was so scared my finger slipped off the light button and the light came on in the pickup and I grabbed for it and we both ducked down and looked around the neighborhood. But nothing happened. And Brad was pressed against me and his blond bangs hung in his face and his eyes were alert like a scared animal. Then he started grabbing stuff. He jammed the whiskey in the front of his pants and shook a couple packs of cigarettes out of the carton. He put the gun back behind the seat and eased the seat-back until it clicked. Then he took the light button from me and shut the door, slowly and quietly and just until the door latch caught. And then, oh my God, *did we run*!

10

I FELL IN LOVE WITH BRAD THAT NIGHT IN a numb way, in a physical way, like I knew he was the one. And that night in my bunk I could still smell him on my hands and on my shirt where I pressed up against him. And I laid my head on my pillow like it was his chest and stared at the wall and thought of what a hard life he had and probably nobody loved him when he was a child. And the next day I walked by the shop and looked in and Brad and Mr. Fitch were working on the riding lawn mower. Brad saw me and when Mr. Fitch turned away he grinned and gave me thumbs-up and he just seemed like the cutest boy.

But after lunch I felt differently. I felt like Brad was a hick. I mean, like a hick in his actual face, like his face was a little too narrow and the smile lines were a little too deep for being seventeen and he had this toughness in his shoulders and his bony arms that wasn't like a jock, it wasn't graceful, it was just hard. And I knew that part of my feelings were because he was here now and afterward I would never see him again and in a way I would have been ashamed if Darcy or Cybil saw him. And when

I saw the preppie counselors I didn't feel so superior anymore, I felt like I had fallen somehow, that they were hanging on to something that I had lost my grip on.

That night I sat on the steps with Rita and watched her smoke and we talked about men and sex but even that was weird because with my perfect teeth and my nice clothes I must have seemed as rich to her as the counselors seemed to me. Not to mention what Brad must have thought. But then in my bunk all I could think about was Brad. I hugged my pillow and imagined us making out and I was practically delirious with lust. And then when I saw him the next day I was suddenly all nervous. And at lunch I was just babbling like an idiot and teasing him about the stupidest things. And then later we were cleaning the horse stalls together and at first it was awkward but then he threw some hay on me and I threw some back and we were laughing so hard and chasing each other around and I swear, it was the funnest time I ever had with a boy.

And then one night I was sitting on the steps trying to write to Darcy and all of a sudden I looked up from my pad and I knew I was not going to be a virgin anymore. Brad was inside reading a comic book. Rita was sitting on the porch, smoking and reading and drinking some of Brad's whiskey out of a coffee cup. And then Brad came out and stood on the steps above me. He had his hands in his pockets and he mumbled something and he was trying to ask me out. My heart was pounding and Rita cleared her throat like, *Say something.* So I said, "Do you want to go for a walk?" And Brad said okay and he ran inside and got his coat and his whiskey bottle and off we went.

We walked around the lake to this old cabin that was boarded up and full of mice and had ferns growing out of the window sills. We sat on the dock in front of it and Brad lit a cigarette and took a long drink of the whiskey, which was pretty scary like he probably drank a lot and he was only seventeen and his parents were probably alcoholics. But he still smelled good and he hung his feet over the water and I guess he was just trying to calm his nerves. And he gave me the whiskey bottle and I tried to drink a little but God, it was awful. It burned my throat and choked me up and made my eyes water. "Rancid stuff," he said. He always said anything gross was *rancid.* So I handed it back and he took some more and I got the feeling that he was too scared to do anything. And it occurred to me that I might be rushing it and maybe he didn't even like me that much and why had I assumed he did? So I just tried to relax and enjoy the pretty night, the moon and the trees and the stillness of the lake.

Then he laid back on the dock and leaned on his elbow and started talking about his mom and stuff, out of the blue, how he had a stepfather and a sister in Montana and it was this long sad story that I sort of didn't want to hear but fortunately it didn't go too long. Then he asked me about my family and I told him my dad was a dentist and about my friends Cybil and Darcy and how Cybil shaved her head which I knew he wouldn't understand. And I told him a little about Mark Pierce but not too much. And he handed me the whiskey and I took it and pretended to drink some. And then I scooted closer to him and picked at the splinters on the dock and we were talking really soft and whispery and then I sort of tipped forward, right into his chest, right into his flannel shirt, like I just stuck my face in it for no reason. At first nothing happened but then he touched my neck and pulled me on top of him and I kissed him and straddled him and I could feel him through his pants and I was pressing against him before I could even stop myself.

After a while he got up and ran behind the cabin and came back with a sleeping bag. So I guess I wasn't rushing it. I guess we were both thinking the same thing. He untied it and spread it on the ground and then we laid down and started kissing again. Then he took off my shirt and my pants and he pulled the sleeping bag over us and took off his own pants and he even had a condom and everything. And I just laid there and he got on top of me and tried to put it in and it felt really strange at first, like I didn't quite know where it was. But then he got it in. And I just held my breath and then he started doing it and it felt so weird. And I waited for something to happen but nothing really did except he made these little grunting noises. And then I thought of stuff I should do like grab his butt but I couldn't really reach. And I wondered if we were going to do positions or stuff like in magazines but he just kept doing it and getting faster and faster.

And then it sort of hurt and I closed my eyes and tried to shift my position and then I got this warm shiver up my back and it felt pretty good. So I shifted again and that felt even better. So then I pushed back against him and got it in this one spot and that felt great. And I was sort of describing it to myself in my mind and also to Darcy but then he stopped and it was over. And I just laid there staring up at the stars and the tops of the trees and I thought, *My life, my real life, has just now begun.*

After that Brad smoked some cigarettes and we talked for a while and then we made out again and this time he kissed my breasts and licked me and he was even going to lick me down there but I couldn't stand it because it tickled too much. And then he got on top of me and started doing it again but this time he was propped up on his arms and I touched his chest and grabbed his butt. And I mashed up against him and got him right in the right position and did it really hard and I was like "Oh! Oh!" which probably sounded totally corny. But then it was over and I was buzzing so hard and squeezing him between my legs and trying to keep him inside me for as long as I possibly could. And I could hear myself telling Darcy: "Oh, you have to do it, it's the most wonderful thing!"

The next day was so weird. Brad was nowhere to be found. It was okay in a way because I wanted to be alone and think about things and try to get used to myself, my new non-virgin self. In the morning it rained and I swept and mopped the main lodge and it was quiet and you could hear the raindrops hitting the roof and echoing in the rafters. In the afternoon I worked in the laundry room and I was getting these weird pangs and then I started to cry for no reason. Then at dinner I was so excited and nervous and I wore my favorite shirt but Brad wasn't there and Rita didn't know where he was. And all day I'd been so hungry but now I just stared at my food. It seemed so weird that he wasn't there and I couldn't understand why he'd be avoiding me. So I left and started back to the cabin but then I heard Brad's boots in the gravel behind me. And he said, "Hey, Andrea," and it just floored me, the sound of his voice, saying my name. And I turned around and he was grinning so big and I walked up to him and slugged him in the arm. He was like, "What?" and I was like, *"You know what,"* and he said, "I don't." Then he said he'd been helping Mr. Fitch with the tractor and he'd been in town all day getting parts. I was like, "Really?" He said yeah. And then he said he thought about me all day and Mr. Fitch yelled at him because he kept spacing out. I said I'd felt sort of weird too and he said, "It was your first time, wasn't it?" I said, *"No, it was not!"* He didn't say anything and then I wanted to kiss him so bad or go riding on his motorcycle or go to the lake or just anything as long as he was with me, in my sight, in grabbing range.

What I didn't understand that first couple days was if sex was so fun why didn't people spend, you know, like six or eight hours a day doing it? I felt like I could have. And I looked at all the grown-ups and older kids and the counselors and I thought how everyone on earth complains they can't get sex but why can't they? Just go meet someone and do it. Everybody wants to, how hard can it be? And even if you don't like the person that much you'll be having sex with them and sex is so fun of course you'll start to like them. I even thought about Mark Pierce and how if he had been halfway nice about it we could have done it all last year except of course he was not as cool as Brad. He was just a spoiled suburban boy and Brad was much more worldly and his hard life had educated him so that he *understood* what he was getting and wasn't a jerk like Mark or Scott Haskell and always getting drunk and bragging about every girl he ever made out with.

The next night Brad was sitting on the porch and I tried to sit close to him but he was acting shy. But then Rita went inside and we made out and I tried not to gush too much but I couldn't help it and I just sighed, "Oh, *Brad.*" And the next night we went back to the lake and I couldn't wait to get started but he was acting weird and not saying anything and it was just a lot of waiting around. And I tried to kiss him and get him interested but you could tell something was wrong. And finally we stopped and he started talking and saying how I didn't really like him, I was just like the other camp girls, just having my vacation and that's how everything was in Harper's Ferry, just summer people getting drunk and getting laid and going back home to their real lives. And then he said how much he hated Harper's Ferry and he was going to move to Spokane or Montana except his mom needed him or something, it didn't really make sense. I didn't know what to say because I thought that's what he wanted, to have sex with me because it didn't seem like I was really his type, I mean, not bad or good, just different, like we were friends for the summer and lovers. Then I started talking and I told him he was right, it was my first time and I would always remember him because he was so sweet and then I started to cry because it all seemed so sad. And he just sat there, looking out at the lake and drinking his whiskey but I guess he felt better because after a while he leaned over and kissed me on the cheek. And then we laid down and made out and he pulled off my pants and I was getting so horny. And then he put it in and we did it for a long time and it felt so good my whole body was humming with pleasure.

11 THE OTHER THING I LEARNED FROM BRAD WAS how to smoke. I started that night at the lake. At first it made me dizzy and sick but it was so fun holding it and having it burning in your hand and it was the perfect thing to fiddle with while you're talking, especially a deep conversation about feelings and love. And I could feel how it calmed you down and I understood that contented look Rita got on her face and how she would stare off into space. That's how I was, sitting naked in the sleeping bag, Brad on his elbow beside me, and the lake so smooth and the stars and the

satellites and the moonlight on the water. And when something splashed in the lake I was totally calm and unafraid and I realized that cigarettes weren't just about being cool and having a prop but they also made you really still inside and you could understand things and accept things better than you could before.

During the final week Brad gave me the bullet he stole from the gun in the pickup. It was gold and gray and the top was soft and you could make marks on it with your fingernail. He gave it to me at the lake. The camp had pretty much emptied and the woods were especially dark and quiet and we had sex and then he told me about this Krokus song called "Destiny" that he wanted to be our song and he made me listen to it about six times on his Walkman. And I kept saying I liked it but he never really believed me. And he asked me what kind of music I liked and I said, "Lots of different kinds," though to be honest heavy metal wasn't my favorite.

And then the last couple days were really hard because there was so much work cleaning up the camp and then we didn't sleep because every night we went to the lake to have sex. And by the last morning I was so exhausted from everything and it was about a hundred degrees and I could hardly crawl out of my bunk. But I did and I started packing and I felt so gross and all my clothes were filthy and they wouldn't fit in my bag and then I got so mad I had a fit and threw my stuff on the floor and then I started crying. And when I finally made it to breakfast Brad was there and I could hardly look at him. But he stayed with me and drank coffee while I ate and that made me feel better.

After breakfast Brad gave me a big hug outside the lodge and we held hands on the gravel path and by the time we got back to the cabin I was so happy. Brad sat on my bed while I packed and when I was done I sat on his lap and kissed his face and brushed his bangs back so I could look into his eyes. Then I rested my head on his shoulder and he rocked me back and forth and I closed my eyes and I could have stayed just like that forever.

But somewhere in the back of my mind I was relieved. I wouldn't let myself think about it but in some far back part of myself I was already back home telling Darcy about my adventures and sitting with Cybil at Taco Time and wearing vintage dresses and being a junior at Hillside and meeting new boys and all with a new confidence because I was not a virgin anymore.

I got packed and we took my stuff over to the main lodge where Mr. Fitch was driving us to Harper's Ferry to get the Greyhound. Brad carried my duffel bag and then we got pops from the machine and Brad got me an orange pop, which was my favorite. And we sat on the log bench on the porch and other people started coming, including Karen, who was the last of the counselors. She looked tired too but clean and showered and with perfect clothes and she smiled up at Brad and me like we were an official camp couple, which I guess we had become. And then Brad gave me the Krokus tape and I told him he should keep it but he said he had the CD and he could make his own tape. And then he wanted me to take his Walkman on the bus but I wouldn't and then he got really weird like did I think he couldn't afford another Walkman? And Karen was watching so I took the Walkman and thanked him and touched his blond hair and he kissed me and it was so sad.

And it was so hot. And my jeans were so dirty they were making my legs itch. And my T-shirt was totally pitted and stinky. And then Mr. Fitch didn't show up and everybody was waiting and me and Brad had already said good-bye so many times there was nothing left to do but sit there. And I was wishing Mr. Fitch would hurry up but when I saw the van come around the corner my heart just sank. The van stopped in the gravel and everybody stood up and Mr. Fitch opened the side door and started putting bags in. I reached for my bag but Brad took it from me and carried it to the van. I followed behind him and watched him put it in and then we were just standing there and I didn't know what to do so I leaned into Brad and put my face in his chest just like I did the first time. And then I started to cry and he pulled me aside and hugged me with so much love I just started sobbing. And I hated myself for thinking of being back at school and for being so calculating and caring about my virginity and thinking he wasn't cute when he *loved* me and I loved him and what kind of person was I? The whole thing was killing me and I squeezed him so tight and when I lifted my head up there was snot on my face and tears and he kept kissing me and holding me and the snot was going down my chin and I tried to wipe it on my shirt and it was so awful.

Somehow I got in the van. It was like an oven. And everything smelled of dust and gravel and hot upholstery. And I wiped my eyes and everyone stared at me and Brad stepped back from the window while Mr. Fitch shut the door. And Brad was brown in the sun and I watched his deep smile lines and his blond hair and freckles and the sad skinniness of his face. And he kept backing away from the van and then his expression turned hard and he stared straight in at me and then he ripped himself away, he jerked himself around and ran up the lodge steps. And I watched his bony shoulders and his denim butt and the heels of his boots disappear into the lodge and then the van jerked forward and I just cried. And it was so embarrassing but Karen was nice and of course she had some tissues and she gave me some and then she whispered to me, "You are so lucky to have someone to love."

At Harper's Ferry the Greyhound bus was late and then it was so crowded some people had to stand up. I sat with a fat woman who was all sweaty and the toilet was spilling or something because the whole bus smelled like restroom disinfectant. And then I tried to sleep but my head kept tipping over and waking me up. At Evanston I was supposed to call my parents but the pay phones were all taken and I didn't feel like talking to anyone. So I went outside and sat on the curb and tried to smoke a cigarette but it tasted terrible and people were frowning at me so I put it out.

When we finally got to Seattle everything was totally fouled up. All the buses were too full or breaking down and everybody was stuck and it was hot and miserable and I sat in one of those TV chairs and fell asleep. Finally I got the 11:30 bus to Portland but it was totally packed and it kept stopping to deliver packages. I dozed off again and when I woke up it was 1:00 and we were only halfway there. So then I watched these army guys play cards behind me and they talked to me and gave me bites of their donuts. And then I curled up in my seat and listened to Krokus and watched out the window, which was mostly trees and sometimes a barn or the streetlight of some tiny town. And when "Destiny" came on I held Brad's bullet in my hand and I would have cried but the air-conditioning was on and the air was so dry and processed it numbed your brain and dried all your tears.

Then it was 2:00 a.m. I was like in a trance, just so tired and cried out and used up. And we stopped at an overpass and I stepped off the bus and the night was so clear and cold and I stood over the highway and watched the cars and my brain was like a huge echo chamber, totally empty except for the last fading sounds of Brad and camp and the summer. But then back on the bus I could suddenly think again and I thought about Hillside and if there were any boys I could like. But even with millions to choose from it was so complicated and there was so much politics about cliques and who your friends were and who was your type. And as we pulled into Portland I had this horrible feeling of wanting to go back to Brad because what if that's all there was? What if that's as close as you got? And I called my dad from the station and he was freaking out because I hadn't called. So then I just sat there waiting for him, staring at my dirty tennis shoes and thinking how incredibly stupid I was if I expected life to be anything else but failed love and mindless sex and crying all night in bus stations.

PART TWO

12

I HAD THREE DAYS TO GET READY FOR SCHOOL.
The first day I slept and then did laundry and then slept some more and then watched TV. The next day I went to the Sunset Mall to visit Darcy at the Gap. And it was so weird because we had always made fun of retail types but that's exactly what she had become. I mean, not in a bad way, just how professional she was and how efficient she looked running around in her little outfit. The last day I drove downtown to HOP! and there were lots of people there and it was intimidating because I'd been out in the woods all summer and everyone else had been downtown getting cooler by the second. I still hadn't called Cybil and I was sort of afraid to, but also I was saving it, like these were the last days of my isolation and I was enjoying how anonymous I felt. And as I walked around downtown I imagined I was with Brad and I was showing him around and explaining my life to him and how I did love him but we were just too different and it never would have worked.

I didn't mind going back to Hillside. I felt at home there. On the first day of school I rode with Darcy and everyone in the parking lot was honking and waving to each other and there was a big gang of people gathered around Renee Hatfield's car, and me and Darcy rolled our eyes because the only thing worse than Renee Hatfield in general was Renee Hatfield, *senior*. And it was weird walking through the parking lot because so much happens and people change so much and you could feel the difference in your status immediately. Now we were juniors. Now we were upperclassmen. And the first couple freshmen we saw looked like little toy people, like little kids at camp except scared because this was the real world, this was *high school*. And we saw this one freshman boy who had really beautiful dark eyes and a cool skater shirt, and me and Darcy whispered that he would be the cutest freshman boy, which was great for freshmen girls but wasn't going to do us any good.

And then we got our lockers and everything had my name on it and not just Andrea Marr but Andrea N. Marr because I had had a little moment of pretentiousness when I filled out my stuff at the end of last year. So now I was Andrea N. Marr and I peeled the tape off my locker and looked down the hall and there was Cybil talking to Rebecca Farnhurst. Cybil had lots of hair now and she had a cool bead necklace and her shirt said "Butt Rock." And she looked taller and her face looked older and sort of strained. But then she saw me and she smiled this big smile and came running over. And she told me about Color Green, who played twice over the summer and their guitarist was named Luke and he was from California and the scene was getting really big and there were all these new people and I had to come to Outer Limits to their next show. And then Richard came over and his hair was long and he had a moustache, sort of, and all these straggly hairs coming out of his chin. And it was weird because I was dressed really normal for first day of school and I wasn't really thinking about Outer Limits. And then Cybil pushed Richard away and said, "You have to tell me everything about Brad." And it was weird because it seemed like she was trying to act really girlish and high school and it wasn't like her and it didn't really work.

At lunch me and Darcy and Cybil and Richard went to Taco Time and I told about Brad and I got the bullet out and Cybil and Richard passed it back and forth and they were quite fascinated by it. Then I told about the lake and when we rode into town on his motorcycle and everybody was totally amazed and impressed at how daring I was. And nobody said it but poor Darcy was still a virgin and when I showed her the bullet she hardly looked. All she cared about was Michael, who was the gay boy at Sunset Mall, and everybody said he was gay but Darcy wouldn't accept it because she was obsessed with him. And then Cybil was going on and on about Outer Limits and then Richard said, "Have you guys seen Greg?" We hadn't and he said Greg had dyed his hair and hadn't taken a shower all summer and they didn't know if he had even come to school or if Mrs. Katz would send him home or what.

But it wasn't Greg who had problems that first day. It was Cybil. During last period Mrs. Katz announced on the intercom that no clothing with obscene words or phrases would be allowed at Hillside. And when I got out of class Cybil wasn't at her locker and people were talking about how Mrs. Renault threw her out of French because of her "Butt Rock" T-shirt. One girl said it was Cybil's own fault for talking back. And everybody asked me but I didn't know anything and another girl said that Mrs. Renault was totally picking on Cybil and everybody saw it and they couldn't do anything because it was going against her rights. But people just scoffed and said this was high school and we didn't have any rights.

And then I went home and my mom was being weird and then she said we had to have a talk when Dad got home. I went to my room and tried to figure out what happened because I had gone to camp and done everything they told me. And then I thought they must have found out I had sex but how could they unless Brad called or got murdered or something? So I started making up this speech about how I used a condom and I was sixteen and that was the national average and everyone at Hillside had done it. But when my dad came home I was totally panicking and hiding in my room and then they called me down and we all went in the living room and my dad turned off the TV. The story was Mrs. Katz had called my mom as a "preventative measure" because my friend Cybil was disruptive and a discipline problem and wore obscene clothing. And Mrs. Katz had said how smart I was and how I wasn't living up to my potential and they were afraid I was getting in with the wrong people and they weren't trying to criticize me, they were just letting my parents know what the situation was. After my mom explained all this I was like, "That's it?" They said yes and I was so relieved I almost started laughing. But my parents were not amused. They were totally serious. They asked me if it was true about Cybil wearing obscene clothing. I said she wore a T-shirt that said "Butt Rock" on it. My mom looked into her lap and my dad looked at me with this pained expression and he said, "What exactly is *Butt Rock*?" And I said it was nothing and anyway it was just part of the feud between Cybil and Mrs. Renault. But my parents said Mrs. Katz wouldn't be calling them if it was nothing. And I said yes she would because that way she could scare people and cut off Cybil from her friends. But that upset my mom. She said I was showing bad faith and I was getting a bad attitude. And then my dad asked me if Darcy was into Butt Rock and I said no and I honestly tried to explain to them that Butt Rock wasn't anything, I had never heard of it before and Cybil probably just made it up. And anyway you could say "butt" on TV so who cares? And then I got mad and said how the real problem was Mrs. Renault and how she hated Cybil and everybody knew it but Mrs. Katz of course had to take the teachers' side. And then I tried to explain that Cybil was a free spirit and she didn't do drugs and she was in her band with Richard and how Richard was the smartest boy in our whole class and they just did their music and ate carrots, and if Mrs. Katz had a problem with them it was because she hated anything different and it was her own problem that she was so mean and such a bitch.

My mother told me never to say "bitch" in front of her again. I said I was sorry. Then we all sat there in silence. My poor parents. They didn't know I wasn't a virgin anymore or that I could smoke or anything really about my life. They looked so old and pathetic sitting there worrying about Butt Rock, I just felt sorry for them. And the truth was, they were too old to have a teenage daughter. They were already old when they had James and then they had a baby who died and I was an accident and all of this was just extra grief they hadn't planned on and didn't deserve.

So our meeting was over. Dad turned on the news and Mom went back in the kitchen and I went into James's room to look through his books because I needed *Sister Carrie* for English class. But then I found James's old Hillside yearbook and I looked at all the people from 1985 and the girls with their New Wave outfits and the boys with no sideburns and their hair sticking up. And I tried to guess which girls were virgins by looking at their faces but I couldn't really tell. And then I dug through some other stuff and I found a *Penthouse* magazine and I started looking at it and reading the letters in the front and they were totally about sex. I mean like every detail. So I immediately called Darcy and tried to read them to her but she was getting all weird and not wanting to talk. And it was like she thought I was making fun of her being a virgin but I wasn't at all, I just wanted to read her the stories but she acted offended and then we hung up.

13

THE NEXT DAY CYBIL WORE A BUTTON-DOWN shirt and preppie shorts and was obviously trying her hardest to avoid any more trouble. At lunch I went with her and Richard and Rebecca Farnhurst to Taco Time. And it was weird because Darcy didn't want to come and Cybil wasn't eating and Richard looked perturbed and Rebecca Farnhurst wouldn't shut up. Rebecca had seen Color Green at Outer Limits last summer and now she was the big expert on the downtown music scene. I ignored her and asked Cybil what happened at home. Cybil said Mrs. Katz called her mom and made this big deal out of it and her mom was pretty pissed. And she gave Cybil this talk about how you had to choose which things in life to take a stand against and that high school dress codes probably weren't the thing and French class wasn't either and that you had to save yourself for the real battles. And everybody knew that Cybil's mom was a big feminist and protested in the sixties and just by the way Cybil said it, it sounded pretty profound and Richard nodded and even Rebecca shut up for a second.

Back at school I noticed Darcy was talking to Wendy Simpson, who had also worked at Sunset Mall over the summer. I noticed they were both wearing Image stuff, which was supposedly so chic and downtown but was really just suburban. I mean, I liked Image stuff too but I wouldn't wear all Image from head to toe and I especially wouldn't wear those little caps like Wendy did because to me it was too cute and too obviously fashion magazine-ish, especially with lipstick to match. Not that I didn't like Wendy. She seemed okay and she had gone out with a cute freshman boy when she was a sophomore so people knew who she was. And when I saw Darcy by Wendy's locker I thought I'd go talk to them but as I was walking up Wendy looked at me over Darcy's shoulder, just the briefest glance and her eyes wouldn't acknowledge me at all, they looked right through me like I didn't even exist. And I was so stunned I hesitated and changed direction and pretended like I was going to the drinking fountain. And then Wendy slammed her locker shut and they hurried off down the hall really fast like they were afraid I would follow them.

And then the next day Cybil came running up to me in the hall and she was so excited. She and Richard were playing at Outer Limits on October 9 with Color Green, Pax, and a band called Bender from San Francisco. It was going to be their first show as Sins of Our Fathers and she was so excited and hanging on my arm and bouncing around. And I asked her if she knew what night October 9 was and she said Friday and I said yes but did she know what was *happening* that night and she didn't. Which showed how disconnected she was from Hillside because that was the night of Homecoming.

Homecoming was a big deal at Hillside. Obviously. Every year we played Camden, which was our big rival because they were the next suburb over. Freshman year I went with Darcy and afterward there was this huge traffic jam in the parking lot and everyone was screaming and honking and standing on top of cars. And I remembered how shocking it was and how the senior boys were like *men* with whiskers and deep voices and the senior girls were these beautiful sex goddesses in their tight jeans and sweaters. And then sophomore Homecoming was the beginning of my friendship with Cybil. She was still in her jock phase and playing soccer and no one really knew her except that she was friends with Marjorie, who smoked cigarettes. That year, after the game, we saw Cybil and Marjorie and it was the usual traffic jam and everyone was going to Julie Cavanaugh's. Marjorie went with Betsy Warren but Cybil didn't want to because Betsy was drunk. So Cybil rode with us and I sat in back with her and she started talking to me in this super direct way. Like talking about Marjorie and how damaged she was and if she would ever heal. And the weird thing was, she assumed I would understand and she asked me what I thought and I was like, *How would I know?* But I could tell she wasn't just putting Marjorie down, she was telling the truth. And I remembered looking over at her in the dark car, the girls in the front singing to the radio, the boys in the other cars hanging out the windows and Cybil was so quiet and watching everyone and smiling at me and then she told me she loved my name, "Andrea Marr," and how she wished she wasn't Cybil.

And it was so weird because at that time Cybil gave me the creeps a little bit. Like I liked her but I didn't want to get too close because she seemed too weird and why was she friends with Marjorie? And also I didn't like the way she would talk about people, just saying exactly what she thought and naturally you wondered what she would say about you. But now, a year later, it was the reverse. Now I liked her and she was the one who kept me at a distance. And it was so weird because I always thought I would go to all the Homecomings because it was the one big event that everyone went to all four years. And now Cybil's band was playing and of course I would go to Outer Limits but it sort of stung me somehow, like something was slowly going wrong with my life and I couldn't stop it. Like maybe Mrs. Katz was right, maybe I was going astray and getting in with the wrong people.

Then Rebecca Farnhurst called me. She wanted to go see Sins of Our Fathers and I asked her why she wasn't going to Homecoming and she said it was stupid and she was getting into culture now like reading and seeing bands, and football was so violent and immature and did she think we'd miss any parties? I didn't know. But she didn't care about Homecoming parties anyway because they were just a bunch of drunken idiots, and Outer Limits was so much more interesting because there were people from every high school and older people and cute boys and everyone was creative and she loved the bands and how everybody supported each other and had I ever seen Color Green? She knew I hadn't. So she explained how Color Green was her ideal of what boys should be because they weren't macho but they also weren't acting gay, not that she didn't like gay guys but she didn't like how everyone was acting gay now just to be cool. I was like, "Everyone is acting gay?" But she meant guys *downtown* because of course Hillside was so stupid and sexist unlike the guys in Color Green, who were really powerful in their music and not oppressing women and against pollution and censorship. And then she said how she was totally behind Cybil's right to free speech about Butt Rock, and how Mrs. Renault used to hassle *her* when she took French and what language was I taking? Spanish. And that Luke of Color Green was probably the coolest boy she had ever seen and had I met any of them? I had met Todd Sparrow. Oh I did? Well he was definitely extremely cool too and he was smarter than Luke and they met in California and had I heard that story? I hadn't. So she told it to me and a couple other stories in case I hadn't heard them and the end of the conversation was that she wanted me to come to Outer Limits with her, she'd pick me up. And it was weird how she said it, like she didn't hint or ask me how I was getting there or any of the normal ways you would suggest it. And it sort of bugged me and I said no, I was going with Darcy and she said, "Darcy's not going." I said, "How do you know?" She said, "I just do. She's friends with Wendy Simpson now and Wendy would never go to Outer Limits." And I said, "Oh, really?" And then she was suddenly quiet, like she felt sorry for me and that just made me more mad and I told her I wasn't sure how I was getting there and I hung up.

And then Greg showed up at school one day with his hair dyed green. The only problem was it was so short it didn't really look like anything. And he was taking showers now and dressing pretty normal and his green hair was like when he shaved his head, it just gave part of a message, it didn't make a whole statement like when Cybil did things. And I decided it was because he had conflicts in his heart. He didn't know if he wanted to be grunge or alternative or just be weird or be a clown and I guess he didn't know what he wanted to say.

And Marjorie was around and seemed a little more visible than last year. Mostly because she was hanging around with Betsy Warren, who did bong hits in her car every morning and who was into punk and heavy metal and wore these really trashy black jeans where you could see her underwear and her butt cheeks. And Betsy had these huge speakers in her car and some days after school there would be stereo wars in the parking lot and she'd put in her punk tapes and blow everyone away. And Marjorie was adjusting her look to be like Betsy and they would drink quarts of Old English 800 at lunch. And it was weird because Betsy could pull it off but when Marjorie got drunk she'd slur her words and stumble around in the halls and everyone said how amazing it was she never got caught.

And Renee Hatfield and Scott Haskell were now the Queen and Prince of the senior party crowd. And Scott Haskell started going out with this sophomore girl named Asia, who was this rich girl from Weston Heights. Asia was really noticeable because she dressed really hippie and had this bizarre accent and she was from New Jersey. Actually, when I first figured out who she was I wondered if I should tell her what a creep Scott was but then I saw her at lunch one day and she had this little entourage of sophomores following her around and she seemed really pretentious and I thought if I tried to say something she might just snub me so I didn't.

And of course Darcy was still avoiding me and she was friends with Wendy Simpson now and it looked like I was out. They were going downtown to dance at Monte Carlo and apparently that was the new thing and all the Hillside and Camden people were going there now. Especially the Weston Heights crowd. And it made me think that Outer Limits was second-best compared to Monte Carlo and all this time I thought I was so cool and daring to be going there but Monte Carlo was where the truly cool people went and the beautiful people and Outer Limits was more for misfits and so far my junior year was not going well.

And to add to my social problems all these weird guys started getting crushes on me. Bob Zeigler invited me to the Homecoming dance and practically begged me to go. I said I wasn't going for political reasons since that's what Rebecca Farnhurst was telling people. John Maruyama kept asking me to movies but I said they gave me a headache which was what

Cybil always said. And then weird Earl, who was into philosophy and never washed his hair, started leaving me notes and squishing flowers through the slits in my locker. And the worst part was that even when normal guys talked to me I would never be nice to them. I don't know why. And the whole thing was so frustrating because it's like, you're sixteen and as cute as you'll ever be and you're in this school full of boys and it's really yourself that stops you. It was like Greg dying his hair, I didn't know what I wanted to do or what kind of people I wanted to be with. And one thing I was already noticing: senior girls were in a terrible position. No one was good enough for them and they had known the senior boys for so long they were sick of them. And there were no older guys. And the younger guys were stupid. And some of them, like Renee Hatfield, seemed so adult and mature they were totally out of place and I realized there were two directions in social life and not only could you go too far down, you could also go too far up.

14 HOMECOMING CAME CREEPING UP. THE RALLY girls were hard at work making signs and blowing up balloons and stretching crepe paper everywhere. And I remembered how freshman year the whole thing had seemed so impressive but now it seemed sad and sort of pathetic. And my freshman year I couldn't imagine what brilliant sophisticated girls invented these wonderful

slogans and this year I saw two cheerleaders at a lunch table, bored, with paint brushes in their hands, staring off into space while GO HILLSIDE dried on a huge sheet of construction paper. And it was weird for me because all week was this big count-down and it was for me too but not for Homecoming. And in a way I was much more nervous about going to Outer Limits than I would have been about the football game. That would have been easy. Outer Limits might be really hard. And that alone made me think I was doing the right thing. At least I was pushing myself.

Then I heard Renee Hatfield was having a party on Homecoming night and it seemed like a safe thing to talk to Darcy about so the next time I saw her I asked her if she and Wendy were going. But she got this attitude and pretended like she didn't know. So then I said I was going to Outer Limits any-way and I wasn't inviting myself. And she was like, "I didn't say you were." And then I told her I didn't care if she was friends with Wendy Simpson but she didn't have to act so weird about it and avoid me all the time. And then she told me all this crap about how she wasn't avoiding me, she was just chasing this boy that Wendy knew from Bradley Day School. It was such an obvi-ous lie. I said, "You don't have to pretend about some boy." And I sounded really snotty all of a sudden and I didn't mean to. And then she said she wasn't pretending at all, his name was Peter and at least he wasn't some redneck boy from Canada who gave girls *bullets*. And I said, "Well at least Brad likes *girls*. At least I'm not a *vir*—" But then I stopped. And we both looked away and I guess we were shocked that we hated each other so much. And then she saw Gary Tisdale and went running after him and I just stood there and it was so awful.

At lunch Rebecca Farnhurst came to my locker. She looked at my face and said, "What's wrong?" I wouldn't say and she said we'd go to Taco Time and she'd get Cybil and I said, "No, do *not* get Cybil." So the two of us went and I talked about Brad and how I tried to love him but I was too mean in my heart and now he was gone forever. She said, "You talked to Darcy, didn't you?" I said I had no problem with Darcy and if she wanted to be friends with Wendy that was fine with me. Rebecca said Darcy was stupid. She said Gary Tisdale was pretentious and Wendy hated men unless they were gay or younger than her and how lame that was. And then she said how lame Image was and she told me all the cool stuff girls wore at Outer Limits over the summer, like long T-shirts with boxer shorts underneath or this one girl who wrapped flannel shirts around her head like a turban. And she told me what the Metro Mall girls were wearing and stuff she had seen in British magazines and then she really got going about how in England they had this whole new scene of rave parties and smart drugs and bell-bottoms and girls wearing the ugliest floppiest clothes they could find and it was a whole movement and did I know what they were rebelling against? I didn't. Girls like *Wendy Simpson* and that whole super-clean, super-uptight, mall-bitch look with all Image clothes and if one thread was hanging down they had to throw it away. And I had to cheer up then because if I didn't start talking Rebecca would yak at me for hours.

And then Friday came, the big day, and Cybil and Richard made a rare appearance in the cafeteria and I sat with them while they planned their afternoon. First they had to take the bus to Greg's stepmom's house to get his station wagon and then they had to go back to Greg's and then over to Richard's to get the drums and then they had to borrow some extension cords and at some point Cybil had to go to Captain Whizzy's to get a microphone because the one at Outer Limits smelled like beer and puke and was full of germs. It sounded pretty complicated and I knew I couldn't go with them and when Rebecca Farnhurst came over I told her I needed a ride. She was so glad. She wanted to plan our outfits and she told me what dress she was wearing and what coat and what shoes. And she wanted to know what I was going to wear and I said I had a dress with cows on it. And everybody thought that was cool and Richard asked me why I never wore it to school and I just shrugged and Rebecca wanted to know what color the cows were.

Rebecca came to pick me up. She was wearing a cool fifties dress and a raincoat and I had my cow dress and my gray cardigan and my mom said we looked like a couple of grannies. And Rebecca immediately started yakking to my mom about HOP! and how vintage clothes were cheaper and made of better materials and better cut and they were more modest and respectful of a girl's sexuality. My mom just stared at her. And Rebecca was talking so fast my mom couldn't answer and she even let me say "around one o'clock" for coming-home time. And then my mom asked Rebecca why we weren't going to Homecoming and Rebecca launched into this thing about how a person should have different experiences and try to meet all kinds of people and not just do the obvious things all the time and . . . I grabbed her and pulled her out the door.

But outside, the whole neighborhood smelled like Homecoming. And I remembered other Homecomings and seeing the stadium lights from the parking lot and hearing the people cheer and running in to see what happened. And I thought of the green grass and everybody wearing sweaters and that smoky October smell and everybody talking about parties and which boys were cute. And now, getting into Rebecca's car, I looked in the direction of Hillside and I could feel the pull of Homecoming. And when we turned on to Shelby Road it seemed like every passing car was people going to the game or parents taking their kids or maybe old people who went to Hillside when they were kids. And at the light we stopped and there was a man raking leaves in his yard and he had the radio on and I couldn't really hear it but I imagined it was the game and that everywhere in the world people were sitting outside and listening to Homecoming and watching the distant stadium lights and hearing the people cheer whenever something good happened.

We drove. When we got downtown we cruised by Outer Limits and there were so many people outside on the street Rebecca had to slow down and wait for them to move. And these boys were guzzling a quart of beer and everyone was smoking cigarettes and acting really cool and tough. But then on the next block we saw Greg's station wagon which made me feel better. We parked beside it. And I didn't have any makeup on and Rebecca had a little mascara and she looked at herself in the rearview mirror and asked me if we should put on lipstick and I said, "I guess we better." So she put some on and I put some on and then some eye pencil. And then she asked me if I ever smoked and I said I knew how and she said good and got some cigarettes from under the seat. And we got out and ran across the street and then we smoothed our dresses and turned the corner and walked into the crowd.

The first person I saw was the rust-haired girl who was with Todd Sparrow last spring. She was standing against the wall and she had Jackie O sunglasses and a super short bob and she was smoking and talking to a black girl who had huge dreadlocks. And me and Rebecca tried to get by and the girl with the dreadlocks turned and she was so beautiful I just about died. "Holy *shit*," said Rebecca, "did you see that girl?" And I nodded and we sort of stumbled forward, passing the guys we saw guzzling the beer and they said hi to us but we ignored them. And across the street there were some skinheads and their Nazi girlfriends, who looked like they were from a lower-class mall in Idaho or someplace. And Rebecca stopped and I walked right into her and we were both sort of freaking out. And she whispered to me if I wanted a cigarette but I didn't and just then a breeze blew down the street and it smelled like rain and smoke and I thought I could be at Homecoming and at Renee Hatfield's party with all the Hillside people, dancing and meeting cute boys and maybe getting a boyfriend but I was here and it was dark and the people were scary and weird and way too cool.

Rebecca decided we should go in and we didn't have to pay because Cybil had put us on the guest list so at least for a few seconds we felt like we belonged. Over the summer they had changed the inside of Outer Limits. It was bigger and there was a real stage now and big speakers and the walls were painted psychedelic and there were all these dolls stuck on the ceilings and stuff hanging down and flowers and toys and old seventies posters like Shaft and Farrah Fawcett along the walls. There weren't too many people inside yet but Cybil and Greg were setting up his drums and Rebecca and I sat on the stage and I saw an amp with COLOR GREEN painted on the side. And then this weird guy came up and asked Rebecca if she had a cigarette and she gave him one. He lit it and said he was the drummer of Bender and they were from San Francisco and he'd never been to Portland before and what was it like? Well he sure asked the right person! Rebecca yakked at him for about an hour and he must have thought she liked him because he asked if he could stay with us. And Rebecca was like, "No way! We live with our parents! We're only sixteen!" And the guy was like "oh" and he wandered off.

But then Sins of Our Fathers played and they were so great! When they started no one was inside but people started coming in right away. Me and Rebecca were in front and I kept watching Cybil and looking back at the crowd and people were really liking it. And Cybil was so good and Richard and Greg too and they sounded like a real group and even their old songs were a hundred times better than before. And they had great new songs that you could dance to right away like this one called "Oblivion" which was about a girl who runs away and travels all around. And it was so wild because every girl at Outer Limits was swaying with the music and traveling away to the sound of Cybil's voice. And I looked at Rebecca and she just shook her head and said, "Cybil is the coolest girl on the face of the earth."

15 AFTER THAT PAX PLAYED AND THEN IT WAS COLOR Green's turn. And even though Bender was supposed to be the headliner it seemed like everyone wanted to see Color Green. And it was getting really packed and people were pushing and me and Rebecca tried to hold our place and not get pushed away by these dumb boys in flannel shirts who kept shoving each other. And it was so obvious that

Color Green was such a big deal and I was already resenting them because I thought Cybil was the best. And when they came onstage they strutted around and acted so cool. And people yelled at Todd and he ignored everyone and they were such rock stars. And then they played and it was really loud and violent and the flannel boys started slamming and elbowing everyone and knocking into us and we had to move away because they were being such jerks.

We went over to the side and watched from there. Then Cybil came over to us and said we could come into the dressing room if we wanted. So we did and it was this little room with graffiti everywhere and Richard and Greg were sitting on a bench drinking juice and eating rice cakes. And I told them how much I loved "Oblivion" and their old songs too and how dumb Color Green was but Cybil said Color Green was good, it was just more grunge influenced and we should give it a chance. And then some other guys came in and they smoked pot and Cybil waved the smoke away and when they left I smelled my dress to see if the smell got on me.

When Color Green got done they came in and they were all sweaty. We scooted down the bench to give them room but they were just waiting for their encore. And I watched Todd and he asked if anyone had pot and then Cybil gave him some of her juice. And then they went back out and everyone cheered and screamed and it wasn't that much different than a football game, boys smashing each other and getting all the glory, except that the audience was crazier and on more drugs.

After their encore they came back and Cybil told us we should leave but Todd told us to stay and the one named Luke drank the rest of Cybil's juice and he was a very dangerous-looking boy. He had tattoos and long hair and this sort of greasy stoner look in his eyes. And they all flopped on the bench and Todd took off his shirt and he had gross little hairs coming out of his nipples. And he talked to Cybil and she was being so polite and respectful and it made me mad because her band was as good as his.

Then the guys from Bender came in and it got too crowded so we went outside and sat on the curb. And after a while Todd and Luke came out and sat there too, a little down from us and of course they were talking to the rust-haired girl and her beautiful dreadlocked friend and they were the coolest girls there and they knew it. And then this guy came up to me and it was Kevin! Kevin who drove me home the night Mark Pierce cut his head! Wow! He said he saw us going into the dressing room and were we rock stars now? I was so happy to see him, I gave him a big hug. And he had a friend, Doug, who was visiting from college and he was cute and he had a bottle of Jack Daniel's and he offered it around. I took a little and Rebecca took some and she immediately started flirting with him. Then Todd Sparrow came over and made everyone nervous because he was such a *star*. But then Doug offered him the bottle and he took a sip and handed it to Luke and when Luke saw what it was he said, "All right!" and everybody laughed. And then the rust-haired girl came over but she didn't talk and she didn't want any Jack Daniel's. She just stood behind Todd and stared at Cybil and she was extremely weird.

Then Bender played. They were really loud and noisy and everybody was outside anyway and it was such a *scene*, like a party, except it was on the street and no high school idiots and everyone was so cool. Rebecca got out her cigarettes and I decided to smoke one except I was out of practice and I coughed and it was embarrassing. And then Todd reached over and grabbed it out of my mouth and at first I just stared at him but then I was like, "Give it back!" He said he'd show me how, and I tried to grab it and he said I was too young to smoke and I chased him across the street and everybody laughed. So I went back to the curb and sat with Rebecca and she gave me another one and I lit it but I didn't really smoke it because I didn't want to start coughing in front of everyone. And then Todd tried to sit down between me and Rebecca and we wouldn't let him and he said we were lesbians. Then he looked really hard at me and said, "Didn't I see you outside the library one time?" I said, "*No!*" And I got another sip of Jack Daniel's and Luke talked to the rust-haired girl and I asked Todd who she was and he said her name was Carla and did I want to meet her? I said no and Todd asked me if I liked girls and I tried to kick him and my cigarette fell in my lap and almost burned my cow dress.

Then we got in cars to go to a party. It was some people Todd knew and we didn't know if we were invited but Todd said we were. Rebecca tried to get Kevin and Doug in our car but they had their own car so we ended up with Mike, who was the drummer of Color Green. Mike had a quart of beer in a paper bag that was all wet and Rebecca kept telling him not to spill any because she'd get in big trouble. So then we followed Greg, who was following Todd, and we were like a caravan and I looked at my watch and it was already quarter to twelve, I only had an hour. We got to the party and went inside and boy was I glad I had on lipstick because the people were totally weird and underground. Everyone stared at us and Todd led us into the backyard which was a relief. Rebecca and I sat on the steps and Todd sat with us and Kevin and Doug wanted to sit too but there wasn't room so they just stood there and they couldn't talk because Todd was talking. Rebecca gave Todd a cigarette and he demonstrated all the ways to hold it like: "The Intellectual," "The Bitch," "The Bohemian," and I kept laughing even though I didn't want to encourage him. And then I looked up and Cybil was watching all this and Richard too and they weren't talking to anyone or having fun and suddenly I felt like I was being this idiot party girl.

Rebecca and I left at quarter to one and we zoomed through town and then out Highway 27 and onto Shelby Road and at the big intersection there was a car across from us full of people and a boy was hanging out the window yelling "Hillside rules!" So I guess we beat Camden at football. And we raced home and I sniffed myself for cigarette smoke and jammed pieces of gum in my mouth and we got to my house at ten after and I ran in and my dad was asleep in front of the TV. Thank God. I went upstairs and stripped out of my clothes and jumped in bed but I was way too excited to sleep. So I put on Girl Patrol and laid there thinking about Kevin and Doug and mysterious Carla and the black girl with dreadlocks and the stupid flannel boys and scary Luke and the Bender guy from San Francisco and all the weird people at the party and most of all, even though I was trying not to, I kept thinking about Todd Sparrow and the cigarettes and remembering how he touched my hand when he showed me how to hold it.

On Saturday I went downtown with Rebecca and we went to Scamp's and we were hoping we might see someone from Outer Limits but it was all normal people downtown, like no cool people would even go there on Saturday. And we wondered if Kevin and Doug would call and Rebecca said that the real question was Todd Sparrow and I was like what do you mean? She said he totally liked me and I was like, "No way!" And she said *yes* and I told her she was crazy. But then she got really quiet and she was scraping the last of her yogurt out of her cup and not looking at me and I wondered if it could be true.

And then on Sunday Kevin called and his friend Doug was going back to Oregon State and did we want to hang out and see him off? We did and it was fun because we had cappuccinos at Metro Mall and then walked around by the bus station and

Rebecca kept tagging along beside Doug and asking him questions and totally putting the moves on him. And then when his bus came she gave him this big kiss and Kevin looked at me and I knew he wanted to kiss me too but he was afraid so nothing happened.

But then the next day he called me and invited me to a movie and afterward he kissed me right away and then we made out for an hour. We went out a couple more times and then on Halloween we went to a party of Learning Center people and everyone was on drugs except us. And that night we tried to have sex in his car but it was difficult and it was over before it really began. And afterward Kevin was getting all weird about Cybil and the Outer Limits scene and he said he thought it was okay to screw around like that when you were in high school but a real artist had to be more serious and I said that Cybil to me was the most real artist that could ever be since she spoke straight from her soul. And he said that music wasn't really art and we argued about it and I guess he felt bad because he couldn't have sex very long.

And then I had to do this horrible history report and my parents started letting me have the car to go to the downtown library. And I bought a pack of cigarettes to have an excuse to stand outside and I always watched for Todd Sparrow but it was November and cold and raining every day so I couldn't stay out there very long. And when the library closed I'd go to Scamp's and eat frozen yogurt. And I'd sit by the window and watch people and wonder where Todd might be. And it was so weird because with Brad I wanted so badly to love him but I couldn't and with Todd I *didn't* want to love him but it was happening anyway and there was nothing I could do to stop it.

16 AT CHRISTMAS MY BROTHER, JAMES, brought his wife, Emily, to visit. I came home from school and everyone was sitting around the kitchen table and Emily was totally pregnant and she looked like she had a beach ball under her dress. And I always liked seeing James but Emily bugged me and whenever they visited everything started to smell like her. And the way they gushed over her pregnancy was so disgusting. And she kept smiling at me like we were *sisters* and sometimes she'd make fun of James or call him "Jaimie," and want me to go along with it and I was just like, excuse me, James is my brother, *who are you*? And no one said it but they all looked at her belly and then at my belly and I was just like, *don't even think about it.*

Then on the last school day before vacation it went around that this anorexic freshman girl had tried to kill herself and was in the hospital and everyone was freaking out. Mrs. Schroeder, who did suicide awareness, was making all her health classes write in this huge card. But no one wanted to because they didn't know what to write and if they wrote something and they weren't really friends with her wouldn't it seem fake? And wouldn't that just remind her that she didn't really have any friends and wouldn't that make it worse? Mrs. Schroeder didn't seem to understand this and she told everyone how horrible they were and then she sent a bunch of people to Mrs. Katz's office. Everyone was whispering about it and me and Cybil walked by her classroom on the way to lunch and Mrs. Schroeder was practically crying and Mrs. Katz was yelling at people and it was just a mess.

Then I went Christmas shopping for my brother. I wanted to go to Sunset Mall but Darcy and Wendy were both working there over Christmas and I was dressed really stupid and I didn't want them to see me. So I went to the Sherwood Oaks Mall but they didn't have anything good so I went downtown. And after all the times I'd gotten dressed up to go to the library or Metro Mall or even just to drive by Outer Limits, here I was in my boringest pair of jeans and my prissy Keds and this dumb sweatshirt and I was rushing through Kruger's and who was standing there but Todd Sparrow and Carla. Of course Carla looked stunning and Todd had a cool leather trench coat and I tried to sneak past but he *grabbed* my arm and I just about died of embarrassment. And then he asked me how come me and Cybil didn't come see Color Green at a Christmas benefit thing because he thought we'd be there and he looked for us. I hadn't even heard about it and I was getting all nervous and apologizing and explaining why I was dressed so stupid. And Todd was like, "It's all right,

Andrea. Everything is all right." So I calmed down and I told them I was looking for something for my brother and I described James and Todd said, "What kind of music does he like?" I didn't really know and Carla said she got her brother a special pipe from Turkey to smoke pot in and I just stared at her. And then they invited me upstairs to the coffee shop and it was so weird because all these yuppies and suburban types were jammed in there and getting all frantic with the Christmas rush but Todd and Carla were so calm and mellowing everyone out with their cool style. We sat in the smoking section and Carla smoked her cigarette exactly like "The Bitch" that Todd had described but I was so surprised because she was actually very nice and sort of odd. Like we were talking about Todd's benefit show and she seemed like she was listening but then she said, "How about *Love Signs*? Is your brother into astrology?" And she kept shrugging, even when she didn't mean to, like a nervous tick. And you could tell she wasn't just *trying* to be weird. And you could also tell how Todd looked out for her and how they must hang around together all the time.

But then the manager came over and you were only allowed fifteen minutes and he kicked us out. So we went back down the escalator and then they left and Carla waved to me and I couldn't believe how all this time I thought she was a bitch. And then I looked down at my stupid outfit and it was so embarrassing but they didn't even care! And it just proved how suburban I was and how image-conscious and shallow and how cool they were to not laugh at me. And then I went to Poor Boy Records and I felt totally energized and so cool because I had just had coffee with Todd and Carla and I was looking at posters and smiling at everyone and just having the best time!

On Christmas Eve Rebecca came over during the day and we baked cookies with my mom and Emily while James and my dad watched football on TV. Rebecca did most of the talking and Emily argued with us about feminism and said we were "young women" and not "girls" and I was like, *I'll just stay a girl as long as I can, thank you very much.* But I didn't say it. And then James came over and snuck cookie batter with his fingers and Emily whacked him with her spoon like he was a dog. And then she smiled at us like, *See how you train them?* But I was like, *Someone should train you!*

After that I walked Rebecca to her car and we had a long talk in my driveway. I told her about seeing Todd and Carla and I asked her if we could ever transcend our suburban upbringing and be as worldly as they were. She said of course we could and she gave me this little pep talk about how our lives were just beginning. Then we discussed what a creep Emily was and what was James thinking marrying her? Rebecca said she'd love to meet an older man and we talked about sex and how Hillside guys were too boring but Outer Limits guys were too scary. And then she gave me a big hug and said Merry Christmas and she said how glad she was that we were best friends now and I said, "Me too."

That night James got totally drunk and almost fell over the coffee table and my parents pretended not to notice. And then Emily was whining to my mom about her hard life and I swear, just the sound of her voice gave me a headache. And then Kevin called and wished me Merry Christmas and told me Doug was home for Christmas and would me and Rebecca like to do something? I said, "I guess." He said, "You guess?" And then we had a fight because he didn't think I wanted to but of course I did, I was just thinking about other things.

Christmas itself was pretty boring. I got some black jeans, which I needed, and a hundred-dollar gift certificate at Image since my parents didn't realize I had transcended it. James gave me some woolly socks to go with my new granny look which was becoming a family joke. Emily gave me some black leather gloves that looked pretty expensive and I didn't know what to say since I hadn't got her anything. And afterward we ate and James watched football and fell asleep. And Dad read the paper and Mom and Emily made a turkey and I called Rebecca and asked her what she got. And then we talked about our double date with Kevin and Doug and what if Doug had a girlfriend at college and wanted Rebecca to be his out-of-town *mistress*? And then we talked about college and how everyone must have constant sex. And then we wondered if you could have sex when you were pregnant and why was Emily so obnoxious and would we be like that if we got pregnant, which of course we never would.

Later that week we went out with Kevin and Doug. Doug's parents were in Costa Rica so we went to his house. It was in the woods and pretty fancy and they had MTV and this huge living room with a loft and stuff. But there was something sort of cold about it. Like you could turn on these floodlights in the backyard but all that was back there was some scraggly trees and a lot of mud. Doug paid a lot of attention to Rebecca and made us drinks and was very suave and college-ish. And we watched MTV and HBO and part of a sex video. Then we took a hot tub except of course we didn't bring our swimsuits and we had to go naked. So we made the boys wait outside and we got in first and they came in wearing towels and I didn't look at their penises but I think Rebecca did. And then we all sat there and it was really quiet in the house and just the gurgling sound of the bubbles and I smiled at Kevin a lot but nobody really talked.

We had sex of course. That was the whole point of the night. Me and Kevin went in Doug's parents' room and I was so horny for some reason and he went pretty long and then after that I put it in my mouth and tried to get it going again because that's what Rebecca told me but it didn't work. So we just laid there and listened to the rain on the windows. And then it got hard again and I put a condom on it and put it in my mouth just to see what it was like but the condom was all slimy from lubricant and it was gross. Then we did it again and did positions and I got on top of him and he made little whimpering noises. Afterward I got one of Rebecca's cigarettes and sat in the bed naked and did "The Bitch." And then I made one up myself, "After Sex," and I thought about Todd and if I would ever see him again and Kevin was telling me I shouldn't start smoking but I wasn't even listening.

But then driving home Rebecca was totally freaking out because Doug put it inside her before he put the rubber on and even though it was just for a second they told us in health class that a little bit of sperm comes out at the beginning and did I think she'd get pregnant? I didn't know. She also said that Doug was really fast and didn't give her any foreplay and maybe it was date rape. But since she wanted to she guessed it wasn't. And all the way home it rained and Rebecca worried about getting pregnant and I kept sniffing myself and wondering if I smelled like sex or cigarettes.

Back at school everyone talked about what they got for Christmas. Julie Cavanaugh got a car and Darcy got a new Gap dress and I heard these two sophomore girls talking about a big Christmas party at Renee Hatfield's. And Cybil had dyed her hair blond but if you tried to talk to her about it she was like, "So I dyed my hair, big deal." But she did want to hear my story of meeting Todd Sparrow and Carla at Kruger's. And she said, "See? You don't think you're that cool but Todd Sparrow knows you are." So then we talked about how only people who are totally secure in their own coolness can afford to acknowledge it in others. But what about Carla? We talked about her too and Cybil said she was an enigma because she looked so aloof but when you talked to her it was like she was mentally retarded. And I said how she always shrugged and it was like a nervous tick. And Cybil said she seemed pretty intense and I said how nice she was and how she thought up present ideas for my brother. And then we both reflected on how interesting their lives must be and how we were stuck at boring Hillside.

And then the next day all these rumors went around about the anorexic girl who tried to kill herself. It turned out she died over vacation because after she went home from the hospital she wasn't eating and then she went into the woods along Cutter's Ridge and got lost and they found her and she'd fainted from starvation and she was all wet from the rain and she just died. And it was so weird because they announced it at lunch and the whole cafeteria went silent and everyone looked out the windows at the rain falling down.

17 AND THEN ONE DAY AT SCHOOL CYBIL WAS IN study hall and I snuck in and sat behind her and just sort of watched her and it was so weird because even though she was now this cool singer in a band there was still something in her shoulders and neck that reminded you of what she really was. A jock. Everybody forgot about that when she shaved her head and started doing her music. But she

was. The first time I ever saw her was playing soccer in gym class freshman year. This girl Megan Carter was the goalie and I was on defense and Cybil would dribble past us and kick it in from anywhere she wanted. And Megan would scream at us to stop her but no one could. And I remembered how confident Cybil seemed and how graceful she was in everything she did. And it was weird because jocks and cool people were supposed to be on opposite sides but if you watched Todd Sparrow walk down the street or go onstage or do anything he had that same gracefulness. And just like Cybil seemed in slow motion when she was creaming us at soccer, Todd had this perfect relaxedness in his shoulders. Like he could catch anything you threw at him from any direction. Now that I thought about it, Wendy Simpson was in that gym class. She never did anything though. And all the girls hated it because it was first period and they would be all dressed up for school and then they'd have to get all sweaty and take gross gym showers. And they always made us play soccer on the softball field so we wouldn't mess up the precious Football Practice Field. The softball field was at the very edge of the school grounds and every time the ball went out of bounds it rolled down the bank and into the woods and there we'd be, these sleepyhead freshmen girls stepping through the dewy grass looking for the soccer ball. And the sun would be coming up and the birds would be chirping and sometimes we'd just give up and sit on the bank until Mrs. Parmeter would come yell at us. And I remembered one time looking up the bank and Cybil was standing on top of the hill picking dirt out of her shoes and watching the other girls look for the ball she had kicked so hard and so far into the woods.

In the next couple weeks I pretty much went for the "Granny look" as my mother called it. Me and Rebecca were about the same size and we pooled our stuff and Rebecca had her eye prescription put in some vintage horn-rimmed frames, which looked so great that I asked my mom if I could have glasses but she said no. And we went to HOP! every day for a week and we made a pact that we would never wear Image clothes and we traded all our Image stuff in at HOP! because if all you had was cool clothes then you would have to dress cool everyday whether you felt like it or not. And then Kevin started taking us to Monte Carlo and trying to fix Rebecca up with different boys. One night we were there and we saw Darcy and Wendy and they were actually nice to me and I talked to Darcy for a while and she'd finally done it with this boy Troy Lonsdale who went to Bradley Day School. She said how it really wasn't that big of a deal, was it? I said, "I guess not," and we talked about boys and stuff but not too much and I was relieved to get away from her.

And then one day this strange-looking boy came over to Rebecca and me at lunch and he said he was a sophomore transfer student and could he sit with us? We sort of shrugged and he sat down and he had a Cyanide T-shirt and long hair and a silver stud in his nose. He said he was from Seattle and he asked us about the local scene, I guess because we looked more into it

111

than anybody else in the cafeteria. So we told him about Outer Limits and Sins of Our Fathers and described Cybil to him. And he kept asking us stuff so we told him about hanging out with Color Green and he totally did not believe it and he scoffed and said, "Like Todd Sparrow, like *that* Color Green?" We acted very offended and said, "Yes, *that* Color Green." And he was totally impressed and he said Color Green was practically his favorite band. And he apologized and said he thought by how we were dressed we would be more into folk-pop or English stuff and that Color Green was more influenced by eighties Hardcore groups like Cyanide and Hammerheads or industrial stuff like Mirage or Positive Space. We didn't know those bands so we said we weren't into labeling people or putting them in categories and we liked Color Green because they were our friends and they took us to cool parties. And he was like, "They take you to parties?" and he still didn't quite believe it but he said, "Okay. Sure. Cool."

His name was Matthew Frohnmeyer and the next day he sat with us again. He told us he played guitar in a band called Seed Machine in Seattle but they weren't for real and he'd like to get in a real band here in Portland and what should he do? We said go to Outer Limits or talk to Cybil. He did. And then Cybil called me that night and asked me about him because he just walked right up to her and asked if he could be in their band. And Richard was already thinking they needed a bass player and he wanted to try him out. But Cybil was nervous because then it would be three boy musicians with a girl lead singer which was the worst kind of band and made you feel like a stripper or something.

And then I called Rebecca and she had just got off the phone with Matthew and he had asked her out! And the reason he gave was because he liked her glasses! I told her that he was already trying to get into Cybil's band and did she think he was cute and what about the stud in his nose because the only other Hillside person who had a nose ring was skanky Betsy Warren and Rebecca said that Marjorie had one too and it was just so small you didn't see it and that she had seen a freshman girl with one and lots of people at Monte Carlo had them. So then we had a long discussion about nose rings and if they left a scar and how could you blow your nose? And then we talked some more about Matthew and how bold he was and if he was cute or not and we couldn't really decide but it was clear he was not going to be just another Hillside student.

Rebecca did not go out with Matthew right away because she thought she should make him wait. But then she saw him talking to Wendy Simpson and everybody knew she went for younger guys. So she invited him to a movie and she was nervous and nothing much happened except they talked a lot and mostly about music and Matthew kept saying what a great guitar player he was. And the next day Cybil came with us to Taco Time to discuss Matthew Frohnmeyer and what his deal was and we all agreed he had a big ego because he came from Seattle which had the hugest scene and about a million famous bands. And Cybil said Richard talked to him on the phone and they were going to set up a practice to see if he could play bass. And then Cybil said one of *us* should learn to play bass, that Richard could teach us and it was easy. But Rebecca flunked piano lessons and I got stage fright so bad I couldn't even sing in the choir. And Cybil frowned and swirled her ice around in her cup and you could tell she thought we were chicken.

And even though I had lots of cool clothes now, my cow dress was still my favorite and I was always fixing it because it was falling apart. And all these years my mom had tried to teach me about sewing and I would never learn but now I was always asking her stuff and I was getting to be an expert. And I always wore it downtown and the people at the library probably thought it was the only thing I owned. I was going there a lot now because I was getting my parents' car all the time and the reason for that was I had finally found the ultimate parental bargaining chip: college.

My parents had never really thought about where I'd go to college but then our college counselor, Mr. Perry, called them and with my grades and my PSATs he said I could go to a good college. And it was weird because James went to University of Oregon and everyone assumed I would too. But people at school were talking about going back east or to California and Mr. Perry was doing these little presentations about different colleges and it sounded sort of fun. But then Mitzi Berkowitz's parents came in and yelled at Mr. Perry because stupid Mitzi *had* to get into Stanford and there was this big controversy because more people at Camden went to good colleges and they were our big rivals. And that started a rumor that Mr. Perry would get fired if he didn't get people into the Ivy Leagues. And then Cynthia Carmichael wrote an editorial in *Hillsider* about how cool Mr. Perry was and would students please keep their parents on a leash when visiting the college counselor, which was a total face on Mitzi Berkowitz and almost got Cynthia Carmichael kicked off the paper.

But the main thing was that my parents were supposed to encourage me, which I convinced them meant giving me the car. I'd say I had to go downtown to study or look at catalogs or do some "outside reading" which was another thing Mr. Perry told them I should do. And really, I felt bad because my parents were so proud and getting so hopeful and all I did was go to Scamp's and eat frozen yogurt. And wear my cow dress. And hope Todd Sparrow would walk by. And I was almost seventeen and my parents were getting old, especially my mom, and my brother, James, was stuck with Emily and her new baby and everyone was looking at me like I was their last chance to do something good.

And then one day I saw Carla in the Metro Mall. She was having coffee and smoking a cigarette and talking to this weird man with slicked-back hair. I had my cow dress on and I was coming out of Scamp's and the minute I saw her I almost chickened out because even if Carla was nicer than you thought she was still pretty scary. But I walked over and I said, "Hi, Carla," as nice as I could. She sort of looked at me and the man with the slicked-back hair looked at me and he had pockmarks and he was extremely scary. And then she remembered who I was and she said hi and I asked if Todd was around. She said he was over at Poor Boy Records and he was coming back if I wanted to hang out. But I said I had to put money in my parking meter and maybe I'd catch him on my way out. And she said okay and I smiled and waved and casually walked away.

Outside I just ran. I ran down the steps and around the corner and almost crashed into two heavy-metal boys. I got across the street and hurried along the sidewalk toward Poor Boy Records. I checked myself in the windows and decided I looked pretty cute. At Poor Boy I opened the door and the little bell jingled and there was Todd. His back was to me and he was flipping through records and my heart was racing and I couldn't think of what to do. So I circled around the row he was looking at and came up the other side until I was right in front of him. His face was so serious and concentrated I didn't want to disturb him but then he looked up and he jumped and he said, "Jesus, Andrea!" And he looked at me and I tried to say something but it was hopeless. My brain was in total confusion. And I looked at the ceiling and the ground and twisted around on my heel and it was so embarrassing. Then he asked me what I was doing and I said I didn't know and he said, "You really don't, do you?" So I said I was going home and I saw Carla and I just wanted to say hi and I was just heading back to my car and Carla said he was here and I was just walking by and blah blah and I was babbling like the biggest idiot. He said, "It's all right, Andrea, everything is all right."

So then he started showing me record covers because this guy named Buzz Mitchell in Seattle wanted to record his band. I said, "Like a record contract?" which was perfect because he started talking about Buzz Mitchell and explaining all the politics and I could relax. And I went over on his side and he showed me stuff and told me about cover art and asked me which covers I liked. And our shoulders were touching and it was so obvious something was going to happen. And then I drove us to his house and he took me in his room and took off my cow dress and put it inside me so fast I hardly knew what was happening.

18 **AFTER SEX, TODD TOLD ME HIS LIFE STORY.** He was born twenty-two years before in San Diego and his dad was in the Air Force and they lived in San Diego and Virginia and Seattle and Texas. Then his parents got divorced and he lived with his mom in Fresno and he went to high school there and it was all these

redneck types and he always got in fights and then he dropped out his senior year and moved to Chicago with an older woman. Then he moved to Seattle to play music and he got a new girlfriend who he really loved but she was sort of crazy and into drugs and she started doing heroin. And it was getting too weird so Todd left and moved to Portland to try to forget her. In Portland he got a job at a bakery and he met this rich guy who took him to L.A. where he met Luke at a Cyanide show. And Luke's dad was totally brutal and would beat him so he latched onto Todd and they came up to Portland and formed a band called Coma. Coma played some places but they weren't very good and Luke was only seventeen and he was freaking out so he went back to L.A. And then Todd went back to Seattle because he still loved his girlfriend and he thought he could help her but she was still on heroin and then one night these guys came and tried to get money out of her and they put a gun to Todd's head and he had to give them all his money and his guitar and everything he had. So then he left, he just walked out into the streets. And he had no place to stay and nothing to eat and then these skinheads found him and fed him and showed him how to hop a freight train back to Portland. And at first he was panhandling and stealing food and sneaking into basements to sleep but then he met Carla and he lived with her. Then he got a job at a health food store where this hippie woman was always trying to seduce him. Finally he saved up enough money to get a new guitar and then Luke showed up with a bunch of money he stole from his dad. So they re-formed Coma and wrote some songs and went back to L.A. to get signed to a record contract but everyone there was full of shit and on drugs and trying to rip them off. And Todd had a job cleaning pools and he'd see all these rich people having sex with their maids and then this black guy who was an ex-baseball player was totally on crack and started chasing him around the pool with a golf club and Todd had to dive over a fence and he broke his arm and the baseball guy gave him $10,000 not to sue. So then he and Luke tried to make a record but they just got ripped off and then they started doing drugs and blowing all their money on clothes and stuff and then one night it was pouring down rain and they were on mushrooms and standing on top of their building and they saw the police shoot this black guy about twenty times for no reason. And then they started getting paranoid that the cops were after *them* so they snuck out of L.A. and came back to Portland where they would be safe and they could do their band in peace. And this time they were just going to concentrate on the music and forget about all the record industry stuff because they already saw where that road led. And besides, if it was in your soul to do it fate would take you there and everything else was just a test to see if you were the real thing.

And all the time he talked I held his head and stroked his hair and the stubble on his face was scratching my breasts. And it must have been a couple of hours because the room had become totally dark and outside the streetlights had come on and Todd was just a dark shape beside me on the bed. And then we started kissing and he touched my breasts and I was getting so aroused. And then we started doing it and he held my hips with his hands and gripped me really tight and it was like he was squeezing all my senses into one place, into the place where he was inside me. Then he held my wrists above my head so I was totally trapped and I could feel something starting to happen and I wanted it to but I was scared and it didn't. But he kept doing it and I knew I was getting close and then I felt my brain turning off and he kept going and going and then it happened, it just poured through me and I pushed up against him and tried to hold it right there and it was so intense I was practically blacking out. And then I tried to slow him down for a second but he kept pounding into me and holding me down and just *fucking* me. And then he pinned my arms down by my sides and got really intense and he squeezed so tight it hurt and then he came and it was over. And I could feel the blood going back in my arms after he released me and I was damp and cold and my brain was swimming and I felt like I'd been hooked up to electric wires and had my brains blasted out.

At home that night I was in a daze. I wore a long-sleeve shirt to dinner so my parents wouldn't see the grip marks on my arms. And I was so spaced out I was sure they'd think I was on drugs. But they didn't notice. After dinner I went upstairs to do homework. I didn't do any though. I just laid on my bed and listened to tapes and then I took a shower and combed my hair and I felt like I'd been totally fucked. It was so weird. With the other boys I had sex. But now I'd been fucked. It was a lot different. When someone fucked you it made you understand that you were female. They were male and you were female and they fucked you. You did not fuck them. And it seemed so weird and grim and scary it made me want to cry. But I didn't. I wouldn't let myself. I just kept combing my hair. And all night my brain was like mush and totally empty except for Todd Sparrow, who was haunting me and no matter what I tried to think about it always came back to him.

At school Rebecca could see something was wrong in my face. She followed me to my locker and she kept asking me what was the matter so I finally told her I had sex with Todd Sparrow. I was bending down for my Spanish homework when I said it and she was standing over me and there was just total silence. And when I stood up she whispered, "Were you drunk?" I shook my head. I said it was in the daytime and in the afternoon and then at night too. She just stood there with her mouth open and finally she said, "Are you glad?" I said I didn't know, would she be glad if Todd Sparrow fucked her, I mean really *fucked* her? Then I showed her the marks on my arms and she just stared in disbelief. And then tears started coming in my eyes and I couldn't help it and Rebecca moved in front of me so people wouldn't see and she held my hand and she said, "Oh, Andrea!"

And the thing was, all this time I had convinced myself that something had happened between Cybil and Todd back when she first shaved her head. That they had made out or something and that she never told anyone because she was afraid it would freak out Richard. But at Taco Time at lunch, Cybil just shook her head. "I was afraid to let him touch me," she said. "That's why I shaved my head. Because I felt like I'd been so boring." But then she said she might have if she'd known him better. And that he seemed okay. And that anyway, I shouldn't be too freaked out about it. But she could tell I was. They both could. I was so freaked out I could barely hold my taco. I was totally freaked out. And then Wendy and Darcy came over to our table and I couldn't look at them and they were trying to invite us to a party. And when I finally looked up Darcy was staring right at me and I was sure she knew instantly. And she would probably tell everyone. And there was nothing I could do to stop the rumors and all the things people would say: that I was a groupie, that I was a slut, that I had been fucked by Todd Sparrow.

But after a couple days the shock wore off and nobody found out and I felt safe again and then, duh, *of course*, I started thinking about Todd. Actually I had never stopped. And I found myself talking to him in my head and every night I hugged my pillow and imagined his stubble on my chest and my tummy and all over me. And of course I wanted to see him again but what could I do? Go to his house? What if it was just a one-night stand? Which it probably was. But couldn't we still be friends? And if we were friends, couldn't we maybe have sex again? And what about Carla? Was he having sex with her? Was he having sex with all the girls downtown? And if I had sex with him more would I become his girlfriend? Was it socially possible that I could be his girlfriend? Was

I old enough? Was I cool enough? Would I need different clothes? And maybe he didn't want someone who was still in high school. Was it even legal for us to have sex? And maybe it would be best if we were secret lovers and we could meet on Sundays to make love and talk and do kinky stuff but not too kinky. Or maybe I could be like his kid sister because that's how he acted, sort of teasing me and stealing my cigarette that time, and even after sex he joked around like it wasn't anything. And I discussed it endlessly with Cybil and Rebecca and it was weird because for the first time, Cybil was really impressed with something *I* did, and everyone was trying to figure out what *I* should do next and all of a sudden I was the center of attention.

And then one day at lunch Rebecca was grilling me on the *exact* details and just what *exactly* Todd did and what *exactly* did it feel like and I was telling her *some* parts and I guess I was sort of bragging but I didn't mean to. And Matthew was behind us and he heard part of it and asked us what we were talking about and Rebecca told him I was "dating" Todd Sparrow and I said no I just went on a "date" with him and we were sort of grinning and Matthew said, "You boffed him?" Me and Rebecca tried to look shocked but Matthew got all excited and said, "You boffed Todd Sparrow? Tell me, Andrea. Did you? Did you boff Todd Sparrow?" I shook my head *no no no* but I was giggling and Rebecca got milk up her nose and then we both cracked up. And then Matthew told us gossip about Nick Pax and how all the Outer Limits crowd was boffing each other and that was the whole point wasn't it? And he said how hot Cybil was and did Sins of Our Fathers get groupies and did she boff a lot of guys? We said of course not but he was so funny and we had never heard anyone call it *boffing* before. And I could tell Rebecca was starting to like him again and now that I had sex with Todd she probably felt pressure to do something dramatic.

Then on Thursday me and Rebecca went downtown and we drove by Todd's house but we didn't see anybody. Then we went to the library and stood under the awning and looked for him and tried to smoke cigarettes and I had on my cow dress and some eye shadow but then I thought I looked like a slut so I wiped it off. Then we walked around Metro Mall and we were getting nervous and thinking up signals I'd give Rebecca if we saw him and she would pretend she'd left her books in the car and she'd leave us alone. And then we went to Scamp's and got frozen yogurts and it was so weird because I could feel what a stupid high school girl I still was, bringing Rebecca with me and making up signals and being so scared to even walk down the street. But in another way I felt this lust toward Todd that felt very *mature*. Like real *desire*. That part of me wanted to send Rebecca home and walk over to Todd's and bang on the door and tell him to make love to me *now*.

19

WE STILL HAD WENDY SIMPSON'S PARTY TO GO to. It was on Saturday night and Rebecca's parents were gone and we went to her house and goofed around and listened to a tape of Sins of Our Fathers that Greg made us. And we danced around and got some Peppermint Schnapps out of the liquor cabinet and we took little sips and put on lipstick and eyestuff and tried on hats with our new winter coats we got on sale at HOP! And when we got to Wendy's we were already tipsy and we went in and everyone was standing around with beer cups and listening to boring dance music. And so we lit cigarettes and everyone freaked out like "You can't smoke in here." And we were like, "Oh yeah?" And then we went downstairs and Darcy was there and she looked awful. And Wendy was really drunk and it seemed like a bad sign when the person who was having the party was drunker than the guests. And Renee Hatfield was there and she was looking over at Wendy with disgust and there were all these really popular people there except they looked bored. And then Scott Haskell tried to talk to us and I turned my back on him. And then Darcy came over and talked to me and I swear, it was like she was on drugs because she had this dazed look on her face and it turned out her Bradley Day School boyfriend had broken up with her. I was like, "It happens Darcy, jeez." But she was moaning about it and being really weird and *clinging* to me. Then Matthew showed up and he hung out with us and he said how lame the party was. And we drank beer and Rebecca almost fell off her new platform shoes and then she took them off and stuck them in her coat pockets and the heels were hanging out and Matthew kept teasing her and stepping on her toes. And then these Camden boys tried to talk to us but we were being rude. And then Betsy Warren and Marjorie showed up and Betsy was drinking a quart of Old English 800 and smoking and Marjorie was all made up and she looked like a total slut. And then some senior boys tried to bug Matthew about his nose ring but he wouldn't take it for a second and he told them to go listen to their Garth Brooks records and he totally faced them. But then he got nervous and he thought they might beat him up and he wanted to leave but Rebecca was like, "Leave? Where would we go?" But then it seemed like a good idea because all we were doing was being rude and making fun of people and it seemed like something bad was going to happen or we'd get bad karma or something.

So we got our stuff and started to leave. Darcy followed me up the stairs and asked me where we were going and I lied and said we were going to get cigarettes and she collapsed on the stairs, she just plopped down and put her head in her hands and I was like, "Darcy, stand up!" But she wouldn't and everyone was watching and then Matthew grabbed my arm and said, "Come on," and pulled me up the stairs.

We went in Matthew's car. I sat in back. And I was getting the creeps so bad from the party and then Matthew put in a tape and it sounded familiar and then Todd's voice came on and I jumped forward and turned it up. Matthew said it was a bootleg of Coma, which was Todd's first band, and I sat back and listened and pulled my coat tight around me and I was so happy. So then we drove by Outer Limits but there was no one there so we went by Monte Carlo and Matthew talked to some people outside and they told him about this place called Zoso. So we went there and it was this coffee shop/art gallery thing and we walked in and there were all these supercool downtown types and people in winter coats and girls with dyed hair and it was sort of intimidating. But Matthew grabbed us and pulled us along. We sat in a booth and everyone ignored us and I tried to think about Todd and remind myself that if I was cool enough for him I had to be cool enough for these people.

Matthew ordered us tea and we drank some and that perked us up. And they were playing a tape that I knew and me and Rebecca were bopping around in our seats. And then Rebecca kicked me and pointed toward the door and it was Kevin. He was with another guy and some trendy girls. I tried to hide behind Matthew because Kevin had been calling me and I never called him back. But there was no way to avoid it and he saw us and stopped by our table and everyone said hi and it was really awkward and weird.

They sat at another booth and Rebecca snuck looks at them and I peeked over the seat to look at the girls he was with. And then when we started to leave Kevin came over and asked if he could talk to me for a minute and I said sure and Matthew and Rebecca sat back down and we went outside to Kevin's Volvo. It was cold and he turned on the heat and he told me how cute I looked and how much he liked my coat. I told him it was from HOP! and I showed him the label that said Kings Road, England. And then he tried to kiss me and I didn't know what to do so I let him and we made out for a while and I thought if I didn't see Todd Sparrow again maybe I should go out with Kevin for sex or to have a boyfriend. But was that too mean? So I told him that I had sex with someone else and that I sort of hoped I'd see that person again but I didn't know exactly what was happening. And Kevin said how could I have sex with a person if I didn't know what was happening? I didn't answer and then he asked me who it was and I told him it was Todd Sparrow.

He let go of me then and moved over to his own seat. I told him it was only one time and he hadn't called me and it was probably over anyway. And then Kevin sighed really loud and ran his hand through his hair and asked me how stupid could I be, did I think someone like Todd Sparrow ever called the girls he fucked afterward? I just shrugged. And I stared straight ahead through the window and I thought I saw a snowflake. And Kevin shook his head in frustration and said how if you're nice to girls they blow you off but if you're Todd Sparrow and you treat them like shit and use them and dump them afterward they all fall in love with you and how unfair it was and why were girls so stupid? And he was getting really mad and it seemed pointless to talk anymore. So I got out and then I did see a snowflake and when I got back inside Rebecca asked me what was happening and I sighed and said, "I think it's starting to snow."

It did snow and the next day everything was white and it was so beautiful. I got up early and helped my dad shovel the driveway and I thought about what Kevin had said but I knew Todd wasn't that type of person. Even if he did have sex with lots of girls he still liked them as friends. After shoveling I made hot chocolate and studied in my room but mostly I looked out at the snow in the yard. And everything was so quiet and peaceful and all I could think about was *Todd* and I imagined him appearing in the snow and yelling up to me and crawling in the window somehow and we would kiss and he would undress me and take me to the bed and we'd make love and talk and spend the whole day just getting into each other.

By Monday morning the snow had melted and it was raining and everything was gray and depressing as usual. And Matthew got in a fight in the parking lot before school and he got suspended because this dumb freshman girl said he started it. And Cybil said they had practiced with Matthew for three hours on Sunday and she had to admit it sounded ten times better with a bass player and Matthew had really good ideas and she even gave him some of her lyrics to think up music for. And then there was this big announcement because this couple at Camden committed suicide by running their car in their parents' garage and they had written the lyrics to a Krokus song on their suicide note and it was a big controversy. And I was really nervous that the song was going to be "Destiny" but it wasn't, it was one off their second album called "Nowhere to Run." So then after lunch we had to talk about our feelings in all our classes and this football player got in trouble because he said he was glad they did it because if they couldn't take the pressure they should get weeded out and it was just natural selection like we learned in biology.

After school me and Rebecca went to Matthew's to see how he was doing. He had a black eye from the fight. But he was joking around and his mom was totally weird, like she didn't even care that he was suspended and she was like, "Oh, you are such *nice* girls! Oh, Matthew, aren't they *nice* girls!" And her makeup was weird and she reminded me of Ms. Simms, who was the crazy art teacher at Hillside and always wore capes and stuff to school. And we went into Matthew's room and I had never seen a room with so much stuff. He had posters and magazines and stereo stuff and electrical wires and tape players and video stuff and skateboard wheels and about four answering machines and a bunch of guitars and amplifiers and everything else you could imagine. And he pushed stuff off his bed and we sat on it and it smelled just like him. And he played us some Coma tapes and some other obscure bands and he even had a tape of Cybil singing her songs by herself. It was all very impressive and Rebecca was totally having a crush on him and I just sat there and listened to Cybil whose voice sounded so pure and sad without any instruments. And then we went to Sunset Mall and had frozen yogurt and I talked about how horrible Darcy looked and Matthew said she was anorexic and I was like, "Do you think?" and he just laughed at how naive we were. And the other thing we found out about Matthew that day was he was actually as old as us because he was held back when he was little because he had been immature and hyperactive as a child.

And all that week weird things kept happening at school. Like Cybil and Wendy had a screaming fight in the hall. No one would say what it was about but I knew it was something about Darcy. And then these psychologists came and told us it was the rain that was making us suicidal and we should get our parents to buy these special sun lamps for our rooms. And then someone wrote MATTHEW IS A FAG on Matthew's locker and since he was suspended it stayed there the whole day and then when he came back on Wednesday he thought it was funny and he left it there and then he got in another fight after school in the parking lot. And Betsy Warren got suspended for smoking pot and then they had anti-smoking day and this horrible man came to our class and tried to act really hip and *speak our language* and *relate to us* and he told us he *knew* how bad we wanted to be cool but having lung cancer wasn't worth it because *he had it* and he was *going to die*, but he had blow-dried hair and the fakiest tan and nobody believed him. And then Richard, who was usually with Cybil or off studying somewhere, actually ate lunch with me and Rebecca and Matthew and it was so weird because the way he acted around Matthew it was like Matthew was the leader of the band now. And later that day I saw Richard in Mr. Perry's office and he said he wanted to go to MIT. And I thought about next summer and what I wanted to do and I definitely did not want to get stuck in Harper's Ferry again so I was being really serious about my college stuff and getting as much ammunition as I could so my parents couldn't send me away.

And then Darcy got a bob and I thought it looked pretty cute and I saw her in the bathroom and I told her how nice it looked. She sort of smiled back in the mirror and she was trying to put this headband on and she couldn't seem to get it right. And she had lots of zits and her wrists looked awfully skinny and I asked her how she was doing. But I guess that was stupid because there were all these other girls there and she gave me this weird look like, *What are you talking about*? and I didn't know what to say so I left.

At lunch I told Rebecca and Matthew about Darcy, and Matthew said she was taking speed. We asked him how he knew and he nodded toward Betsy Warren who was sitting at the next table. And then Jerry Kruger came up behind Matthew and called him a faggot and Matthew pretended like he didn't see him and waved his hand like, *What stinks*? And Jerry slapped him on the side of the head and Matthew started swearing and grabbing his ear and everybody thought he was joking but it turned out his eardrum was broken.

And that weekend me and Rebecca were downtown at Poor Boy Records and we saw Carla. I asked her about Todd and she said Color Green had been in Seattle meeting with Buzz Mitchell about their record contract. She told me an address and I wrote it down and thanked her and it was weird because when we went outside I felt relieved like that explained why I hadn't seen him. And also I felt sort of free like I could walk down the street and I didn't have to worry about what I was wearing every second or which corner Todd might be around. And it made me think that love was best when it was in your mind, when it was imaginings on a snowy day or doodled names in your notebook or dreaming in your bed at night. Except for sex of course, which was obviously the biggest part, once you figured it out.

20

MY FIRST LETTER TO TODD SPARROW I wrote in my room and it was my life story and it was five pages long and it was so boring I threw it away. My next letter I wrote at school and it was about the music scene and all the news about Sins of Our Fathers and how Matthew was playing bass and making us tapes of Coma and bootleg Color Green shows. It had a long part where I admitted that I didn't know that much about music except that I liked the energy of it and the weird people at Outer Limits and all the stuff Richard used to say about a new generation and teenagers having their own music. My third letter I wrote in the downtown library and I tried to sound like I *did* know about music and I mentioned obscure bands Matthew had talked about but then I thought Todd would see through it. So I dug out the second letter and recopied the parts about Cybil and Matthew but left out the stuff about how I didn't know about music. Then I went to Scamp's and wrote another part about how I hoped I wasn't being weird but I sure liked hanging out with him and going to his house that time. And then I felt daring and I wrote how Carla had been so nice and how me and Rebecca thought she was such a bitch because we were afraid of her and how people always hate other people if they're dressed cooler than them or if they're artsy or pretentious or whatever. But then I crossed the Carla part out and recopied that page but then I decided to leave it in and I had to recopy it again. It took two frozen yogurts and three coffees to get it all done but I was so excited and I signed it "See you" and kissed every corner of every page. And then I ran down to the post office and kissed the envelope ten more times and drew some flowers on it and dropped it in. And the minute it fell through the slot I felt sick from nerves and caffeine and yogurt.

The next day at school me and Cybil had lunch at Taco Time, just the two of us, and we talked about Todd Sparrow and how with him you had to be honest because he could see right through any lies or games and how when you were with him you felt like anything could happen and how exciting it was. But also how vulnerable you were with him because he had all the power and you were in "his movie" and how only people like Carla could be equal to him because they had movies of their own.

And I tried not to think about Todd but of course the whole reason I wrote to him was so he would write back. And every day after school no matter where we were going, Rebecca and I would stop by my house and look in the mailbox. And Rebecca was having a major crush on Matthew now and even Cybil was admitting he was cool. And since he broke his eardrum Matthew couldn't take a shower and he looked so scruffy and when Mrs. Katz tried to say something he told her he had been assaulted in *her* lunchroom by one of *her* students and it wasn't his fault he couldn't take a shower, his doctor wouldn't let him. And then during spring break Girl Patrol played at Outer Limits and Cybil and Matthew and Rebecca and I went. Matthew was so daring he just walked right into the dressing room and started talking to Girl Patrol. And it was so weird because I thought they were going to be these wild young girls but they were actually sort of old and beat-up looking. The drummer was fat and the singer looked really sickly and pale and afterward Matthew said she was on heroin.

And then on Monday it was raining and I went home and there was a letter in the kitchen and it said my name and it was

135

from "T.S." in Bellingham, Washington. I sat down and opened it and started reading. At first it was really nice and he was glad I wrote him because it was so boring where he was, which was not really in Seattle but in this boring suburb. And I was reading pretty fast to get to the part about me and I thought I found it but then I had to back up and it was about someone named Jessica. She was in another band that was rehearsing in the same studio and she was really talented and Todd liked her a lot but she was so hostile and competitive that it was turning into a disaster. And they were all stuck in this little town and she was ruining everything. And I started skimming really fast for parts about me but there were none. Except at the end where he said he wished more girls were like me, laid back and willing to let a good vibe develop and not immediately putting all men down like Jessica did. It was signed "See you soon" and when I got done I read it again and when I got to the part about Jessica I threw the paper on the floor and stomped it with my foot.

And then Sins of Our Fathers finally played again at Outer Limits. Everyone was there. It was the usual line-up with Pax on last but you could tell Sins of Our Fathers were getting the most attention from the crowd. And when they came out Cybil had this great miniskirt and a cardigan over a T-shirt that was cut off so you could see her bellybutton. It was very risque for Cybil and I knew right away that Sins of Our Fathers was going to be a different band with Matthew in it. And they were. They started off with Richard playing this little waltz on guitar and then they all started pounding this super heavy beat, really loud and hard and everyone started dancing instantly. And Cybil grabbed the mike and did this chant and it was:

> *We are all*
> *Prostitutes*
> *We are all*
> *For sale*
> *We are all*
> *Pretty candy*
> *We have all*
> *Gone to hell*

And then she turned back toward Greg and Matthew and they were totally getting into it and Richard was doing his little hopping thing and Matthew's hair was flying all over and everyone was totally rocking out.

After the first song I heard this boy tell his girlfriend that Sins of Our Fathers was the best band in Portland. And these other boys said, "That singer is so hot!" And then the next song was really smooth and fast and everyone went spinning around and dancing and going totally wild. And boys were moshing and girls too and it was this big swirl of people and me and Rebecca looked at each other and then we both ran right into the middle of it. And everyone fell down and we were getting kicked and smashed and falling over everyone and rolling on the floor and then we got up and we were dancing like crazy and whipping our hair around and it was the wildest time!

After Sins of Our Fathers were done Rebecca and I went out to the curb and drank some mineral water and everyone was talking about Sins of Our Fathers and how great they were. Nick Pax was sitting in the Pax van and telling people he didn't want to follow Sins because they were too good. And then Cybil came out and she had this huge overcoat on and she was so hot and sweaty you could see the steam coming off her head. We were like, "Cybil, you were so good!" and we hugged her and we all sat on the curb and Cybil rested her chin on her knees and picked at her shoes and tried to ignore all the people that were staring at her.

Then Kevin showed up but he had missed Sins of Our Fathers and he was drunk. And then Pax played and they were good too but in their usual goofy way and not as intense and you could tell right away that people lost interest. That was really the difference because Thriftstore Apocalypse used to be goofy like that but Sins of Our Fathers sure weren't. Because what people wanted was something intense and real and not just someone making a joke out of everything. But I still went in and Kevin was dancing around and I started dancing too. And then we started making out and he was pretty drunk and we fell over the front of the stage and Nick

Pax dedicated a song to us. And then we went to Kevin's car and made out and he put his hands in my panties and kissed my neck and he was making me really horny. He had a condom and we tried to do it but we couldn't get a good position. So then I made him sit in the back seat and I straddled him and that worked, sort of, but it wasn't that comfortable and it never really felt that good.

Driving home I told Rebecca what we did and she started scolding me for being a slut. But I said I still liked Kevin and we were friends and maybe he was my boyfriend since Todd Sparrow wasn't around anymore. She said, "Did you really think Todd was going to be your boyfriend?" I said I didn't know, how could I know? And she said I better be careful because I might be getting conceited. And when I got home my ears were ringing from the music and my dad was asleep in front of the TV and I was just about to sneak upstairs when my mom called me into her room. It was dark and she had stuff on her face and she looked so awful no wonder my dad slept on the couch. She asked me where I'd been and I told her about Cybil and how Sins of Our Fathers were getting really big and she was like, "Sins of Our Fathers is the name of a band?" I said yeah. She said that was a horrible name. I tried to explain they didn't mean their *real* fathers, it was just an expression, but my mom shook her head and said how everyone blamed everything on their parents nowadays and didn't we understand how hard they had tried? And then she asked me about college and if I was really serious about it because she couldn't tell anymore when I was being sincere. I said I was serious about it because if I had to go to college I might as well go to a good one. She said I didn't *have* to go. I said I wanted to but I didn't sound very convincing. And then she asked me if I had a boyfriend and I told her about Kevin but she didn't seem that interested and after a while she let me go.

It was cold in my room and I took a shower and hid my underpants because they were all gross from sex. I got in my nightie and the wind was blowing outside and the window was rattling and I put on a tape and got deep under the covers. But then I couldn't sleep because all these ideas were coming into my head, like I was a terrible person and conceited and a slut and I hadn't even tried to help Darcy, who was anorexic and on speed. And everything in the world seemed like it was pressing down on me and I started to cry and I swore to be a better person and get interested in college and not smoke cigarettes and not have sex except if I really loved the person. And also not to wear eye shadow or go in the slamming pit or be insincere to my mother. But it seemed so hopeless because I had already changed so much and broken so many pacts and it just seemed like the older you got the more corrupt you became and really, if you thought about it, in terms of your morals and stuff: you were dying from the day you were born.

21

THEN I TURNED SEVENTEEN. IT WAS SO depressing. I couldn't even look at anyone. At school nobody cared because most of them had already turned. At home my mom made a cake and my dad was acting weird and trying to make eye contact. And all day I kept studying my face in the mirror and wondering if I would have jowls someday like Mrs. Schroeder. And everything old was bugging me like Lizzy Rosen's grandpa who went on these pathetic walks to the corner that took him half the day. That night I took my Coma tape and sat outside on the steps with Brad's Walkman and listened to it all the way through twice. And I knew my parents were wondering what my problem was and then my dad came out and stood over me and asked me what I was doing. I said nothing. He asked me if I was sad about my birthday or if it was something else and I couldn't answer and I couldn't look at him. So he sat down and said it was hard being my age and no matter what happened he still loved me. And mom too. And after a while he gave me a hug but even then he was holding back because I was seventeen and my breasts were touching him.

On Friday Cybil and Rebecca and I went to Monte Carlo. I was trying to be into it but mostly I just sat there in a daze. Then Matthew showed up and he flirted with Rebecca and later they went off somewhere to have sex. And then the next day Rebecca was being so aloof and she wouldn't tell what happened but Cybil told her Matthew had one-night stands all the time and that broke Rebecca down pretty quick. And then later we went to Taco Time for lunch and Jerry Kruger was there and he was throwing ketchup packets at us and we waited for him to stop or go away but he wouldn't and so we finally gave up and left.

After school I saw Richard in Mr. Perry's office. He was sending off for stuff from MIT and we talked and then we went for frozen yogurt at Sunset Mall. And Richard was being so nice and cheering me up but then he started saying how bad he wanted to get out of Hillside and away from Portland and go back east and I was like, "What about Cybil? What about Sins of Our Fathers?" And he shrugged and said it was fun and that's all a band was for and it didn't matter anyway because Matthew was taking over and Cybil could stay with him if she wanted to keep going. And I knew that he and Cybil weren't a couple in the traditional sense but the way he was talking made it sound like they weren't together at all. And I wanted to ask him about it but it didn't seem like it was any of my business which was weird because the whole fun of high school is that everything is supposed to be everybody's business.

The next day I had a meeting with Mr. Perry and we talked about where I could go. And poor Mr. Perry, because last year Camden got four people into Stanford and we didn't get any. And they had people that went to Harvard and Yale and we only had one person, Jim Dietz, who went there. So Mr. Perry wanted people to apply "early decision" and he said I should figure out over the summer which one was my favorite and he suggested Berkeley or Brown or maybe Wellington which was a good small school. And I was relieved because I thought he was going to make me try for Stanford, which everybody said was all computer nerds and law school types.

And I had written Todd another letter but I hadn't heard back from him and I went downtown to the library just about every day and I always looked for Carla to see if she had any news. And then one day Matthew came running up to Rebecca and me in the parking lot and he said Color Green was opening for the Astral Planes from England in a club in Seattle and we immediately started plotting ways to go.

And then one day in the cafeteria, Greg and Cybil and me and Matthew were sitting at a table and Jerry Kruger came up to Matthew and started picking a fight. Cybil just got up and walked away. Matthew told Jerry he was going to kick his ass and Jerry said he was going to kick Matthew's ass and Greg started to say something but everyone told him to shut up. And then Cybil came up behind them and she had a folding chair and everyone saw her except Jerry and she lifted the chair up and smashed him right on the head. And then Matthew tackled him and Cybil kicked him and Matthew kept punching him in the face until Mr. Angelo dragged him off. All of them got in trouble and they were going to be suspended but there had just been this big assembly about sexual harassment and everyone said how Jerry harassed Cybil and other girls and she was only defending herself. So Cybil got out of it and only Matthew and Jerry got suspended.

Then in Writing Concepts we practiced writing college essays because all the teachers said how stupid we were and how bad the essays were last year. Mr. Boswell told us to write about a role model so I wrote about Cybil but he didn't mean like that, he meant a *real* role model, someone like Mrs. Katz. So I wrote about Rita at summer camp and even put in a little about Brad, not the sex but just how their life was up in Harper's Ferry being close to nature and dealing with tourists and all that. But it was boring so I made Rita Hispanic, which might have been true since she had a dark complexion. Then I put in some stuff about how she was from Honduras and her brother was in the army and her family were chicken farmers and had escaped to America blah blah and Mr. Boswell thought it was so brilliant he read it out loud in class and I was so embarrassed I practically crawled under my desk. And after class everyone was laughing and Betsy Warren told me what a great bullshit artist I was. And it was the first time I ever talked to her and she seemed pretty nice but then she asked me if I wanted to buy some LSD and I was like, no thanks!

Meanwhile, we figured out how to see Color Green in Seattle. We told our parents we were going to the University of Washington to visit the campus. We made up some friends of Matthew's that went there and we were set. It was me, Cybil, Rebecca, and Matthew. And Friday after school we went to

Matthew's and his mom gave us cookies and we got in his car and got on the freeway and it was so exciting! And Matthew played Color Green tapes and me and Cybil bopped around in the back seat. And after a while we settled down and talked about stuff and Cybil said Richard would probably get into MIT and the way she talked it was like he was already out of the band.

Then Matthew wanted to check out a truck stop so we stopped at one and sat at the counter and had coffee and all the truckers talked to us and asked us if we were flower children because I had my cow dress on and Cybil was wearing her Pax T-shirt with the big peace sign on the front. And the waitress was being mean and filling our cups too full and you could tell she was jealous. And then outside the sun was going down and the sky seemed so big and beautiful and we skipped around the trucks and they were like these huge hissing monsters. Me and Cybil climbed up on one but there was a man sleeping inside and he got all pissed until he saw we were girls and then he was like, "Hey! Come back!"

Back in the car we talked about the new image of Sins of Our Fathers and the new songs and were they switching to a more anger thing instead of peace-and-love type stuff? Cybil just shrugged. She didn't know. But Matthew did and he told us the new philosophy of the band and it sort of bugged me that Cybil was letting him take over. And Rebecca was agreeing with everything Matthew said and being the biggest kiss-ass. And all the time nobody mentioned Todd but I kept thinking about him and what I would say to him and how I'd act like we were just friends which was probably all we would be, if even that.

Seattle was so cool. And we were pissing our pants and looking around at everyone and it was Friday night and there were people with leather pants and skanky heavy-metal girls and about ten million bums. And we were freaking out because Seattle was so much wilder than Portland and would people think we were just a bunch of dumb high school kids? And then we got lost and even Matthew was losing his cool and he finally stopped and asked this couple where the club was but they were tourists from Germany and they didn't know anything. So we drove around and looked for someone to ask but we couldn't find anyone and then we saw the Germans again and we gave them a ride because they were students and they wanted to go too. So we drove around some more and found some yuppies and they gave us directions and we finally found it. We parked but then the Germans had pot and Matthew wanted to smoke some so we had to walk around and find a place and it was totally scary because if we got in trouble our parents would kill us. They found this little park and I kept looking around and the Germans were smoking their pipe and handing it to Matthew and being so casual and saying, "It is good bud, yes?"

So then we went back to the club and got our money ready and got in line and I knew something was wrong. First of all, people were being really pushy and rude and Rebecca had to push this guy and the Germans yelled at him with their accents and that saved us. But then when we got to the front the bouncers were like, "Where do you think you're going?" They said it was over twenty-one only and we were like no way and they said *yes way*. And people behind us were pushing and calling us jailbait and Cybil stomped on somebody's foot and then the bouncers told us to leave. So we ran back to the car and looked in the newspaper we had and it said *all ages* and we ran back and tried to show the bouncers but they just pushed us away. And then it was sold out and all these other people were shouting and arguing and we couldn't believe it. We were in shock. And the bouncers told everyone to clear the sidewalk and we walked away and the streets were dark and it was starting to drizzle and all these bums and drug dealers were lurking around and we all turned to Matthew like what should we do but he was totally stoned on pot and he couldn't even remember where the car was.

22 IT WAS CYBIL'S IDEA TO TRY TO SNEAK in. Me and Rebecca were like, *yeah right*, but Cybil thought there must be a back entrance so we walked around the block and sure enough there was an alley with a locked fence across it. Matthew went first. He crawled up on a Dumpster and climbed the fence and jumped over to the other side. Then he snuck down the alley and around

a corner and we waited while he checked it out. And Rebecca was freaking out like what if there were dogs or Matthew got shot, how would we get home? Cybil got on the Dumpster to look out and me and Rebecca were supposed to be watching the street but it was too scary so we climbed up with Cybil. And then Matthew came back and did thumbs-up and Cybil immediately started climbing over. And me and Rebecca were like, *Cybil*, but she said, "You wanted to see the show, didn't you?" And there was no way we were going to get left behind on that dark street so we started climbing. And the fence was all wet and gross and I immediately caught my tights and got a big run and Rebecca caught her dress but Cybil had jeans on so it was easy for her. And then we ran down the alley and it was misting and dark and spooky as anything. We gathered at the corner and peeked around and there was a loading area with a van and a rent-a-truck and we all ran behind the van and hid. And then a door opened and we could hear the music inside and this guy ran out and got something from the truck and hurried back in. Cybil ran after him and tried to catch the door but it locked. So we stayed behind the van and then a different guy came out and he lit a cigarette and he just stood there and we peeked through the van windows at him and then Cybil whispered that we should try to talk to him, it was our only chance. But it didn't matter because he heard us and he stepped around the van and there we were.

His name was Ian and he was English and he was the singer of the Astral Planes. We told him we were friends of Color Green, besides being big fans of his of course, and he said Color Green was playing right now and it was almost over. He knocked on the door and asked the man if the supporting act was over yet and the man said yes. And when they opened the door we could hear Todd saying good night to the audience. And then Ian told us to wait in the truck because we were going to catch cold. So we squeezed into the truck and we were all wet and I looked down and I had this huge rip in my cow dress.

It got worse. When Todd and Luke and everybody came out there was an extra person and it was female and it was Jessica. I knew it was her. She was dressed like she was grunge but it was totally fake because she was super clean and her face was creamy smooth and you could tell she was *a star* and probably a total bitch. And I was so embarrassed and jealous of Jessica I didn't want to get out. But Ian had told Todd we were there and he opened the door and very slowly and very reluctantly we came down from the truck. And Todd looked at us and Jessica looked at us and they said we looked like drowned rats. I stayed as far away as possible from Todd but he saw me and smiled at me and I just turned away. And everybody was looking at Jessica and she knew it and she just laughed at us and told Todd we were his fan club and weren't we cute? And it was so embarrassing and Matthew was stammering to Todd about what a big influence he was and finally Cybil took charge and asked Ian if we could leave through the club so we wouldn't have to climb the fence. Ian got a bouncer to escort us and we said good-bye to Todd and the bouncer marched us through the club. It was hot inside and loud and packed with people and then we were outside again, back on the cold side-walk and we were all wet and Jessica was right, we were like drowned rats.

But at least Matthew wasn't so stoned now. We got in his car and cranked up the heat and we didn't know what to do and I suggested going to the University of Washington. So we asked some people and we found our way there and we found the main drag of coffee shops and stuff and we went into a cafe and had tea. And then Matthew talked to this girl with a Cyanide T-shirt and she told us about this lounge on campus where we could maybe sleep. So we tried to find it and we got lost and then we found a party of the University Hiking Club and it was all these drunk guys with beards. And then we found this passageway to another building and we walked around and looked at all these classrooms and offices and read the cartoons on the doors. And then we met two hippie guys and they told us about another party and we tried to find it but we got lost. And then we found these women with dreadlocks and they were checking us out like they didn't believe we were prospective students because we were so dirty and wet. But they showed us where the party was and we went in and it was this dark room with all these cool people dancing and a band playing and we were like, *wow*. And the people were dressed like HOP! except even better and it was like Outer Limits minus the skinheads and the jerks, and just the coolest people. And even Cybil was excited and we pushed up toward the front and the band were these cool punk boys with sunglasses and ripped shirts. And we started jumping around and dancing and all the college guys were noticing us and trying to meet us but we ignored them and it was so fun!

Cybil found some girls who were in a sorority and me and her slept there and Rebecca and Matthew slept in a lounge somewhere and had wild sex all night. According to Rebecca. And back at school she told everyone about our wild adventures, which freaked me out because I didn't want Mr. Perry to hear about it. And I told my parents that I liked the University of Washington but I didn't know if it was good enough academically and it seemed like too much of a party school.

And then a couple weeks later Cybil was downtown and she thought she heard two girls talking about Todd and it sounded like he was back and living with Carla. I had not heard from him or written to him and I had gone out with Kevin a couple times and we had pretty intense sex. But I didn't love Kevin. I loved Todd. Maybe not in a practical way but definitely with all my heart. And in a way it was easier to love him because he was safely out of reach and always in Seattle and I didn't have to worry about loving him too much or playing hard to get. I went to Taco Time with Cybil and I asked her what I should do and she told me not to get my hopes up because Todd was a big shot in cool Seattle and we were nobodies in stupid Portland.

Then Sins of Our Fathers got their first headlining show at Outer Limits and Matthew was so excited and we all went to his house to help make posters. We picked out cool pictures and lettering and then the next day we went postering down-town and we ran around and stapled the posters on telephone poles. And I swear, if you want to meet people putting up posters is the best because pretty soon these two skater boys were helping us and letting us ride their skateboards and then we met their girlfriends and these other boys came and pretty soon there was a whole mob of us. And everyone loved the poster, which was this Vietnamese guy shooting another guy in the head and beneath it huge letters that said: SINS OF OUR FATHERS. And other people came up to us and we gave them posters out of the stack to put up in their rooms. And then Rebecca came running up the street and she had just given posters to Carla, and Carla said Todd was in California seeing about his record but he'd be back and she'd bring him to the show.

The next day was Matthew's seventeenth birthday and we celebrated by putting up posters at school but of course the teachers ripped them down immediately and Mrs. Katz made an announcement saying there would be no unauthorized political advertisements allowed at Hillside. But we had already given out a bunch so some people had them in their lockers and in general it seemed like people at Hillside were finally noticing that something cool was happening. At lunch we had a little birthday party for Matthew at Taco Time but he was really stoned on pot and it was sort of weird. And then after school I went over to Cybil's to try on some miniskirts and help her figure out her outfit for the big show. And we listened to Girl Patrol and talked about school and going to Seattle and it was the nicest time I'd had with her in a long time.

The show was on Friday night and Outer Limits was total chaos. There were four other bands, Party Hats, Curmudgeon, Nation of Pain, and Drano. And there were people running all over and everyone was nervous including Richard and Greg, who were arguing with another guy about where they could put their stuff. Me and Rebecca sat outside on the curb and there were all these skinheads across the street and some redneck flannel boys and one boy kept puking in the bushes and it was definitely not a University of Washington party.

And then when Party Hats played we went inside and Jerry Kruger was there. He was in the front and he was slamming and so was Bobby Wingate, who was a Hillside football player, and they were totally smashing people. And me and Rebecca exchanged looks like, *What are they doing here?* And everyone was bumming out and trying to get away from them and Elaine of Party Hats even said in the mike that they were assholes and to go back to the suburbs. And me and Rebecca were so embarrassed because if it wasn't for our posters around Hillside they wouldn't have even known about it.

And then Todd and Luke and Carla showed up. They were outside on the sidewalk and I was afraid to go out there but then Matthew wanted to smoke pot and Rebecca wanted to go with him so I went too. We went out and walked down the street a little ways and I didn't even look in Todd's direction. Matthew found a doorway and he lit his pipe and smoked it and Rebecca smoked some too. And I just watched and then Todd and Luke came running over and it was so embarrassing because I thought they were coming to talk to me but they just wanted pot. And Todd was ignoring me and smoking pot and Matthew was trying to ask him about record contracts and how did he meet Buzz Mitchell. And then Todd offered me the pipe. I shook my head but Matthew was like, "Go ahead, Andrea." But I had tried pot once and it made me so stupid I couldn't talk. And then Rebecca took it from Todd and told them I was allergic and that saved me. And meanwhile Jerry and Bobby Wingate had come outside and some girl was yelling at Jerry and he just laughed and when her hippie boyfriend tried to say something Bobby Wingate pushed him over a car hood and dropped him in the street.

23 JERRY KRUGER AND BOBBY WINGATE HAD found freak paradise. There were hippies and faggots and punkers in every direction. And then they saw the skinheads across the street and they started saying stuff to them and then they saw Matthew and they were

like, "All right, look who's here!" And we were heading back inside and Matthew whispered to Luke and Todd to watch out and I thought something would happen for sure but Jerry just said, "You guys better be good, we want to slam!" And Luke sort of pushed past Bobby Wingate and *nobody* pushes Bobby Wingate but the way Luke did it, so casual, like he didn't even notice that Bobby weighed about a thousand pounds, Bobby didn't even do anything.

I tried not to look at Jerry but there were all these people jammed around the door and I was stuck and Jerry was grinning at me. So finally I said, "Why don't you just go home." And Jerry was like, "But Andrea, we like it here!" and I was like, "You do not!" And I turned away and tried to ignore him and then I saw the skinheads. They were coming through the crowd and they were bouncing and whooping like Indians and they were going for Jerry. And then this other boy backed into me and people were pushing to get out of the way and then I saw Jerry's head jerk down and all the other skinheads swarmed around and then everyone was falling over and I got tripped and a girl fell on me. And I was trying to get up and then Matthew appeared and he grabbed my wrist and yanked me up so hard I thought he was going to break my arm. And then someone screamed and everybody ducked and Matthew grabbed me around the waist and dragged me inside. And everything was in total confusion and everyone outside was trying to get in and everyone inside was trying to get out. And then it was like this electric shock went through the crowd, like something really bad was happening and we all knew it together at the same instant. Our fun night was gone. And Matthew let me go and I was rubbing my arm and looking around and everyone had the same horrible look on their face. And Todd was looking for Carla, and me and Rebecca went back to the dressing room and Cybil took one look at us and said, "What? What is it? Andrea, *what is it*?" I just shook my head and said it was a fight. And then we all went to the front door but the commotion had moved down the street and the Outer Limits guys were trying to keep people inside and then Todd came running down the street and he couldn't find Carla and his face was white as a ghost. And Rebecca was in shock and I turned back and looked at the stage and all I wanted was for Cybil to sing and everybody to dance and have fun and why did boys always have to wreck everything?

And then police came and ambulances and the Outer Limits guy told us to stay calm but he was so freaked out he was scaring people worse. Matthew stashed his pot, and Todd and Luke went looking for Carla. Rebecca and I stayed in the dressing room with Cybil and everybody talked about who got hurt and what happened and if someone got killed or not and it was so awful. And then Todd came in and got us all together and he told us that he couldn't get in trouble with the police and that they would ask us everything that happened and we should tell the exact truth but don't mention his or Luke's or Carla's names.

And he was right. The police kept everyone there and we got trapped in the dressing room. Todd found Carla and of course they all got away. And then the police wanted someone who knew Jerry and Bobby and we had to talk to them. And the police were such assholes because they wouldn't tell us anything. But they made us talk and I said that I knew Jerry and Bobby from high school but I wasn't friends with them and they were pushing people and being obnoxious and everyone was getting mad. After that, Matthew and Greg got the station wagon and loaded their stuff and all this time Richard was sitting on a bench in the dressing room and not talking to anyone. And the police took everyone's names but he was so quiet they missed him completely.

Jerry Kruger was dead and Bobby Wingate was in critical condition at the hospital. By Monday Bobby was in stable condition and it was so horrible because everyone at school asked me what happened and all I could say was they got in a fight with some skinheads. And everyone acted like this confirmed how bad Outer Limits was and it was so depressing and Darcy and Wendy Simpson even came up to me and they were like, "Are you still going to hang out there?" And everyone's parents freaked out and there was an editorial in *Hillsider* by Cynthia Carmichael about how violent and hopeless our lives were. And a reporter from *The Oregonian* called me at my house and asked me a bunch of questions. My parents hadn't heard about it but after that I had to tell them and they were so shocked and my mom said how much she hated the whole idea of Sins of Our Fathers and how I wasn't going to associate with those people anymore. But I just shrugged and said I didn't associate with people like Jerry Kruger. Those were exactly the people I was trying to avoid.

Then in the middle of school on Wednesday the police came to school and took Matthew away for questioning. After school me and Cybil and Rebecca waited for him by his car in the parking lot and people stared at us as they went home. We waited an hour and then another hour and it was six o'clock when the police car finally came back and let him out. He looked so tired. We didn't even say a word, we just all gave him a big hug and held it for a long time.

Every day there was stuff in the newspaper about the police chasing the skinheads. And it was so weird because in *The Oregonian* Outer Limits was "an informal gathering place for disaffected teens, street youths, and skinheads." And "Jerry T. Kruger, 17, and Robert Bryant Wingate, 18," were "tragic victims of a rising tide of gang violence, hate crime, and anarchy that has overtaken our city streets." Bobby was getting better and they had a picture of him in *The Oregonian* sitting in his hospital bed with his head all bandaged. And then they caught some skinheads in Idaho and they brought them to Portland and the Chief of Police went on TV and promised they'd get a fair trial even though everyone wanted the death penalty. But then it turned out the skinheads were only fifteen and they'd been at school that day and they were the wrong ones.

And then there was a funeral for Jerry and an assembly at school and Matthew didn't go because he was scared of Jerry and Bobby's friends. At the assembly me and Cybil and Rebecca stood in the very back and Mrs. Katz made a speech and said what a tragic loss it was and how we were a troubled generation and we should look out for each other and all the rally girls cried and had to leave and it was like mass hysteria. When it was over we went straight to Taco Time where Matthew was and he said he was going to drop out because the football players would kill him or Bobby would when he got out of the hospital.

And in all the excitement people had forgotten that school was almost over and Cynthia Carmichael wrote an editorial about how life goes on and we should keep Jerry Kruger in our hearts but we also owed it to ourselves to think toward the future and toward Prom and it was pretty confused reasoning and everyone said it was one of her worst editorials. And then people wanted to dedicate the yearbook to Jerry but Mrs. Katz thought it was too controversial. And then Mr. Perry called me into his office and he was acting really weird and trying not to mention about Jerry Kruger and he told me that it was very important that I get an interesting job over the summer or do an internship and he gave me some pamphlets. They came in pretty handy too because that night my parents were about to ground me from downtown forever but I showed them the stuff and said how I needed to get an interesting summer job and could I please not go to camp?

About a week after that me and Rebecca were downtown having frozen yogurt and we walked over to Outer Limits and it was totally closed and shut down and you could look in the window and they had torn down the stage and all the stuff was taken off the walls and a big sign said FOR LEASE. We went into the Shoe Repair across the street and this old man said the city closed it down. He said it was a place for Nazis and that he remembered World War Two when he was a boy and how he never thought people in his own country would turn into that and how terrible America was now and how the young people scared him to death.

The next day at school I went with Cybil to Taco Time for lunch and she told me that Richard had quit the band. I guess I wasn't shocked. The way things were going it made sense. Richard was really smart and a good student and he would prob-ably go to MIT. And in a way, all the stuff he used to say about new music for a new generation didn't make sense when people were killing each other at the shows. I asked her if they would still go out or be friends or whatever. She said they'd stopped doing that a long time ago. I said, "You did? Why didn't you tell me?" She just shrugged. And it bugged me how Cybil never told you what was happening in her life and for once I told her that.

She didn't answer and so then I told her how I supported her band and I always tried to be her friend and she wouldn't even tell me if she was still going out with her boyfriend. And then I sort of lost control because there was so much tension inside me and I yelled at her and I didn't even mean it really. And she told me I was her best friend and she appreciated everything I did and she didn't mean to be so closed off. And it was so embarrassing because then I started to cry and she got me some napkins. And then we were late for fifth period but Cybil said we should take the rest of the day off, we'd earned it. I had never skipped before but I didn't even care and we got coffee and relaxed and then I felt a lot better.

The last couple weeks of school were the worst. People were totally cranky and the teachers thought we were evil and me and Cybil and Rebecca became sort of infamous, like everybody knew we were there when Jerry got killed. And Matthew was never at school and I was sure he would flunk but then it turned out he had some deal with the school psychologist and he was doing outside homework. And when Bobby Wingate finally came back everybody treated him like this big hero and there were all these cards stuck on his locker welcoming him back which Mrs. Schroeder made everyone write. And then Mrs. Katz called Bobby and Matthew into her office and they talked to the psychologist and it must have been embarrassing to Matthew but they had to do it because Matthew was getting so paranoid and he really thought they would kill him.

Then my mom got me a summer job. It was at this community radio station and they would actually pay me and I couldn't believe it. And I had to call this woman Ms. Caliban and she really grilled me but I was so excited I was like, "Yes ma'am, no ma'am," which made her mad and she told me to call her Sondra so I did. And I told her how I was really into radio and everything and she said I'd be emptying wastebaskets and I was like, "*Cool!*"

So I was all excited but it didn't start until June so I just finished off the year and studied really hard because Mr. Perry said the last term of junior year was the most important. So I went downtown to the library a lot and I even dressed more conservative because the scene was totally dead now. And Todd was back in Seattle and I didn't feel like I needed to impress anybody. And when I saw Carla on the street one day I just waved and kept walking. And I still went out with Kevin sometimes and had sex with him sometimes and Rebecca was still chasing Matthew and I guess the most interesting thing was wondering who Cybil would go out with next.

24

WHEN SCHOOL GOT OUT MATTHEW AND
Cybil started auditioning bass players.
Matthew was going to play guitar. It was
clear he was taking control of things now but Cybil insisted
she still had her power and I guess she proved it when they got
a girl bass player. Her name was Fiona and Cybil said it was
good for everyone because she was female and a good musician and she liked all the stuff Matthew liked like grunge and
punk and heavy metal and now they would rock super hard.
And me and Rebecca went over to Matthew's where they practiced now and it was weird because Fiona was twenty-two and
she just looked at us like we were little girls. She had her own
six-pack and she drank and smoked cigarettes and we looked
at Cybil like, *Isn't she kind of rough*? But Cybil was totally into
her and they were teaching her everything and being very
careful and serious and you could tell they had big plans for
Sins of Our Fathers.

And then I had my first day at my new job at KBAN. It was
like public TV except it was radio and it was actually pretty dirty
and gross inside. I had to empty all the wastebaskets and vacuum and then I had to sort all the mail and write up these lists of
advertisements and write down all the messages on the answering machine. Ms. Caliban wasn't very nice but other people
came in and they would say hi and introduce themselves and
some of them were nice but not all of them. And everywhere you
went you had to listen to the radio because there were speakers

everywhere and it was mostly boring jazz and talk shows about nuclear power and women's issues and the black coalition. After the first couple days they let me sit at the desk I was supposed to sit at and this black guy named Jamaal, who did the jazz, made me go across the street and get him iced coffee and I was scared because Ms. Caliban told me to stay at the desk when I was being the receptionist. And the dumb lady at the store was weird and she gave me the most evil looks and I didn't even know what iced coffee was.

But the great thing was when the day was over I was free! KBAN was on East Burnside where all the bums were but I could walk over the bridge to downtown and I could hang out and do whatever I wanted. Rebecca was working at this day-care place in the mornings and she'd pick me up and we'd drive around. And all of June was really hot and Rebecca and I mostly went to air-conditioned movies or to Scamp's for frozen yogurt. And one day it was 105 degrees and we took our swimsuits and drove down to Riverside Park and found a rope swing. These boys were there and they told us how hard it was and all the rules of how to do it but I just grabbed it and went and it was pretty scary and I did a belly flop. And Rebecca went and the boys were so impressed and they wanted us to meet them later but they were East Side types and kind of greasy and we said we already had boyfriends.

That night we went to Matthew's and watched Sins of Our Fathers practice and Fiona had learned all the songs and she was trying to get Greg to do things with her, like in "Oblivion" she wanted' to leave a space in the middle of the chorus and at first nobody understood what she meant but then Greg figured it out and they started doing it and it sounded cool and everyone was very impressed. A couple days after that I saw Richard downtown and he asked about Cybil and Sins of Our Fathers and I told him how good they were getting and how Fiona was a real musician and they were sounding really heavy. He smiled and he was happy for them and he said he'd go see them when they played.

On the Fourth of July me and Rebecca and Cybil and Matthew and Fiona all drove down to this big rock concert jam that Matthew had heard about. It was in this big field by the river and it was all these heavy metal bands and heavy metal people in low-rider cars and the skankiest girls. The bands were these horrible poser guys with poodle perms and spandex. Matthew had a bunch of pot and me and Rebecca smoked some and we got so stupid we were giggling like idiots. And we went and sat by the river and these two studly metal boys tried to talk to us and get us to drink some of their Black Velvet. But we were just giggling and then Fiona came and started talking to them and being really sarcastic which made us laugh even more. And then these groupie girls came and they had total cleavage and the boys forgot about us pretty quick. Back at Matthew's car Fiona said the groupie girls had fake tits and we were like, *no way*. But she explained how you could tell and then Rebecca asked her how she knew so much about it. Cybil glared at us but we were so stupid from the pot we didn't care. And Fiona said don't worry, hers were real and did we want to see? And Matthew said, "Yeah, show tits!" and Fiona started undoing her shirt and we just collapsed in the grass laughing.

And then one night I went downtown after work and no one else was around and I was walking down the street and someone came running up behind me and I turned around and it was Todd. And I had sworn to myself that I was going to be so cool and aloof when I saw him again but he had this big smile on his face and he seemed so happy I just had to give him a hug. And he hugged me back, sort of, and we walked along together and talked and it was so exciting and then he asked me where I was going. I said nowhere. He said he was going to pick up a check at Carla's and did I want to come and I said sure!

Carla lived in an old apartment building in Northwest. Todd had a key and we rode up in this clunky elevator and he opened the door and I swear, I had never seen a place as trashed as Carla's apartment. There were clothes piled up in mountains and this huge vanity was totally covered with jewelry and makeup and sunglasses and all this cool stuff. And there were about a hundred pairs of shoes spilling out of the closet and all these cool magazines spread around and books and candles and about ten million tapes around the cassette player. Todd got an envelope off the refrigerator and sat down on the bed. And I was just standing there, trying to look at everything and Todd said,

"Sit, Andrea." So I did. And then he asked me if everything was okay and I said everything was okay. He opened the envelope and looked at the check and asked me what I wanted to do and I told him I wanted to kiss him. He looked up from the check and he had the biggest grin on his face. So I kissed him once, really soft on the lips and it was just heavenly. Then we made out and he rolled me back on the bed and took off my pants and started to put it in. But he didn't have a condom. So then he ran all over Carla's with his penis bouncing around looking for a rubber and I didn't have one because I was always afraid my stupid parents might find it. Then he picked up the phone and started to call Carla to ask her if she had any rubbers but I didn't want her to know so I told him to come to the bed and I put it in my mouth and started doing that. At first I was sort of nervous but then he started moaning with pleasure and stroking my hair and it was sort of fun. And then he started to come and I didn't want it in my mouth so I put it on my chest like I saw in a video. After that Todd told me how sexy I was and kissed me all over and then he went down on me and at first it tickled so much but also I was getting super horny. And then he licked it right in the spot and it felt *so good* and I squeezed my legs so hard I was afraid I was going to break his neck.

But then we had to leave because Carla was coming back. So we walked back downtown and it was dark and all the bums were on the streets and even they looked at Todd like he was so cool. And it was too late for him to cash his check so I bought him a frozen yogurt and then we went to Poor Boy Records and I bought him a tape of Bender. And then we walked up to Sweeny Park and he got some beer and we drank it and laid in the grass and looked at the stars. And he told me about Seattle and all the politics of the music business and how they always rip you off and how pathetic people are when they get old, they forget their own dreams and just try to suck off other people's. I said how I hated watching Lizzy Rosen's grandpa walk down to the corner and how sad it was that everything that's beautiful fades away. And he said he thought about that all the time and he felt like right now he saw the world through a perfectly clear glass but as the years went by it would get more clouded and murky and he would forget his ideals and that's why he always kept a journal so that when he was old he could look back and remember. And I said how my dad always fell asleep in front of the TV. And he said that your parents probably believed everything you believed when they were young but life had broken them down and made them lose their dreams and once you had lost your dreams you were adrift and defenseless and the first adversity that came along would destroy you. And all this time we were laying in the grass and holding hands and it was just a perfect moment. And then he leaned over and kissed me and then we started making out and then he took off my pants and took off his own pants. But we still didn't have a condom so we were just touching and rubbing against each other and then I wanted him inside me so bad I couldn't stand it anymore and I reached down and put it in myself. And then we just laid there for the longest time. And we whispered to each other and he told me how beautiful I was and I told him I wanted him inside me every second of every day. And we tried to be still and not make him come and my legs were all the way around his back and it was in so deep and we were kissing so soft and slow. And then we couldn't help it and we started doing it and then he started coming and he pulled it out and put it on my stomach and it was squirting all over. And then he laid down on top of me and the stuff was gooey and warm and sticky, like glue holding us together.

"You are so nasty!" was Rebecca's reaction when I told her. I guess it was true but the thing was I loved Todd so much I didn't care. And when he went back to Seattle I wasn't even sad because I knew I was in his heart and he was in mine. And I didn't care if we weren't officially boyfriend and girlfriend or if he lived with Carla or if he hung out with other girls because my feelings were beyond possession and whining and the usual girlfriend stuff. And if I was sad sometimes it was the best kind of sadness, just lying in your bed and dreaming of someone or imagining he's sitting with you on the bus or talking to him in your head while you're going through your day. And it was true I was totally in lust and we were pretty nasty but it was love too and love was like that and made you *desire* with all of your being. And anyway it wasn't like you could be with someone like Todd every day. He wasn't that type of person. And I mean, even if it was bordering on groupiness, that was hardly an excuse to give up the funnest person you ever met.

And then at KBAN Jamaal was bugging me if I had a boyfriend. I said sort of and I told him about Todd and how he was a musician and a free spirit and then Jamaal dedicated a song to "Andrea and Todd" and it was this woman with this super deep voice and it made you think you were in a smoky train station and your lover was leaving forever and how the world was so full of tragedy and sweet sadness. And then Jamaal sent me across the street to get iced coffees and when I got back Ms. Caliban was there and she was being such a priss and asking me if I vacuumed yet and I had but obviously it wasn't good enough. So I got out the vacuum and turned it on and then she yelled at me to turn it off because she was on the phone. Fortunately I hadn't done the wastebaskets yet and so I did that and when I was done she was still in my chair so I went and sat with Jamaal and he showed me how to turn the dials to fade out the music.

25

WHEN FIONA FIRST JOINED SINS OF OUR Fathers, she said she didn't do drugs that much. But that didn't last long. She and Matthew were smoking pot every second. And also drinking. Greg was still totally straight, except for his addiction to hair dye, and so the band was starting to divide between him and Cybil on one side and Matthew and Fiona on the other. Cybil didn't seem too worried about it though, the real complainer was Rebecca, who would say how much she hated pot and drinking beer all the time but when she was around Matthew she would always do it. And she still liked Matthew but she was so afraid of Fiona she wouldn't try to challenge her or ask Matthew about it and everybody was beginning to suspect that Fiona and Matthew were doing more than just bong hits in his basement after practice.

Then Greg got a girlfriend. Her name was Barbara and she was this trippy girl from Outer Limits and she had hair extensions and a nose ring and she smelled like incense. And she came to every practice and smoked cigarettes and wouldn't talk to anyone. And Cybil said how weird she was and one time me and Rebecca tried to ask her questions but she wouldn't answer and she acted like she was too cool for us and she seemed sort of pathetic. And then one day she didn't come and Matthew said they had broken up and even though nobody liked her that much we all felt sorry for Greg.

But at least he got laid. I guess sex was all anyone thought about during the summer. I know it was all I thought about. And every day I went downtown to the Metro Mall after work or hung around Scamp's or sometimes sat at the tables outside Kruger's Department Store. And everywhere I went boys looked at me and tried to talk to me and sometimes I would be tempted but they were always boring or on some ego trip or something. Todd was really the only person I could think about. And I'd sit outside Kruger's and write letters to him or poems or just little notes and sometimes I would draw him or I'd make a chain across the page with "Todd Sparrow" on one end and "Andrea Marr" on the other.

And then one day I saw Luke at Metro Mall and he said they were all back at Carla's. I talked to him for a while and then gave him my number really casual-like in case Todd wanted to call. He did. That night during dinner. And he sounded so weird on the phone, really raspy and far away. And the conversation was awkward because my dad was yelling at me to get off the phone because he gave somebody a root canal and their face was supposedly exploding. I pulled the phone cord into the next room and tried to ignore him. And poor Todd, because their van got towed and everyone was sleeping on the floor at Carla's and he was calling from a pay phone and they were all broke and everything was going wrong. And I tried to be there for him and make him know how much I loved him without actually saying it. And I guess it worked because he started talking really sexy and I said things and I could tell how horny it was making him. And when I hung up I was blushing and my dad grabbed the phone and hung it up but then the root-canal guy didn't even call.

The next day Todd called me at work and wanted me to come over. I was lusting so bad. And as soon as work was over I jumped on the bus and went to Carla's and buzzed her apartment. Todd came down and we snuck into the basement to this little storage room. We got inside it and Todd locked the door and he didn't say one word, he just backed me to the wall and kissed me and reached under my dress for my panties. And he was feeling me in this really aggressive way and then he lifted me up against the wall and put it inside me and started doing it and all this dust was getting on me. After that we laid on these old rugs and he was being really quiet and it was weird. And then we started kissing again and making out and I kept trying to look in his eyes but there was all this dust and stuff and he kept sneezing and then we did it in this sideways position and I couldn't really tell what he was thinking. And then he had to go back upstairs and I started to leave but then he called me back and gave me a hug. But it was weird because it wasn't a happy hug, it was sort of sad and desperate and like trying to hold on. And then he seemed embarrassed and he tried to smile and I just left really fast and walked to the bus stop. And my mind was racing and I kept telling myself that everything was okay but it wasn't okay because I was just craving Todd and loving him more than ever and I was getting in such a panic I had to stop and sit down and take ten deep breaths.

The next day Rebecca called me at work and she was hysterical. She had been talking to Matthew and he had casually mentioned that he'd had sex with Fiona. And she was so shocked and I tried to tell her it was pretty obvious but then she started yelling at me like, why didn't I tell her? How could I let her be so humiliated? I tried to explain that maybe Matthew hadn't considered her his girlfriend and that really set her off. She wasn't some dumb slut! She wasn't some *groupie*! I said of course she wasn't though she was in a way. We all were. Except Cybil. And then she said that Matthew was only a junior and we were *seniors* and how dare he! And that was funny because it made me realize that high school did not matter anymore. Now that we were seniors, now that all the high school rules worked in our favor, we had transcended them. And I was trying to calm her down but all the time I kept thinking about Todd and what I could do to prevent this from happening to me.

What I did was, I started rationing Todd. Or at least I tried to. I had a big desktop calendar at work and whenever I saw Todd I put a "T" on that day and if I had sex with him I put a circle around it. If I called him I put a T with an arrow pointed toward it. If he called me I put a T with an arrow pointing away from it. And I made up rules like I would never call him three days in a row. And I would never call him the day after we had sex. And if he called me I could call him back if for some reason we hadn't talked enough but I never invited myself over or suggested we go out unless he had called me or unless two days had gone by since we last had sex. And after only two weeks I had this huge chart and all these rules diagrammed out like math formulas. And naturally all of this was a secret but then Jamaal saw me working on it and he started bugging me to explain it. So I finally did and he cracked up and said how white people always had to organize everything into charts and graphs, even their love lives.

And all this time Jamaal was getting me addicted to iced coffee and I would always have one with lunch now and they were so delicious, especially when it was really hot. I had finally made friends with the lady at the store across the street. Sort of. I think she was prejudiced. Not just against black people but against everyone at KBAN. Probably Sondra Caliban had given her a hard time. But I would be really sweet and I would trick her into talking to me by asking her really stupid questions and then agreeing with everything she said. Her favorite thing to talk about was the horrible Mexicans who were always sleeping in her doorway and going to the bathroom on her garbage cans. And one day it was like 102 degrees and I was getting iced coffees and her fan was broken and she was sweating and her perm had totally fallen over. And she tried to give me some gum that was melting and she seemed sort of crazy and it was so depressing because she was old and she had no friends and what could she possibly have to look forward to?

And then one day Todd called me at KBAN and asked me about Sins of Our Fathers and if they were any good. I was like, "Sins of Our Fathers? They're the *best!*" He said he saw them a long time ago but they didn't have a bass player and he thought they were pretty bad. So I told him about all the changes they had made and they were a totally different band and they were really heavy now and Fiona was the bass player. Todd said, "Fiona Carlisle?" I said yeah and he laughed and I said what's so funny and he said she gave Luke herpes. I was like, *what*? But he just laughed. And then he said everyone was talking about Sins of Ours Fathers lately and he was going to give them a shot at opening for his band in August at this big show. But that made me mad and I said, "Give them a *shot*? Don't you even know who Cybil is?" And then I told him about when Cybil shaved her head for *him* and how he was a legend to us for *years* because of Cybil and he had never heard any of this and he was like, "No shit?"

I hung up and immediately called Rebecca. I told her that Fiona had herpes and she about died. She started inspecting herself while we were on the phone and she was like, "What does it look like?" I said, "How would I know?" She said she always used a condom with Matthew and didn't that protect you? But I didn't know and so she called some other people and I called Cybil and she said herpes was no big deal but still don't tell anyone because it would make the band seem sleazy. So then I told her that Todd wanted to play with them but Cybil didn't seem that impressed. She said, "Tell him to call Matthew."

Todd didn't have to. Matthew called him. And they set it up. So then everyone was getting all excited about the big show of Color Green and Sins of Our Fathers, especially Matthew. Meanwhile Rebecca didn't get herpes and she forgave Matthew and she wanted me to come to a practice with her. So I did and we hung out and it was really loud and Cybil was screaming her brains out and Fiona was really cool the way she head-banged like a boy. Afterward we all drank beer and I even smoked pot because I had made a pact with myself that I could smoke pot a couple times during the summer but not during the school year. And Fiona told dumb-blonde jokes and smoked cigarettes and then Greg came over and asked me about Todd Sparrow and what he was really like and I was so stupid from the pot I just laughed at him. But then I noticed that everyone was waiting to see what I'd say about Todd. Matthew especially and Cybil and even Fiona leaned toward me and waited to hear. It was so weird. And I was too high on pot and I was getting paranoid and I told them all to stop staring at me.

And then Todd called me at KBAN and he was going to Seattle to see Buzz Mitchell and he wasn't going to be back until the show with Sins of Our Fathers. I was at my desk at work and looking at my calendar and it was August 5 and the show was August 14 and when I saw all those blank spaces in a row I couldn't think of what to say. Todd was trying to be nice and I said, "Couldn't you just come back for a day in the middle?" He started to say why he couldn't but I said, "I didn't mean that. I know you can't," or some dumb thing. All I wanted was to get off the phone before I turned into whiny girlfriend. And as soon as I hung up I went and got iced coffees and the crazy lady was there and yakking at me and I didn't hear a word she said. And then back at the station I sat in the studio with Jamaal and I drank my iced coffee so fast it made my head spin.

26

IT WAS SO WEIRD WHEN TODD LEFT. FOR one thing I was walking through Metro Mall one day and this girl I never saw before came up to me and asked me if I was Andrea Marr and was I going out with Todd? I said I was and she introduced herself as Lisa and she wanted to know if Luke had a girlfriend. I started to answer and she said, "I mean a girlfriend in Portland." She said that she knew they were always going up to Seattle and stuff. And I wasn't sure what she meant but she smiled a certain way and then I knew. And I was taking the bus home anyway so I had coffee with Lisa and she was weird and her hair looked really damaged like it had been dyed a million times. And then it turned out she went to Camden and she had just graduated and we talked about graduating from high school and she said the whole thing was stupid, it was all this build-up and the next day nothing happens and you're just hanging around Metro Mall or maybe looking for a job. She was pretty depressing. And then when I went to the bus stop she followed me and she asked me about Todd and had I heard any of the tapes from the new record but I didn't even know there were any. And she told me about her friend Vanessa and how all her friends had crushes on Todd and they had heard about me and she was really glad to meet me. And I said me too and I shook her hand and then she hugged me and it was extremely weird.

And then Rebecca had this idea that we should all go to Monte Carlo and look for new boyfriends. Cybil was not into it and she hated Monte Carlo because it was just a bunch of girls

178

like Wendy Simpson. But it was summer and there wasn't anything else to do or any place to go since Outer Limits closed. So we all went and it was Rave Night and everyone was dressed British and trying to be fashionable. We sat in a booth and boys immediately started coming over and asking us to dance and Cybil was being such a snot. But when girls came over and asked her about Sins of Our Fathers she was totally nice to them. This one girl stood there for fifteen minutes telling us about the band she was starting and how great they were going to be. Then Lisa walked in. I hid behind Rebecca. And then Kevin came in with his new girlfriend, Celeste, who was the most beautiful blond hippie spirit you ever saw. And I was trying to be mature and be happy for them but I sort of hated her. And the music was totally pounding and all the boys were jumping up and down like monkeys and Monte Carlo was okay but compared to being with Todd it just seemed like a big waste of time.

Then Carla walked in. She was by herself and Cybil waved to her and she came over and she acted really shy even though she was the coolest person in the whole place. She asked if she could sit with us and we were like, "Of course!" So she got in the booth and then she looked straight at me and said that Todd had been arrested in Seattle and he was in jail. We were all in shock and then she looked at Cybil and said, "You're Cybil." And Cybil said, "You're Carla," and then they had mutual admiration society and Carla said how much she liked Sins of Our Fathers and Cybil said how much she liked Carla's fashion ideas. And I told

Carla how I loved her apartment and how cool she was to let Todd stay there. And Cybil asked her about her hair and where she shopped. And Rebecca was getting pissed and she finally blurted out, "I thought we came here to meet boys!" And Carla looked around and said, "Are there any interesting ones?" And Cybil said, "No." And Carla lit a cigarette and me and Rebecca both took one but I was coughing and I couldn't really smoke it.

Rebecca found a boy. He was from Learning Center and Kevin sent him over and Rebecca danced with him. And Carla turned to me and said, "I don't know if you know this but when Todd goes to Seattle he stays with a girl named Tori and if you want to call her and find out if he's out of jail, I'll give you her number." I said okay and I took the number and sat back and we all watched Rebecca dance. And all these boys kept coming up to us and it was annoying and Carla wanted to go outside. So me and Cybil went with her and it was a lot better outside because everyone leaned on cars and sat on the curb just like at Outer Limits. And I asked Carla what Tori was like and how old was she and Carla said she was pretty weird and she was twenty-five and she was manic-depressive. And all the time we were talking guys were staring at us and girls too and I remembered Outer Limits and how Carla was always the coolest girl and whatever people were with her were always the coolest people.

The next day at work I wrote Tori's number on my calendar. But I didn't call her. I was too scared. I called Cybil and she agreed that it would be too weird for me to be dealing with Todd's Seattle girlfriend. Like we were the various chapters of the Todd Sparrow girlfriend club. And she hadn't said it before but she thought my relationship with Todd was definitely bordering on groupiness. So we talked about what I could do about it and we decided it was just the nature of Todd and the only thing I could do was not act like a bimbo. And then we talked about Carla and Cybil said she really liked her and I told about her apartment and how trashed it was and how much cool stuff she had.

Then some skinheads beat up two black kids in the neighborhood by the radio station and then the next night some black guys beat up some white skateboarders I guess because they couldn't find any skinheads. And then at the radio station everybody was all upset about it and having big arguments and screaming at each other right over my desk. And everybody was there even when it wasn't their shift and Jamaal did the news and went on these rants and the white news guy was having tantrums and Ms. Caliban was on vacation and for once I wished she was there.

The next day Cybil called me and she had gone shopping with Carla and I was so pissed, like why didn't she call me? She said Carla was a genius at a clothes rack and how Carla told her about going to Los Angeles, where her sister lived, and all the incredible shops they had down there. And Cybil was wondering if she was a lesbian because she had never had sex with

Todd. And it was so weird because it seemed like Todd *adored* Carla and they must have had sex at some point. But it scared me too because what if Todd liked her more because she didn't have sex and that made her more mysterious and exotic? Like he just wanted me for sex and she was his soul partner and the one he really loved.

Meanwhile Doug was back in town and he and Rebecca started going out and having sex all the time. Then she called me and Doug had a friend and she wanted to double-date. I didn't really want to but I said okay. My date was named Trevor and he thought he was so cool with his Astral Planes T-shirt. So I told him how we met Ian of Astral Planes in Seattle and the whole adventure with Color Green. And he had heard that Color Green were really good but he hadn't heard them so I told him about Todd and Color Green and how they were up in Seattle but they were coming back except Todd might be in jail. And then I told about Buzz Mitchell and how I helped Todd with his cover art and how Todd and I had talked about getting old and how Todd kept a journal so he would always remember. And I guess it was bumming out Trevor's ego because he was getting cranky and he didn't want to hear any more about Todd and when they took me home he didn't even try to kiss me.

The next day Cybil called me at KBAN and Carla had told her that Todd had *not* gone to jail but just got hassled by the cops one night walking back from the studio and Buzz Mitchell was trying to exaggerate it and make it into a controversy so Color Green would get in the music papers. Carla also said that Todd might come to Portland a couple days before the show. I was ready. With my first couple paychecks I had gone straight to HOP! and also Ragtime, which was a new vintage store, and I had a great new dress that was like my cow dress except it had fishes and it wasn't falling apart at all. And I had these white-and-black saddle shoes which were pretty daring since the only girl in Portland who wore saddle shoes was Carla. And every day I wore my best clothes to work and had all my stuff and plenty of money and everything I would need if Todd called. But he never did.

The big Color Green/Sins of Our Fathers show was on a Friday night and it was a drag because I had to work and the funnest thing before a Sins show was to go to Cybil's and help her get dressed because then when she came onstage you could see all your decisions and you could see the audience's reaction. But I didn't have time to get the bus all the way home and then come back because the show was early because it was in a Youth Center underneath a church. And when I got there at seven, it was still hot and nobody wanted to go inside and poor Party Hats were playing to no one. And then Rebecca and Doug and Trevor came and Trevor was acting surprisingly nice. So I went with them and we drove to the store and got some beer and listened to tapes and it was fun in a college sort of way.

When we got back to the church Greg's station wagon had arrived and Fiona had her old smashed-up Toyota and they were moving all their stuff and there was still no sign of Todd or Luke or Carla or anybody. So we stood around and then Lisa showed up with her friend Vanessa. Lisa made a big deal of introducing me but Vanessa just glared at me and then asked me if I had heard the new Color Green record yet and of course I hadn't and she just rolled her eyes at Lisa like, *Who is this idiot?* I just tried to get away from them. But Lisa followed me around and then Trevor came over and Lisa sniffed at him like he was *so uncool* which was true. And as soon as I talked to Trevor she lost all respect for me and walked away but I was glad to get rid of her.

Now I just had to get rid of Trevor. I pretended like I was going to the bathroom and then I snuck over by the stage where Cybil was and hid in the back hallway until Trevor went back outside. Then I hung out there but Cybil was being cranky and Fiona was arguing with Matthew about which side of the stage she was going to stand on. And poor Greg was trying to get his drums ready and everybody kept knocking his stuff over and ignoring him. So I helped him and talked to him and I asked him what he was doing over the summer and he said, "Nothing."

Then I felt something. It was like a sudden tingle in the air and it meant that Todd Sparrow was here. I stuck my head around the corner and I saw two guys carrying a big amplifier and it had COLOR GREEN stenciled across the side. But I stayed

184

where I was. I watched them put the amplifier on the stage and go back to the door. And then Fiona came barging through the hallway with her huge bass and I had to back up to the stairs. And since there was nothing else to do, I went up them. I wandered through some hallways and up some steps and then I opened a door and I was standing on the stage of the church. It was huge. It had tall arching ceilings and my first thought was, I sure hope none of the skinheads find their way up here. And even though you could hear the noise below, the room was so big it kept its own silence. And the rows of wooden benches looked so orderly and everything was so neat and clean and polished. And I sat down on the steps by the pulpit and rested my head on my hands and just sort of enjoyed the silence and not knowing what was going to happen with Todd or with school next year or going to college. And it was probably totally sacrilegious but before I left I thanked God for Todd and the music scene and for all the fun I was having and at least my youth wasn't being totally wasted. At least I found someone to love. At least when I was old I'd have one good thing to remember.

27

CARLA MET ME COMING DOWN THE STAIRS. She had just got there and she was looking for the bathroom and I had to go too so we looked for it together. The one we found was really nice and it must have been where the priests put on their robes and stuff

185

because it had a lighted mirror and it was really fancy. After we peed Carla was doing her lipstick and I was sort of watching her and she said, "Todd's here." I said, "I know." And she put on more lipstick and she looked at me in the mirror and she said that what Todd really liked on girls was big hair. And I complained how boring mine was and she started grabbing it and bunching it up on my head. And then she said I should do darker lipstick and she gave me some and then she held my hair up and started putting pins in it. After that she put some eyebrow pencil on me and she was standing so close her breasts were touching my arm. And when she tipped my head forward to fix my bangs I could feel her breath on my forehead. And I was worried she'd think I was too much of a groupie so I said I didn't really care what Todd liked. She said, "I know, it's just an excuse." And I watched her face while she fiddled with my hair and I thought what a strange and mysterious girl she was.

Downstairs things were not going well. It was so packed you couldn't even see back to the door and Sins of Our Fathers were onstage and Matthew and Fiona were yelling at the sound guy and the P.A. was all screwed up. And when Cybil tried to talk into the mike it did feedback so loud everyone had to plug their ears. And people were shouting at them to play and Greg started hitting his drums and Matthew yelled at him to shut up. Cybil was getting really pissed and the whole fun of the first moment, of Cybil making her entrance, was already spoiled. And all the time I kept glancing toward the front to see where Todd was.

And I kept touching my bare neck and sort of wiggling my head to feel my hair which was piled on my head like I was the Queen Of Siam.

Sins of Our Fathers played exactly one song and then the fire trucks arrived. And then the police came. And then more police came and they had riot gear and it was so weird because everyone just looked at them like, *what*? We were watching all the commotion from the back hallway and then these two hands covered up my eyes and someone kissed my neck and I spun around and threw my arms around Todd and gave him the biggest kiss. And Todd was like the antidote to all the bad energy because as soon as he and Luke showed up everything was fun again. And the cops were talking in megaphones and telling people to clear the building and we all snuck up the steps and hid in the priests' bathroom. Todd sat in the sink and popped a zit on his chin and then we went back downstairs and started carrying out the amplifiers and when the cops asked us what we were doing Todd said, "We're leaving."

And then outside this guy came up to Todd and said we could have the show at his farm. Todd was like, yeah? The guy said he would be honored. So everybody started whispering the directions to his farm. And then Todd started organizing everything and getting the equipment loaded and everyone helped and we did it really fast. And we all hopped in the Color Green van and everybody else got in their own cars and off we went.

And when we got there it really was a farm with fields and tractors and everything. And the guy was there at the gate waving us in. And Todd drove the van into the barn and we all jumped out and unpacked the stuff. And it wasn't even dark yet and all these people showed up and Color Green set up their stuff and started playing. Right in the barn. It was so hilarious! We danced and jumped on the hay piles and Todd tried to sing his lyrics but there was no mike so you couldn't really hear. And then Matthew and Greg were jamming and Cybil played drums and some boys hit a washtub with a stick. And the guy who owned the farm was so happy because he had saved the day and all these people were having such a great time. And when it got dark he built a fire and people got beer and then we all sat around the campfire. And I had hay sticking out of my hairdo and Todd ran around but whenever he walked by me he kissed the back of my neck. And then he took me in the van and he had a rubber and we did it really fast but it was still really sweet. And then we went back out and I was laughing so hard and skipping around and my dress was falling off and everybody was singing and it was such a blast!

The next day at KBAN Jamaal bugged me that I'd done something kinky because I had scratches all over me. I was wearing my hair down normal but every time I went by the bathroom I would run in and push it up and my neck was all scratched but it still looked so glamorous and sexy I couldn't stop doing it. Then Todd called and he wanted to go see this French movie but he didn't have any money so I took him. And then we had sex in Sweeney Park because Carla was home but then I had to walk to the bus stop by myself and I got home after midnight and my parents yelled at me.

But all that week I kept going into bathrooms and pulling my hair up into a bunch on my head and stray bits would hang over my face and I looked so sexy I could hardly believe it. And it made me mad that I had wasted so much time wearing it down in the most boring of all possible ways. And one night I was trying on different tops and looking at my breasts and sort of talking to Carla in my head, asking her questions, like which way should I pin my hair and would Todd like this blouse or that shirt. And I knew Todd liked my breasts but I pretended that Carla was advising me on what was the sexiest top to wear and if I should go braless or show cleavage or just be totally covered and mysterious.

And then Todd called me at work and he was going back to Seattle. I was like, "Todd, you practically live there." He said, "What do you mean, I *do* live there." I tried to stay calm and I asked him if I could come with him to the bus station because he usually took the bus but he said he was getting a ride and he had all these excuses and then I started to cry, silently of course, and I was still going "Uh-huh" and "Yeah" as we talked but the tears were rolling down my face and splatting on my calendar. And he was being so smooth and charming and just so Todd-like and then I sniffled and he knew I was crying. There was a long silence and I just wanted to crawl through the phone line and curl up beside him. But then I apologized and said what a wimp I was and he said, "It's all right, Andrea. Don't worry. Everything is all right."

It was the last days of summer then and the wind was blowing and the air was full of dust and smoke. And all the fun of summer seemed over, like it was time to get serious again and think about school and worry about things. And Cybil was pissed because in their last two shows Sins had played a total of one song and Fiona was grumbling because Matthew had told her they'd be playing all the time. And then Matthew called me to get Tori's number and he called Todd and tried to get some shows in Seattle. And Rebecca was getting so hot for Doug and saying that she was going to the University of Oregon because that's where he went. They even got me to go out with Trevor again because he had tickets to see this rap group. The four of us went and there were a million cops and they searched you and made you walk through all these metal detectors and everyone was being really paranoid. After that Doug drove us to the store and they got a bottle of wine and I got some Cheese Widgets and Rebecca got gum and Trevor paid for it all. Then we went to Sweeney Park and hung out. And I had made Rebecca promise she wouldn't make out with Doug and leave me alone with Trevor but they did it anyway and Trevor tried to kiss me and I told him I liked him more as a friend and I was getting grass stains on my pants from scooting away from him. And then he started putting down Color Green and saying that *he* was creative and he had suffered more than Todd and he once tried to commit suicide even. Like that would impress me. And he said how guys in bands were all egomaniacs and how easy it was to play music. And I had been so good in the last week at blocking Todd out of my mind but now it all came rushing back, how great it was to be with him, that great feeling of being *free* and having great talks and being a million miles away from mean stupid people like Trevor.

The next day I drove by Hillside on the way to work and all the football players were in their shoulder pads and doing jumping jacks and the sprinklers were on and the faculty parking lot was full of cars. Everyone was getting ready for the new year. And downtown everything was "Back to School" and all the suburban types were invading Kruger's and Metro Mall and all of a sudden I thought very seriously about college. I did not want to turn into Lisa and graduate from high school and the next day be "hanging around the mall or maybe looking for a job."

And then on the last weekend of summer Cybil called me and she was going to Monte Carlo with Matthew and Fiona and did I want to come and Carla was going to be there. I did. I piled all my hair up and pinned it with Carla's pins that I kept in a special KBAN envelope. They picked me up and Fiona and Matthew were smoking pot while they drove and they were drunk too but Cybil wasn't scared so I didn't say anything. At Monte Carlo Nick Pax was in the parking lot with these girls who said how stupid Monte Carlo was. They were from Seattle and they were just laughing at Portland. And then someone was blasting Color Green out of their car stereo and it was their new record. It was out. And then I saw Carla coming across the street and me and Cybil ran to meet her and I thought to myself: *Carla is always alone.* But we were all so happy to see each other and Carla said she liked my hair and we immediately went off by ourselves, away from the parking lot and the stupid Seattle girls.

And then some boys recognized Cybil and they gave us a ride to Tower Records so I could buy the new Color Green tape. We looked at magazines and stuff and Carla told us all the gossip about Buzz Mitchell and his new band, Spank, which Tori started but then got kicked out of. And then we walked back to Monte Carlo, down Broadway by all the shops and department stores and Carla smoked cigarettes and she and Cybil talked and I mostly listened. And I kept looking at the tape and turning it over in my hands and I couldn't wait to go home and turn off all the lights and get in bed and listen to Todd.

PART THREE

28

BACK TO SCHOOL, WHAT A NIGHTMARE.

And I was having the worst hair crisis of my life because I loved piling my hair up and nobody cared at Monte Carlo or Color Green shows, but at Hillside High School? It was a terrible decision because if I just wore my hair normal I was giving in to their mediocrity and if I put it up there wouldn't even be anyone to appreciate it and I would get teased and what was the point? And for the last week before school I had worn it up every day because it was so hot and now it felt weird to let it down. And also, as Carla had pointed out, my whole taste in clothes was heading toward a big hair look anyway and it was like the missing link and I looked like an idiot if I wore my fish dress and saddle shoes and then left my hair hanging off me like a dog. It got so bad that I even contemplated getting a bob just to end the agony but no one was getting bobs now and even Carla was growing hers out. And I was having a total panic so I called Cybil and she said I should shave my head and I was like, *very funny, Cybil.* Then I almost called Carla but she wasn't in high school and I thought it would be too embarrassing to bother her with such suburban stupidness.

But even without calling her, I knew what Carla would do. She'd wear her hair any way she felt like and with Jackie O sunglasses and a scarf and the shortest miniskirt and if anyone said anything to her she would give them her blank stare and they would be totally *faced*! So what did I wear? I wore my plainest black jeans and a T-shirt and my hair down and sunglasses that I was too scared to wear out of Rebecca's car. Cybil wore blue jeans and a button-down shirt and Rebecca was the most daring of us all because at least she wore a dress. And walking across the parking lot that first morning, there were all these *children* getting out of their parents' cars and they looked so small you were afraid you'd step on one. And everyone always said how school is just babysitting until you're old enough to work and for the first time it really seemed true.

At this point the only thing at Hillside I really cared about was Mr. Perry and making sure I got into college. I went right in the first day and said hi to him and got my SAT stuff and he smiled at me like here was a girl with potential. But then Cybil told me at lunch that the all-women's colleges were full of lesbians and I better watch out. And then Greg came and sat with us and he had just come from the parking lot where he had been smoking pot with Matthew. And it was scary because Greg never did drugs and you could see in his eyes how crazy it was making him and how scared he was. So then after lunch Cybil and Matthew got in a fight about Greg. Matthew said it wasn't his fault and anyway what business was it of hers? But Cybil said it *was* her business and how she wished it wasn't, how the last thing she wanted was to be dependent on a bunch of pothead boys.

After school all the seniors were in the parking lot and there was a party at Forest Park and Greg was still stoned and afraid to go home so Cybil and I took him to the party. It was a beautiful day and there was a keg and we all sat on picnic tables and everyone drank beer. And these boys bugged us to come play Frisbee and we tried and I couldn't even throw it but Cybil of course was a total expert and was whizzing it around and all the boys were so amazed. And we drank some beer and took off our shoes and this one boy tried to talk to me and he said, "You're friend is pretty good at Frisbee." I said, "Yeah and she's also the biggest rock star in Portland." The boy nodded and looked at Greg and he didn't have a clue what I was talking about.

And it was weird being a senior because people were getting their last chance to switch their friends or change their image or adjust their look. Like Rebecca was now Miss Alternative Fashion with her horn-rims and her Chinese slippers. Cybil, on the other hand, was getting blander by the second. At least at school. It was like she was trying to disappear. Matthew looked the same, scraggly and with a tattoo, but now he hung around with Betsy Warren and Marjorie. Marjorie had dyed her hair blond and was doing a sort of druggy glam look and even wore fake eyelashes for half a day before Mrs. Katz told her it was "inappropriate." And Betsy Warren was still doing bong hits all the time and dealing drugs and getting dreadlocks from never washing her hair. And Greg started wearing these super baggy skater shorts that Cybil gave him. He was still dying his hair and there was now a sophomore boy who dyed his hair all the time and dressed weird and people started calling him "Little Greg." And then

197

Rebecca got a crush on a junior boy named Tom Petrovich. He was a trendy Monte Carlo type and he was going out with this cute sophomore girl but Rebecca decided she wanted him. So she started asking him out and she had a car and the other girl didn't and she was a senior and the other girl wasn't and she would have sex and the other girl wouldn't and so Rebecca got him pretty easily.

Meanwhile football season was going and everyone said we had such a great team this year and Bobby Wingate was going to be All-State. There was a picture of him in *The Oregonian* as well as an interview in the school paper, *Hillsider*, in which he said that Camden had not shown respect to Hillside and it was their mission to make Camden pay the price this year at Homecoming. And then Nathan Roth came over to me one day and told me he wanted me on *Hillsider* and Mr. Perry had told him to get me and would I come hang out with them and maybe write something if I felt like it? Nathan was one of the brains of our class and he was the new editor of *Hillsider*. So after school me and Cybil went to the newspaper office and when we walked in everybody stared at Cybil. Unlike the boys at the keg party, they knew who she was. They remembered her shaved head and her fights with Mrs. Renault and they knew she was in Sins of Our Fathers with Matthew. And it wasn't like they were against her, they just didn't know how to deal with her exactly and it was awkward and they gave us stuff to proofread and we did it and then we left. And then we went to Taco Time and Cybil said she wasn't really into *Hillsider* but she thought I should do it because it seemed pretty cool and anyway it would look good on my college applications.

And it sort of bugged me how people acted around Cybil. Like sometimes I would hear people talking about her and making up rumors and I started to realize that was their revenge. They were boring and Cybil was cool so they tried to isolate her and starve her socially. And the next morning I put my hair up and wore my fish dress and I made a pact with myself that I would wear my coolest clothes and shoes every day for a week to show my solidarity with Cybil. Of course at school everybody had to say something and tease me but not too much because I was a senior. And when Nathan saw me he looked at my hair but then he said he was sorry that everyone gave us a weird vibe and he still wanted me to work on *Hillsider* and Cybil too. I didn't have anything else to do so I went there after school and sat off to one side and proofread some other things and it was pretty weird because I was so dressed up and everyone else was in jeans and sweaters and trying to look newspaperish and literary but they played cool tapes so it was okay. And then Nathan read me his editorial about distributing condoms in school and he wanted to know what I thought and I said it seemed sort of boring. He nodded and I said it might still be good, what did I know? But he said I was right and he went to rewrite it and I could hear people whispering about me and I was sorry I said anything.

The next day Cybil came running up to me and Sins of Our Fathers was going to open for The Sidewinders from Texas at Baker Theater. I was like, "Wow!" And then I went to *Hillsider* and told Nathan and he said I should write an article about it. And I was getting all excited and thinking of what I'd write and then I called Cybil but she was totally against it. She said that she just wanted to get through Hillside with as little waves as possible and it was already hard enough and please please please don't tell Matthew because he'll want the publicity and there'd be a big fight.

So that was that. There was no article in *Hillsider* but there was a little blurb in *The Oregonian* about The Sidewinders with one line about "local rockers Sins of Our Fathers," which upset Matthew since he hated "rockers." The day of the show Cybil was getting so antsy she skipped the last half of the day. And as soon as school was out I drove to her house and we got dressed and Cybil was really nervous because Baker Theater was huge and a real theater. Then we went to Matthew's and loaded the stuff and me and Cybil and Fiona drove in Fiona's smashed-up Toyota. And it was so exciting because The Sidewinders had their huge bus outside and the Baker Theater people looked at us like we were little kids. And then during sound check Cybil sang "Oblivion" to the empty theater and it sounded so incredible even the janitors stopped to watch.

After sound check I tried to leave Cybil alone in their dressing room but she made me stay because she needed me because she felt so alone. So I stayed and then just before they went on we both snuck out to the back of the stage and crawled up the steps and peeked over and it wasn't super crowded but there was still a lot of people. Cybil said it didn't matter how big the crowd was, just that it was a professional sound system and a real stage and it would be good practice.

After that I waited out front and they came out and everybody clapped and Cybil looked so great in the little-girl dress we had picked out. She had tons of lipstick and her hair was parted in the middle now in a sort of Prince Valiant look and her pale skin looked so white next to her red mouth. And then Greg and Fiona started "We Are All Prostitutes" and all the people in the front nodded their heads to the beat but not too much. The people in the back barely watched. And Sins sounded good and it was fun but people didn't really get into it. They came to see The Sidewinders from Texas and they didn't care about some band of "local rockers."

And just when Sins were playing their last song Nathan appeared. He had pushed his way to the front and he grabbed me and told me how great they were and he couldn't believe Sins of Our Fathers went to *his* school. And I guess he was trying to look cool in his paisley shirt but he looked pretty dorky and he danced around and headbanged and it was embarrassing. And then afterward he wanted to go to the dressing room so I took him and he shook everyone's hand and Matthew immediately started schmoozing him. Cybil and Fiona were trying to change and I told them sorry about Nathan and I didn't know how to get rid of him. Cybil was sort of pissed but Fiona told her she better get used to it. And then Matthew lit a joint and he and Fiona smoked it which made Nathan nervous and he left.

Afterward we drove home with Fiona and I asked Cybil what she thought of Nathan. She didn't think much. I asked her what people at Hillside would think of the music scene if they knew about it but she was too busy listening to a tape of the show and analyzing all her mistakes. And all I could think about was how bad Cybil would *face* Hillside if they did an article about her and all she could think about was if she should scream the last verse of "Love Disease" or just sing it normal.

29 BUT EVEN IF CYBIL DIDN'T WANT SINS TO be in *Hillsider*, Matthew did and Nathan did too. They planned this big spread with pictures and interviews but then Cybil found out and said if they did it she'd quit the band. She told me about it at Taco Time, which was so packed with sophomores throwing food and shrieking at each other we could barely discuss it. And after school Nathan came up to me and we talked about the whole Sins controversy and if Cybil had a right to deny Hillside students a story that might be an important cultural message. And I was like, "If she

doesn't want to be in the paper she shouldn't have to be." And I knew he wouldn't do it because Mrs. Schroeder was the faculty adviser and she would never let you embarrass anyone.

Meanwhile, Rebecca was gushing over Tom Petrovich all the time and she was being so obnoxious and making fun of me for being on *Hillsider*. I was getting sick of her anyway. It seemed like all the seniors were sick of each other but at the same time there was the attitude that this was our *senior year* and we'd completed some *great journey* and weren't we *wonderful* and didn't we have all these *fond memories* and it was so bogus. And people were already getting nostalgic and sappy and when they did senior pictures for yearbook everyone thought up dumb quotes to put with their pictures, like "What a long strange trip it's been," or "I came, I saw, I partied!"

College. That was all I thought about. Getting out of Portland. Getting out of Hillside. And so I kept going to *Hillsider* and Nathan made me assistant editor so I could put it on my applications. And I took my SATs again even though I did really good the first time. And I always checked in with Mr. Perry and we sent away for applications and my parents were getting excited even though my mother was complaining I dressed up too much and I was trying to look like a model. And at *Hillsider* this girl Beth would always come sit by me while I read stuff and she would gossip about the other *Hillsider* people and how all the girls had a crush on Nathan except Amy Brubaker, who hated Nathan because she thought she should be editor. Amy had been Cynthia Carmichael's main assistant last year when Cynthia was editor and Amy assumed she would be next in line. Now Amy said it was sexism that Nathan got editor because they wouldn't allow two women editors in a row. And Beth told me about Cynthia Carmichael and how she would write the whole paper herself because she was a total Virgo perfectionist and she didn't like any of the other people's stuff and how Nathan was so much better because he just told people to write something and he didn't care what. Cynthia Carmichael went to Berkeley, which was where Beth wanted to go because it was the most progressive college in the West and she didn't want to go back east because the people there were too snobbish. She asked me where I wanted to go and I didn't know and I asked her if it was true that the all-women's colleges were all lesbians and she was shocked and she said, "Who told you that?"

And even though I didn't think of myself as being involved in Hillside, I was so busy getting good grades and doing *Hillsider* and talking to Mr. Perry that I was more of a high school student than ever. And when I went downtown to the library I practically hid inside it and I never went to Scamp's or to Metro Mall because I didn't want to see Carla or anybody from the music scene because I was thinking about different stuff now. And some days I would wear my black dress and my pumps and take my umbrella and my trench coat and I would walk around downtown by the secretaries and the business people just to feel what it was like to be a real adult. And I would look around at the buildings and try to imagine real skyscrapers like in San Francisco or New York and what it would be like to be around real cosmopolitan people. Because in Portland no matter how "big city" you felt someone would always walk by with a knife on their belt or a John Deere cap or have the most embarrassing haircut.

And then it was Homecoming and all the underclassmen were getting all excited and it was so weird because if you were a senior it didn't seem like anything. It was just a joke. Even among the corniest people. I still went to the football game though. I went with Cybil. It was at Camden and we sat in the parents section and wore big coats and hid under our umbrellas. And it was raining and cold and the field was like this big mud pit. And Cybil tried to explain the rules and we watched Bobby Wingate, who never seemed to do anything because he was on the line. Cybil said that was normal and he would still be All-State. And all the time we watched him we talked about how he had seen his friend Jerry get killed by skinheads and even if we hated him that was still pretty intense and maybe that was why he was such a good football player because he knew it was just a stupid game.

Maybe that was why I was such a good high school student, because I knew it was just a stupid game. And in my locker I had a little jewelry box with my bullet from Brad and a guitar pick of Todd's and on my door I had an old Thriftstore Apocalypse poster from Outer Limits. That was my real life. And then Beth invited me to go for lunch at Arctic Circle, which was a couple blocks down from Taco Time and was right on the border of where Camden students hung out. So we went and it was all Camden students who were just as dumb as Hillside students except for one boy who was cute and sort of preppie and kept looking at us. Beth was yakking away about an article she was writing about what it was really like to be a cheerleader, besides all the glamour and popularity that people saw on the surface. And then the preppie boy came over and he was like, "You guys are from Hillside, aren't you?" And then he told us we couldn't hang out at Arctic Circle and I guess he was trying to be funny because then he tried to talk to us. But we just blew him off.

Then after lunch Cybil came running up to my locker and said there was a new club in Portland called K Club. And Matthew had already got them a show on a Saturday night. So after school we drove downtown to check out K Club. It was across the river and in this warehouse building down by the train tracks. And it was raining so we got our umbrellas and walked around and tried to look in the windows and then a guy came out and said, "Can I help you?" Cybil said she was in Sins of Our Fathers and he said, "Cybil, wow, come on in." So we did and it was all dark and dusty and there was sawdust everywhere and tools and you could see where they were building the stage. The guy's name was Eric and he told Cybil he was at the church show and what

a drag it was when the police came. So we told him about playing in the barn and he had heard about it and he called it "The
Legendary Farm Show" and he was really bummed out that he
missed it. Then he offered us some beer and we said no thanks
and he offered us pot and we said no thanks and so he made tea.
And he was playing Color Green on his box and Cybil told him I
used to go out with Todd and he was so impressed even though
I told him I didn't really. And he cleared off a board and set up
a little table with the teapot and the cups and everything. And
he told Cybil how he saw her with Pax at Outer Limits and they
talked about bands and shows and I sipped my tea and it was
really fun in a mature having-tea sort of way.

Matthew must have told Nathan about Sins playing at
K Club because the next day Nathan wanted me to write something about it or at least get some pictures because everyone at
Hillside was talking about Sins of Our Fathers now and they
had to do something. But that wasn't true. The only people who
cared about Sins were the *Hillsider* people and their only interest
was to try to be cooler than each other and none of them were
very cool to start with so it was like a race of slugs. And Beth
asked me what you wear to a Sins of Our Fathers concert and I
explained to her that it wasn't a "concert" it was a "show" and
you could wear anything you wanted except if you went near
the slamming pit it would probably get ripped off you. That
scared her and she said she'd wear a sweatshirt or something
that wouldn't get ruined and I told her if she did that no one

would talk to her. And it was very confusing to her so I said, "I can't explain it, you just have to go a couple times."

And then Eric K Club called up Cybil and asked her out. We were so shocked because Eric was older and obviously rich if he was starting a club and Cybil didn't know what to think. So we went to Taco Time and tried to talk about it but all the Hillside *children* were there so we went to Arctic Circle, which was not quite as bad and at least they were from a different school. Cybil debated it and I tried to be objective even though in my heart I was afraid of her getting a boyfriend because Todd was gone and it didn't seem like I'd ever get a boyfriend at Hillside. But Eric *was* very cool and maybe older men were the solution. And anyway I could tell she was curious about him so I told her to go for it. Not that it mattered what I said. And then I thought I should try harder to get a boyfriend for myself, like not a really serious one but just someone to go to movies with or have sex so I would still be in practice when I went to college.

And it was kind of a drag being at *Hillsider* because everyone was arguing about Sins of Our Fathers. Like some people didn't even think they were a real band but then other people would say how "important" they were and what they "represented." And they finally interviewed Matthew and there was a big controversy because when they asked him about drugs he said he was pro-drugs, especially pot, and Nathan said they had to take that part out. But then someone else said wasn't that censorship? And it was all pretty pointless since everybody knew that Mrs. Schroeder would never allow it. And then Beth confided in me her plot to get Nathan to take her to the Sins of Our Fathers concert and what did I think was the best way to get boys interested in you? I told her to give him a blowjob and I meant it as a joke but she was totally serious and she said, "Do you think I should?" And then one day Amy Brubaker, who had totally ignored me before, suddenly asked me if I didn't think all this music stuff was pretentious and narcissistic. She was obviously trying to bait me but I told her the truth anyway. I said, "Some bands. But not Sins of Our Fathers. And especially not Cybil."

And then my SAT scores came and they were really high. And Mr. Perry got all excited because this year maybe he could get more Ivy Leaguers than Camden. Nathan scored really high too and he told me he wanted to go to Yale and I remembered Jim Dietz, who went there my sophomore year, and how old and distinguished he seemed and I looked at Nathan, who was nice but basically a dweeb, and it was scary how fast things change. And then this rumor went around that the top two SAT scores at Hillside were Richard Kirn and *Betsy Warren*. Everybody freaked out and nobody would believe it about Betsy but then everybody started watching her in classes and noticing how the teachers were sort of afraid of her and how she got A's even when she was totally wasted and people started to believe it.

The Sins of Our Fathers show was the big opening weekend for K Club so there was lots of publicity. There was a write-up in *The Oregonian* and posters everywhere downtown and by the end of the week someone had put up a Sins of Our Fathers poster in the *Hillsider* office. Fortunately Cybil had her date with Eric to worry about and wasn't paying attention to what was going on at school. They went out on a Wednesday and all that night I tried to study but I just kept looking out my window and wondering what was happening. But then the next day we went to Arctic Circle and Cybil was really quiet and she said it wasn't that great and she probably shouldn't go out with older men, especially if he was the owner of K Club where they would be playing all the time. And she went on like that, thinking up excuses and I ate my ice cream and watched her and thought how Eric K Club was so cute and so nice and if she couldn't like him, who could she like?

30

ERIC HAD K CLUB READY FOR THE GRAND opening. It looked great. It was bigger than Outer Limits and the stage was higher and they had cool blue lights that swirled around and made the walls look like the ocean or the sky or something. And everyone was starving for a new scene and there were so many new people that whatever cliques there were from before were now irrelevant and everything was starting from scratch. And it was so crowded I stayed in the dressing room with Cybil and Eric was smoking pot with Matthew and everyone was acting casual but they were obviously very nervous and excited. Party Hats played first and then there was a new band of all girls that weren't very good and then it was Sins of Our Fathers. I snuck out and hid right at the front of the stage because I didn't want to see Beth or Nathan or any Hillside people. I just wanted to see the show. And everyone was crowding forward and getting excited. And then Cybil walked out and she was wearing baggy skater shorts and this cool striped shirt and she looked very boyish and cute but also you could tell she was nervous. And the crowd at the front shouted, "Hey, Cybil!" but she just ignored them and sort of smiled and then Matthew came out and he hadn't shaved and he looked really trashy and stoned and Fiona looked really tough and even Greg looked like a real drummer. But it was weird because they seemed intimidated by the huge crowd and I could see Cybil shaking when she drank some water. And then something happened to the drums and they had to wait and people yelled and I started to get worried. But then they were ready and they started "Love Disease." Matthew played the first part and Cybil waited by the drums and everyone was watching. And then Greg clicked his sticks 1—2—3—4 and Cybil jumped in the air and when she hit the ground the band just exploded. Just this incredible roar of sound, super fast and super loud and totally pounding. The crowd went crazy. It was like this huge tension was released and the whole room surged forward and then back and people started pushing and slamming and diving off the stage. And I stood there in awe and then these really young girls came crashing into me and I pushed them away and they were laughing and screaming and totally drunk.

Sins rocked so hard. By the middle of the set everyone was drenched with sweat and Eric watered the front row with pitchers of water. And Cybil whipped people with the mike cord and then someone pulled her into the crowd and they passed her around above their heads and then they threw her back onstage and you could see her confidence growing. And when they played "We Are All Prostitutes" the whole crowd was singing along. And people were pushing so hard I was getting squished against the stage and Eric saw me and pulled me out of the crowd and I sat with him on the side of the stage. And then on the last song Cybil looked around in the crowd and then she said, "This song is for Andrea, wherever she is," and it was the Color Green song "Girl" off the new record and I was embarrassed but then when they played it I was so proud I got tears in my eyes.

Afterward everyone hung out. Nathan and Beth were there looking dweebish and very high school. And of course after worrying that half of Hillside would show up and embarrass us, they were the only two. Cybil went back to the dressing room and I sat on the stage with Eric, who was trying to keep people from trashing the place. Because all the old people from Outer Limits were cool but the new kids just wanted to destroy everything. And it was a weird crowd because it was a lot more suburban people and skateboarder types and less the street kids and skinheads that used to be at Outer Limits. There were even a gang of girls with bomber jackets and perfect hair and I said something to Eric and he said they were slumming. And then I saw the preppie boy from Arctic Circle standing with this really beautiful girl and he saw me and tried to make eye contact but I wouldn't.

On Monday nothing much had changed at Hillside since no one had come to the show. Cybil was glad of course and she was now trying to study more because she didn't know what she was going to do after high school. And I knew there was tension between her and Matthew because he definitely wanted to keep the band going. And it must have been a weird situation for her, having to commit herself to someone like Matthew, and probably for him too, because Cybil was very hard to predict and she did not have the usual ego motivations of most musicians, which was probably why Sins of Our Fathers were so good.

Meanwhile Mr. Perry was getting people to apply early decision to their first-choice college. I sat with Beth at *Hillsider* and we talked for hours about the various colleges and Berkeley sounded okay but also back east might be fun because of the cities and they had real snowstorms and it seemed more romantic somehow. Mr. Perry wanted me to go for Brown or Smith but I went for Wellington, in Connecticut, because it was smaller and coed and seemed more mellow. So I went around and did all the stuff and sent it in and then Wellington wrote me back and said I had to get interviewed.

Of course Mr. Perry had told us about interviews but I guess I hadn't thought about it and when I got the letter I got really nervous. The interviewer was in Portland. His name was Paul Johnson and he was a Wellington alumnus and his address was a law firm on the twenty-ninth floor of the Pacifica Building. I showed my parents and they had heard of him and then they got all nervous and we started arguing about what I should wear. My mom was terrified I would blow it by wearing one of my "goofball outfits." So she took me to Kruger's downtown and bought me this super conservative dress. Then we went for shoes and a hair trim and I basically let her choose everything and even if I tried to make the tiniest suggestion she was like, "No!" And it was so awful because my mom didn't know anything about fashion, even the most basic stuff, and even my dad understood but he kept whispering to me to just go along and I didn't really have much choice.

So when I showed up at the Pacifica Building I was wearing shoes that hurt and this dumb dress that was poking me and my hair was all brushed and combed and in a barrette and I swear I looked like some Okie farm girl from Idaho. I went up the elevator to the office and the receptionist was totally stylish and gorgeous and I could not have been more embarrassed. And then I went in to see Mr. Johnson and he was this crusty old guy who looked really tough and smart. He was on the phone and his office was sort of dark and with lots of wood and I could see through a crack in the curtain behind him that he looked out over all of Portland. He smiled at me and pointed for me to sit and the chair had such nice leather I almost slipped off it. But I didn't and I settled myself and folded my hands in my lap and tried to smile. And then he hung up the phone and shook my hand and we introduced ourselves and then he sat back in his chair and stared at me. I stared back. Then he smiled. I smiled. Then he grabbed my application stuff and flipped through it and asked me why I wanted to go to Wellington. I said because there were probably a lot of smart people there. He nodded and said there were. Then he asked me if I was smart. I said I didn't feel very smart but I got good SATs. He asked how good and I told him and he said yes, that was very good. Then he threw my application on the desk and said that SATs weren't everything and what else had I done? So I told him about *Hillsider* and KBAN and how I was into music and how I made posters for my friends' band. And all the time it was like this bluffing game and I couldn't tell if he was trying to scare me or if that's just how lawyers acted or what. And I knew he wanted to put me under pressure but I looked so stupid in my dress it was hard to really worry about how I sounded. And also I kept thinking of Cybil and how brave she was and if I couldn't go onstage like her, I could at least show some old lawyer guy that I wasn't scared. And really, we hadn't even talked that much and he was just starting to seem nice and then he said, "Okay, Andrea Marr. I think you'll do fine at Wellington. I'll give you my highest recommendation." I was so shocked. I didn't know what to say and then I tried to thank him but the secretary came zooming in to get me. And as she rushed me down the hall I told her I loved her outfit and she said thank you and I said, "My mother made me wear this dress, can you believe it?" But she just smiled and nodded and pushed me into the elevator.

When I got home I told my parents and they were so happy we all danced around in the living room. And the next day I wore my fish dress to school and put my hair up and stuck chopsticks through it and I walked into Hillside like I was the Duchess of Wales. And Cybil wanted to celebrate so after school we went to her house and put on black lipstick and tons of eye stuff. Then we went downtown and walked around Metro Mall and all these boys were looking at us and this one guy looked sort of like Todd from the back but it wasn't him. The next day there was a bomb threat at school and we hung out in the parking lot during third and fourth period and we were all at Matthew's car. He played Color Green on his stereo and Betsy Warren and Marjorie were there and Mrs. Schroeder stared at us and Matthew asked her if she wanted a bong hit and then said, "Just kidding!" And everyone laughed and I did too and for once I wasn't afraid of a teacher.

The next issue of *Hillsider* had an article about Sins of Our Fathers. Nathan wrote it and he said how cool they were and how there was so much talent at Hillside that we didn't see because we were so numbed by corporate rock and beer commercials and music videos. And Nathan came up to me and he obviously wanted me to say what a genius he was but I didn't really like his article that much and I told him. And then about a week later Beth dragged me to Arctic Circle for lunch and she was all upset because Nathan didn't like her and what should she do? And then the preppie guy came in and he walked right over to us and sat down beside Beth and asked me out. And Beth and I just stared at him and he did what Mr. Johnson did, he stared right back and sort of challenged you, so I said okay and I gave him my number.

And then Beth told everyone at *Hillsider* about the preppie guy and Amy Brubaker was teasing me and then Nathan said, "So that's what you like, *boldness*." And then he said, "Hey, I can be bold." And I was like, "Oh, please!" And I knew he was just joking but I could see Beth getting jealous. And then Eric K Club called Cybil again and we went to Taco Time after school to talk about our boy problems like how when you finally get a boy interested in you you never want him. And we discussed if that's how life would always be, giving you what you don't need and always keeping the thing you really want just out of reach.

The preppie guy's name was Steve and he had a Saab, which impressed my mom when he pulled into the driveway. I made sure to wear the exact same clothes I was wearing when he asked me out so I wouldn't confuse him. We went to a movie and then to Scamp's for frozen yogurt and Steve asked me about K Club and the music scene and did I really know the people in Sins of Our Fathers because he thought they were from California. And I ate my frozen yogurt and talked and watched out the window and it was November already and I felt this strange emptiness inside me. And then later in his car we made out and I was feeling really reckless and I undid his pants and pretty much invited him to have sex with me. But it freaked him out and his penis wasn't getting hard at all and then he said why couldn't I just relax and he didn't realize what type of girl I was and he should have known since I hung out at K Club. And he was so mad he took me straight home and when I got out of the car he floored it and left me standing in a cloud of burnt rubber.

I told Cybil about it and she said, fuck him. And then a couple days later she went out with Eric K Club and the next day she was depressed and she didn't think she should go out with older men and especially if they were in the music business. I reminded her how much fun we had when he made us tea but she didn't feel comfortable about it and now Matthew was trying to make a deal where they would play at K Club every Sunday night and get a salary or something and it would be a lot of money. And then Matthew started telling people that Eric was going to be their manager and that Sins were going to make a record with Buzz Mitchell. And then me and Cybil went downtown to look at records and I looked at Todd's CD because I had only seen the tape. There was a big picture of them on the back and Todd was staring down at the camera and I remembered how much I loved him and how I loved having sex with him and lately I had felt like such a big-shot senior but one look at Todd and I realized how boring and empty my life really was.

3 1 **MY MISTAKE WITH AMY BRUBAKER WAS I** didn't stand up to her at the start. And since I didn't she started to pick on me. And then one day at *Hillsider* Beth and I were putting in a picture of Kate Marshall, who was our star cross-country runner, and it was a cool picture, dark and shadowy, but Amy came and took it and said it was too blurry. We said it was okay, it was sort of artsy but Amy just stood in front of me and held the picture and wouldn't give it back. And everyone stopped what they were doing and Amy said how Nathan had broken the rules by making me assistant editor since you had to be picked the year before. And then she said how I thought I could do anything I wanted by having an attitude and thinking I was so much *cooler* than everyone else and how the other people had *worked* to get on *Hillsider* and they *believed* in it and I was just using it to get into college. And everyone was watching and no one said anything and it seemed like people agreed with her. And then Amy said, "Well?" And I couldn't answer and I was totally faced.

Cybil just laughed when I told her about Amy and it made me mad because I was really upset and I didn't know what to do. Cybil said I should fight her and I said "How?" She said, "Punch her in the face." I was like, yeah right. And later I saw Nathan in the hall and he walked right past me and I thought Amy must be right and probably everyone really hated me.

The next day I was afraid to go to *Hillsider* after school and I hung out with Cybil by her car. And Betsy Warren was blasting Color Green really loud but when the song was over a different group came on and after that a disc jockey came on and it was the *radio*. We all ran over to Betsy's car and looked at her stereo and it was KZCK FM Rock. Color Green was on FM radio! Matthew said it was also on the AM heavy-metal station. He said that Color Green had been getting airplay in Seattle for a couple weeks and now it was going national. And he shook his head and grinned at Cybil like, *that could be us.*

And it was such a drag because the next day I had to go to the *Hillsider* office because I told Nathan I'd look at his AIDS article. When I got there I felt so stupid and then Amy came in and she knew how bad she had faced me and she was drunk with power. And she stomped around telling everyone what to do and then she ripped down the Sins of Our Fathers poster and wadded it up and threw it in the trash. And then she told me to proofread her article and she said she wasn't sure if she was going to use it or not. I said, "Then why do you want me to proofread it?" And then Michael Strohecker told her to leave me alone and she said, "What?" And he said, "Leave Andrea alone." And Amy tried to ignore him because he was just a junior but this time people agreed with him because everyone liked the Sins of Our Fathers poster and now they were getting sick of Amy.

Everyone was sick of everyone. But that didn't stop them from having parties. Wendy Simpson had about ten and she had become Party Queen of Hillside. And Darcy had found a new boyfriend from Camden and they were practically married according to everyone. And Rebecca was teaching Tom Petrovich how to give her orgasms. And the football season went on forever because they kept winning and advancing in the big state tournament so the cheerleaders were busy making banners and having rallies and getting sexually harassed by the football players. And then Mrs. Katz had an operation and Mrs. Schroeder got all hysterical because someone wrote "Die bitch!" on the card they were sending her. And then this really wild-looking freshman girl that nobody knew stole her stepfather's car and drove it into the wall by Hawthorne Tunnel at ninety miles an hour and there was a big controversy if it was suicide. So *The Oregonian* ran a big article about how many teen suicides were covered up as accidents and there was a sidebar about if heavy metal was really a cause of suicide or if it was just a symptom.

And then one day there was a thing in *The Oregonian* that said that Color Green was playing at Baker Theater with Mirage from England. The show was December 28. And I was immediately getting nervous like what would I do if I saw Todd and would he call me and would I have sex with him? Of course I would. In a second. Matthew was trying to get Sins of Our Fathers onto the bill as the local act and Eric K Club was now co-manager so he was involved. And Cybil said that Eric kept calling her and she was freaking out because she wasn't sure what he wanted since he wasn't pressuring her for sex or trying to impress her or any of the usual things.

And then Hillside got into the state championship and the whole football fever which had been this annoying rah-rah thing switched into this mystical thing where if a football player walked by everyone stopped talking and looked at him with total reverence. They were going to play in the stadium downtown against Carlton Tech, which was already the state champions from last year and so there were all these articles in *The Oregonian* about Hillside and our poor underdog football team.

And it was getting cold out and raining and the leaves were off the trees and I felt like this was my last autumn and soon my high school life would be over. And I dug out my British overcoat and it was so woolly and wonderful that I'd go places just so I could wear it. And Cybil was always at practice and Rebecca was always with Tom so I'd ride the bus downtown and walk around by myself. I'd go to Scamp's and have frozen yogurt because I could blow off my homework now since it didn't really matter anymore, especially if I got into Wellington. And I would go into bookstores and read *The New York Times* and look at books or *Vogue* or whatever and I'd feel so adult and intelligent. And then I'd walk along Broadway and look in all the shops and let my mind fill up with all the things I could do in my life and how exciting everything was.

32

THE ONLY BAD THING ABOUT HAVING CYBIL for your best friend was she didn't like to talk about boys. I mean she would but she wouldn't gush or discuss sex or gossip like most girls. Her idea of talking about boys was to get really depressed and wonder how anyone could ever connect with anyone else. Or if boys could think past the ends of their penises. And also she never wanted to go boyfriend hunting. Not even in a sarcastic way. Like you couldn't call up Cybil and say you felt horny and let's go down to Monte Carlo. And it was weird because it rubbed off on me and when I would hear girls being really giggly about a guy I would act aloof and think how dumb they were and how shallow. But then other times I would look in the mirror and I would think how it was such a waste to be seventeen and not scamming on boys in a major way.

And then Beth finally got Nathan to ask her out and since she was really my only friend at *Hillsider* I had to go to Arctic

Circle and listen to all the details of their date, how they went to a movie and went for pizza and how they talked about college and marriage and what kind of families they would have. And inside I was like, *oh, please,* but outside I was like, "Really? He said that?" And on Thursdays Amy had swimming practice so I could go to *Hillsider* without worrying about another confrontation. And Michael Strohecker was always there and I hadn't really thought of him as a boyfriend prospect but he was kind of cute and he stuck up for me and he seemed easy to talk to.

Then Cybil made out with Eric. It happened on a Wednesday night when she was at K Club. They were hanging out and he asked if he could kiss her and she said okay and then they made out on the couch in his office. After she told me I was like, "Well?" She was like, "Well what?" I said, "Do you like him more?" She said, "Why would I like him more?" And I gritted my teeth and I said, *"Because you made out with him!"* But she didn't understand and she said how weird it was and she figured it would screw everything up and she was being totally impossible.

So then I wanted to go out with someone and I thought of Michael Strohecker. I went to his locker after school and talked to him about music and I asked him if he felt like going downtown to Poor Boy Records. He said sure but then he looked at me really strangely like he couldn't believe I had asked him out. I drove and he was acting totally weird and his ego was getting so big because he thought I was in love with him. And then at the record store he made me look at horrible jazz records and he didn't even like heavy metal and he was a boy! And then these two really cute skate boys walked in. They were looking at cool stuff and I was watching them but Michael yelled at me to come look at a Grateful Dead bootleg and it was so embarrassing.

And then Eric K Club invited me and Cybil to a party at his parents' house at Lake Oswego. It was this big house and all these older music-business types were there, guys with leather jackets, women with miniskirts and leopard skin tops and too much freckles from tanning machines. Matthew came and we had "cocktails" and acted sophisticated and Matthew told us who everyone was and tried to get Cybil to talk to this woman Ronnie Kincaid who was a big shot in the music business. And me and Cybil were totally dressed and I had my hair up and tons of lipstick and we looked very striking and all the men were staring at us.

Then this cool hippie guy came in and he looked like a male model and he was with someone and it was Carla. I grabbed Cybil and we ran over to Carla and gave her hugs and jumped around and told her about the show with Mirage and Color Green and Sins of Our Fathers. And everyone was looking at us so we went in the bathroom and did makeup and Carla told us all the big news from Seattle. And it was big. Todd had almost got married to Tori but then Tori had an affair with a lesbian named Katrina and Todd got in a fight with Katrina and she tried to have him arrested except she had a warrant on herself from parking tickets and when the cops came she had to hide in her garage. And then Carla said how Color Green was getting so huge and getting on the radio all around the country. They had a new manager in L.A. and they were suing Buzz Mitchell and they had this punk rock lawyer who used to work for Hulk Hogan. And finally I said, "But how is Todd?" Carla said he was okay but he always seemed tired when she talked to him. And everyone said how tiring it must be to be a big rock star. And all the time we were sneaking looks at Carla's date, who was sitting in the bathtub smoking cigarettes like he was in a fashion ad.

Back outside the party was getting crowded. People were in the kitchen and squished in the hallways and Mirage was playing in the living room and people were dancing. And everyone stared at Carla and her beautiful boyfriend, and me and Cybil were sort of following them around and we all sat on a couch in the living room and watched people dance. And then Carla's date handed her a pill and Carla asked us if we wanted to do Ecstasy with them. We said no thanks and watched them swallow the capsules. And then Cybil asked her about Ecstasy and what did it do and Carla said it was like drinking lots of coffee and being drunk at the same time and it was great for dancing.

But then it was really awkward because we tried to act casual but we kept looking at Carla and her boyfriend to see what was happening to them. So then Cybil and I went in the kitchen and

Eric tried to talk to us and Cybil wouldn't even look at him. We moved over to the drinks table and Cybil said maybe we should take Ecstasy and I was totally against it but she said she couldn't deal with Eric and she was going to. I said, "I guess I'll just go home then." Cybil took a big drink of vodka and said don't be like that. But there was no way. If she took Ecstasy I was gone. And she said it wasn't that big of a deal and Matthew had done it and it might be fun. I said, "If it's so fun why are you doing it now when you're depressed and hating Eric and getting drunk on vodka?" But that just made her mad and she walked away and went back to the living room. I watched her go. And the minute she was gone all these guys started talking to me and somebody handed me a drink and I put it down and walked through the hallway and out the front door. I got in my car and slammed the door. I got out my keys. But then I just sat there. I sat there for an hour. And then I went back inside and into the living room and Cybil and Carla and Matthew were dancing and laughing and I knew they were all on Ecstasy. So I went to the couch but Cybil saw me and pulled me into the dancing. So I danced and they were all acting weird and Matthew tripped and almost fell and everyone was cracking up. And I started to worry because what if Todd came to Portland and everyone was getting into drugs except me? And, then Cybil sat on the couch and I sat with her and I asked her what it was like and when she looked at me it was so weird because it wasn't her. It was like there was a different person inside her face. And her voice sounded really high and strained and she said it was really fun.

But it didn't look fun. It looked terrible. And then she said she didn't mind that I didn't want to do it and she understood and she still loved me. And then she asked if she could put her head on my lap and before I could answer she did it and it was so embarrassing except I was the only one who was embarrassed. And then I hated myself for being so uptight and I took a big gulp of her vodka and stroked her hair and watched everyone dance. And then some other people sat down on the couch and they must have been on Ecstasy too because they had that same zombie look on their faces. So I took another huge gulp of the vodka and that helped me relax and Cybil's hair felt really warm and soft and I petted it and remembered when it was stubble. And just when I was getting in a better mood I felt this wet spot on my leg and I realized Cybil was crying her eyes out.

I tried not to panic. I had heard that people got mushy on Ecstasy. And when Matthew walked by the couch I tried to wave him over but he was so high he didn't understand. And then I whispered to Cybil if she was okay but she was just sobbing. And then I asked her if she wanted to leave and she nodded yes and I sat her up. She looked so scary. She had black eye mascara smeared down her cheeks and her lipstick was all smudged. And I got our coats and helped her with hers and she seemed okay but as soon as she got in the car she collapsed into tears again.

Fortunately her mom wasn't home and I got her inside and then I just wanted to leave. But I was afraid to because she was so cold so we went in her living room and sat down and she started pulling all these blankets around her even though she had her coat on and it was already warm in the house. So I stayed and then she was mumbling about her mother and how she wanted to die before her mother and no matter what else happened please God could she just die before her mother. And I was like, "Nobody's going to *die*," but of course everybody was and I knew it and Cybil knew it too and it made me cold just watching her shiver.

Then she wanted to go to her mother's room. I helped her carry the blankets because she was afraid to come out of them because she was freezing and her teeth were chattering. We got her to the bed and she was still cold so we piled all the blankets on top of her and even with her clothes on she was still shivering. And then she asked me to get in with her and I didn't know what to do so I took off my coat and my shoes and crawled in as best I could. And as soon as I did she scooted over to me and hugged me and with her big coat on it was like hugging a bear.

But it seemed to work. After a while she stopped shaking and she whispered to me in nonsense sentences and told me I was her best friend and she loved me and then she stroked my hair and called me her dear Andrea and she pretended we were British and shouldn't we go back to England and would I like some tea and crumpets? I was like, "I don't know, Cybil, would you please stop chewing on my ear?" And she kept saying, "Oh my dear dear Andrea," and it was so hot I was sweating. And then she sat up and took off her coat and her shirt and kicked her shoes out of the covers. And then she started pulling on my shirt and giggling and tickling me and grabbing my bra. And she was on Ecstasy so she had an excuse but what excuse did I have?

I guess it was her smell. And the parts of her neck that I had been watching for so long. And how smooth her skin was and how some parts of her body seemed so familiar and other parts seemed so new. And it was so comfortable and I knew exactly what she meant when she said she loved me because I loved her too. And we sort of kissed each other and touched and chewed each other's ears. And then she pressed against me and we rocked back and forth and it was all so sleepy and dreamy and like we weren't even doing it, like it was just our bodies doing it and we weren't even involved.

Then I woke up. My head hurt like a hangover and I was sweaty and hot and I looked at the clock and it was four-thirty in the morning. Cybil was fast asleep. So I slipped out of the bed as quietly as I could and dug around for my clothes. Then I walked outside to my car and the sky was so cold and black and then I really woke up. And I knew what I had done and I was panicking and trying to find my car keys and get myself home before I totally freaked out.

Back at my house my dad was asleep in front of the TV. I crept up to my room and started the shower and sat down in the tub and let the hot water pour over me. After that I got in my bed and I laid there and when I closed my eyes it was like I was falling right out of myself, right out of my body and into this other world where everything was a dream and when you woke up you were six years old again and nothing counted yet and everything was still to come.

33

AT SCHOOL ON MONDAY I AVOIDED CYBIL ALL morning. After fourth period I looked for Beth so I'd have someone to eat lunch with. When I finally found her she was with Nathan but she could see I was desperate and she invited me along. The three of us went to Arctic Circle. Nathan talked the whole time and Beth gushed over him and the one time I tried to talk they both interrupted. And it seemed like all the *Hillsider* people were snubbing me now that Amy Brubaker had faced me so bad. It was like they were getting back at me for being too cool and all I could do was sit there and take it.

And then after fifth period Cybil came to my locker. I just held my breath. And she was being really shy and she thanked me for taking her home from Eric's and said sorry for any embarrassing stuff and then she said how sick she was from the Ecstasy hangover. I put my stuff in my locker and I was avoiding eye contact but when I actually looked at her I was so relieved to see Cybil and not that zombie face. And then she said how it was so true that Ecstasy made you mushy and weird and wanting to hug everyone. And we both looked up and down the halls like this was our little secret, which obviously it would be.

But the big news of Eric's party wasn't us. It was Matthew. And Carla. Matthew had somehow got her away from her hippie model and they had gone down by K Club and spent the whole night wandering around the warehouse buildings and the train tracks. It was Wednesday when Cybil told me and I was like, "No way!" And we were whispering a hundred miles an hour and she found out at practice because Fiona was bugging him and the way they talked about it it was like something sexual had happened. And we couldn't figure it out because wasn't Carla celibate and what would she want with Matthew? And Cybil said how Matthew was so *proud* of it and it was weird because even though Matthew was sort of slimy his attitudes toward women always seemed okay. My theory was that he wanted to follow in Todd's footsteps. But Cybil said, "Then why didn't he go after you?" I said because I was too boring and Cybil said I wasn't boring but I said I was and I didn't mind because it made it easier to have interesting friends.

On Thursday Cybil and I went to Taco Time with Matthew. And we were pissing our pants and Matthew was totally teasing us and we were like, "Are you going to call her?" "What did she say?" "Does she like you?" "What happened to her boyfriend?" And Matthew laughed at us and said, "To tell you the truth I was a little surprised how *wild* she was." And then we were *really* pissing our pants and saying: "Like what?" "Like sex?" "Was she kinky?" "What did she do?" But he just laughed and he wouldn't tell us anything and then he went to his car to smoke pot before fifth period.

And then it was December and I was getting nervous because my letter from Wellington would come soon. And Sins of Our Fathers were playing in Eugene and Seattle so Cybil was in and out of school, leaving me to hang out with Beth, who was now asking me about the Metro Mall and thinking she'd write an article about street kids and runaways. And then Beth had a party at her house for *Hillsider* people and it was weird because her parents were there and everyone drank sparkling cider and stood around the fireplace. Fortunately Amy Brubaker didn't come and I mostly hung out with Nathan and Beth. And it was like a real adult party and I thought this was what college would be like, very polite and civilized and everyone smiling a lot.

And then one cold day the envelope was in the mailbox. It had my name on the front and in the left-hand corner it said Wellington University and it had a little shield and some Latin words and it looked very Eastern. And everyone said if it was thin that was good and if it was fat that was bad. It seemed

233

sort of in-between. And I said a little prayer and ripped it open and I was accepted to Wellington! I ran in the house and jumped around and I called my mom and told her and she was so happy. Then I called my dad but he was pulling someone's wisdom teeth so I left a message. And then I wanted to talk to someone my own age, like Cybil, but I was afraid to call her because . . . I don't know why. Maybe she would be jealous or think I was a snob or something. So I took the car and drove around and then I went to Hillside to see if Mr. Perry was still there but he wasn't. So then I walked across the street to Taco Time which was totally deserted and quiet inside. And I got a coffee and sat by the window and watched the cars drive by and I didn't know what was going to happen to me but I knew something was.

And then my brother and his wife came for Christmas and I had to ride out to the airport with Mom. But I didn't mind and all the time we were there I imagined myself getting on a plane to Connecticut. And then James and Emily appeared and they had a baby. I guess I knew they had one but I had forgotten. And I had to pretend like I was excited and say how cute it was but actually it was fat and ugly. And it was drooling all over itself and wearing this little baby hat that was falling off. And then Emily did her usual thing of acting like me and her were long-lost sisters. She said to the baby, "Does Andrea want to hold us?" And everybody looked at me like if I didn't it would be the biggest crime of the century. So I smiled and took the baby and it immediately drooled all over my sweater. And all the time Emily watched my face to make sure I was enjoying it.

The next couple days were pretty hectic around our house, which was good because it made me forget about seeing Todd and the Mirage/Color Green/Sins of Our Fathers show which was December 28. On Christmas Eve we went to church and afterward my dad gave me a talk about how expensive Wellington was and the sacrifice it meant for their pension fund. It didn't really sound like Dad though, it sounded more like Mom's words in Dad's mouth. And then to remind me of the terrible cost of Wellington I didn't get anything good for Christmas. And that night we all went out to dinner and talked about what I should major in and Mom seemed to be getting a little too worked up about it and I had to remind her that *I* was the one going and *I* would have to figure it out for myself. And Emily said, "Good for you, Andrea," and gave us all a lecture, which just made my mother more cranky.

And then Beth called to ask me what happened because everyone was getting their early decision things back. I said I got in and she was totally excited and it was so fun to talk to someone who understood. And she told me that Nathan had not gotten into Yale. But Martin Schaap had gotten into Princeton and so far it was just me and him, which was embarrassing since Martin Schaap was a total calculus nerd. I asked her how Nathan was taking it and she said so-so and I felt bad because for someone like Nathan what college you went to was *everything*. So I called him but he sounded really weird and sort of cocky and he made fun of me for applying to Wellington on early decision because it was a "small school" and for early decision you should shoot for the moon. I thought *Shoot for the moon*? And since I had never heard anyone my age say that I figured that's what his parents were telling him to make him feel better.

And then it was the day before the big Mirage show and I drove over to Matthew's to watch Sins practice. Matthew's weird mom let me in and she talked to me and gave me cookies. Then I went downstairs and it was all smoky from cigarettes and pot and Fiona was playing her bass and Cybil had her fingers in her ears and she and Matthew were discussing the set list. Greg was playing his drums and Fiona told him to shut up because she was trying to play something different. And then Cybil told them both to shut up and she pointed out something to Matthew. And then Greg started playing "Oblivion" and Matthew yelled SHUT UP! That seemed to work but then Fiona played a Pax song and Greg did a surf beat and then Matthew ran over and ripped the sticks out of his hands. And Greg started pounding his kick drum and Fiona blew smoke at Matthew and he called her a bitch and it was all very unpleasant.

The crankiness continued. After practice me and Cybil went to Scamp's for frozen yogurt and Cybil said she hated

Scamp's because it was so yuppie even though she knew it was my favorite place. And then there were these long silences while we ate and the only thing I could think was she was nervous about the show. Or maybe she was sick of everything. The band, Hillside, me. And she knew I was going off to fancy Wellington and she hadn't even filled out her stuff for the University of Oregon. But also I thought it might have to do with the Ecstasy night. How could it not? But I didn't want to think about it and I guess I just wanted everything to be normal.

The show was a really big deal because Mirage had a big song that was Top Forty and they had this great video that people kept telling me about but I had never seen because my stupid parents still hadn't got cable. And tickets were sixteen dollars, which is the most Baker Theater ever costs. But it was a drag because the day of the show I got stuck babysitting Emily's baby and then my mom made me go to the store and then we had to have dinner *as a family* and I hadn't even called Cybil yet. But then Cybil called me and my mom answered and she said to tell Cybil we were eating. But I ignored her and took the phone into the other room and Cybil said they were already there and she was putting me on the guest list and I asked if Todd was there and she said, "He's somewhere but I haven't talked to him." And I went back to the table and Emily asked me about the music scene and then she started telling me about "women's music," which sounded totally horrible.

Then I called Beth. It was totally spur of the moment and probably a mistake but I didn't want to go by myself. And I put on my coolest miniskirt and tights and my favorite shirt and pinned my hair up and put chopsticks in it and black lipstick and snuck out of the house before anyone could see me. And when I picked up Beth her mom answered the door and Beth must have told her parents I was going to Wellington because her dad came right to the door and they were all excited to meet me and congratulate me and I guess they weren't expecting me to have black lipstick. So that was really awkward and when Beth came down she was dressed in jeans and this preppie sweater but as soon as she saw me she said, "Oh!" and she ran back upstairs and she came back in black jeans and a T-shirt and her parents were like, "But Beth . . ." And she said, "We're late, Mom, see you!"

And really, Beth was being pretty cool about everything and she knew the whole Todd story and she could see how nervous I was. We got there and all these people were crowded at the door and I grabbed Beth and pushed to the front and the guy remembered me from The Sidewinders show and he let us through. Inside there were a million college students who were home for Christmas and everybody was in a good mood and obviously relieved to be away from their families and out with their friends. And we had just taken off our coats when the lights went down and this huge voice said, "Please give a warm holiday welcome to Portland's own *Sins of Our Fathers!*"

34

FIRST MATTHEW CAME OUT AND PLUGGED in his stuff and then Fiona and then Greg got behind his drums and everything was ready. And then they started playing and Cybil came running out and I knew it was her because of how she ran but it didn't look like her because she had that wig on. That sixties wig. From her mother's attic. And also sunglasses. And she wobbled her head so the wig hair flopped around. And Beth was going *wow* and I looked around at other people to see if they noticed but why would they? They'd never seen Cybil before. She sang "Love Disease" but something was wrong with the sound because all you could hear was the guitar. And people didn't seem that into it but I grabbed Beth and we ran to the front and danced around even though we were the only ones.

And then after only six songs they had to get off. But Cybil saw us dancing and she came to the edge of the stage and yelled to us to come backstage. Poor Beth. So we went around to the stage door and there was this scary security guard but Cybil told him to let us in. And just as we came down the hall, I saw Luke going into the Color Green dressing room. He was wearing leather pants and his hair was really long and scraggly and he looked like such a rock star. We went into Cybil's dressing room and she took off the wig and her real hair was all sweaty and gross. And she asked me if I was going to talk to Todd and I said I didn't know but I hoped so.

Then I was getting really nervous. So I bummed a cigarette from Fiona and stood in the doorway and watched down the hall for Todd. And the cigarette was making me sick but I kept smoking it and Beth stood with me and then the security guy knocked on the Color Green door and said, "Time to go!" The door opened and Luke and Todd had their guitars, and the other guys were different than the original guys, they looked older and more professional and like they'd taken more drugs. And they acted so important the way they walked and me and Beth flattened against the wall as they went by and Todd was behind Luke and he had his head down and his eyes on the floor and he didn't even see us.

They went around the corner and then someone else came out of their dressing room and it was Carla. And she said, "Hey, you guys!" and Matthew must have heard her voice because he came running over and he was like, "What are you doing here?" We all looked at Carla to see how she would respond to Matthew but she just ignored him and got out a cigarette. And then he said, "I didn't know you were here." But she still ignored him and then there was a huge rumble through the walls and it was Color Green starting and we all ran down the hall to watch.

People were into Color Green. They clapped and yelled and somebody threw something at Luke. They started with this long jam thing and then Todd started singing but his voice sounded terrible. It was so raspy and hoarse it made you cringe to hear it. But they kept playing and then Todd sang "Girl" and Cybil nudged me and told me they wrote "Girl" for me and I said they didn't because they were playing it before Todd even met me. Cybil said it still seemed like my song, to her, and I said it was probably for Carla but that didn't make sense either because the girl in "Girl" was a generic suburban type. And I knew that for sure because I had read the lyric sheet.

And then during their encore me and Beth and Cybil snuck behind the stage and crouched on the steps behind the drummer. Luke and Todd were pounding their guitars and the crowd was headbanging and Cybil nudged me and said they were rock gods. And mostly I watched Todd but whenever he turned toward the drums I didn't look at him because I was too embarrassed. And by the end his voice was so ragged he could hardly talk and Luke had to sing the last song. And then when they were done the drummer almost stepped on Cybil's hand and he winked at us like he thought we were groupies.

After that Color Green went back into their room and closed the door. We went into the Sins' dressing room and Matthew was arguing with Fiona and Greg was arguing with Matthew and everybody was cranky. And Carla was probably with Color Green and I had secretly expected to somehow see Todd but now I realized I might not. And then groupies Lisa and Vanessa showed up, don't ask me how, they probably gave blowjobs to the security guard. And worse than that they weren't looking for Color Green, they were scamming on *Matthew*. Fiona smoked some pot, which seemed to calm things down somewhat. And then Lisa started talking to Matthew, and Vanessa was acting so aloof and she wanted some of Fiona's pot but Fiona wouldn't give her any.

Then Mirage went on. The crowd went totally crazy, like way past what they did for Sins of Our Fathers or Color Green and it made you realize how people only cared about what they heard on the radio. They couldn't tell which bands were good, they just liked what they were supposed to like. But me and Beth still went behind the stage to watch and Mirage had fog machines and cool lights and this synthesizer dance beat that was super fast and made the whole building shake. After a couple songs we went to find Cybil and we walked into her dressing room and there was Todd. By himself. And it was so weird because my first instinct was to hug him. But I couldn't. He was untouchable. Then he asked me how I was doing and his voice was all scratchy and raw. I said I was doing fine and I said I didn't think I was going to see him and he said why not? I said because he was getting so famous. He sort of frowned and looked at Beth and he looked so tired and sad I just grabbed him. I just gave him the biggest hug. And Beth left the room and we hugged and hugged and didn't say anything because it seemed like talking would just wreck it.

Then he kissed me. And then he kicked the door closed and really kissed me. And then we went out to their van and it was so weird because we just fucked, it was just pure sex and we didn't dare talk and it seemed like this was the end. And it didn't last very long and after he came his head fell on my chest and his ears were really hot like maybe he had a fever. And I held his head and tried to get his penis out of me before the condom fell off. And then he woke up and we talked a little and he told me about the tour and the cities they'd played in and what the weather was like. And it was so sad because it was just small talk and his voice sounded terrible and it was probably just making it worse.

When we left the van we were in this parking lot, surrounded by fences and barbed wire and floodlights shining down. And I tried to get my skirt straight and keep up with Todd, who was hurrying back because he didn't have a coat. When we got inside Mirage had finished and Todd went into his dressing room and I followed him even though I didn't really know if I was invited. Carla was there. And Luke and the other guys. And horrible Vanessa had found their drummer and she was hanging all over him and playing with his hair and he was feeling her butt right in front of everybody.

And then Matthew came in and he was looking for Carla. But she wouldn't talk to him and everybody stared at him and he asked her to come out in the hall. And Carla was really mean and she said, "What do you want?" Matthew was like, "I just want to talk to you for a second." And then Luke told him that Carla didn't want to talk to him and that he should leave. But Matthew said it was between him and Carla. And then Todd came over and Luke stepped right into Matthew's face and just when they were about to fight, Carla said, "I don't want to know you, I don't want to talk to you, I don't want to fuck you, does that answer your questions?" Matthew was totally faced. And when he left he bumped into Lisa, who was coming in, and she immediately went chasing after him like, "Matthew! Matthew!" and it was so true how Christmas turns everything into a horrible soap opera.

So then I wanted to leave and I went over to Todd and kissed him on the cheek and told him it was nice to see him again. He said, "Yeah, it was." Then I went back to Cybil's dressing room and got Beth and we walked back through the theater, which was empty now except for the security people and all the broken cups and stuff laying on the floor. And looking around I felt this horrible finalness and Beth tried to smile at me and I couldn't really look at her. But outside the theater everyone was hanging out and it was that same atmosphere as when we arrived, all the happy college students and the trendy high school kids and just everyone buzzing and talking and asking where the parties where. And me and Beth sort of paused on the steps to look at them all. And then these cute guys started talking to us and they invited us to a party but Beth had to go home so we left.

Back at my house Emily and James were watching TV and drinking wine. They said to come sit down so I did and they were talking to me and trying to be nice but I just stared at the TV. I was thinking about lightning storms in Texas and snow in the Midwest and all the other places Todd had been. And this horrible ache was growing in my chest, not because I wanted Todd back, but because without him everything would be normal again and there'd be nothing to daydream about. And I wondered where he was, asleep in the van, maybe awake, driving back to Seattle with those horrible people, that horrible drummer and horrible Vanessa and what did he think about all those nights driving between cities? But Emily was asking me something and I finally had to answer her and then I excused myself and went up to my room. And I was so relieved to be alone I just sat on my bed and fiddled with a button on my coat sleeve. And when I took a deep breath my whole chest heaved with pain. So then I got undressed and shut my door and turned off the light. I got deep under the bed covers and curled up in a ball. Then I closed my eyes and let my chest fill up and my eyes fill up and then, very slowly, very gently, like making love, I started to cry for Todd Sparrow.

35 AND THEN THE HOLIDAYS WERE OVER AND IT was January and dark and wet and the clouds were low over Sunset Park and everything was gray and depressing. I took Emily and James and the baby to the airport by myself and I wore my nice black dress and my normal

pumps. And as we walked to the gate they were still talking about Wellington and I felt bad because they really did care about me and they really were excited about me going back east and I didn't know anything about their life and honestly, I didn't want to. I guess because I was young and they were married and stuck with their baby. And after they were gone I walked around the airport and went into the gift shop and this very handsome man was totally staring at me and I got some postcards and I was going to smile at him at the counter where he was buying *The Washington Post* but of course I chickened out. And then I went and sat by the window and wrote a postcard to Cybil pretending I was in New York City but I tore it up because maybe she wouldn't think it was funny. Then I wrote one to Todd, just "Hi, how are you," but also a little bit about how fun it was to see him and good luck with the band and don't let them grind you to dust. I still had Tori's address in my purse so I bought a stamp and mailed it before I lost my nerve. And then I felt energized and I got an espresso in the coffee shop and listened to the waitress complain to her friend about birth control pills and how they made your breasts swell.

Back at Hillside everyone was gossiping about who got into college early decision and Amy Brubaker had *not* got into Berkeley where her *dad* even went so it was a total face on her. Richard Kirn got into MIT of course and Mitzi Berkowitz got into Stanford and that was about it so far. And then at *Hillsider* Nathan was freaking out over his applications. He did a total reversal from before and he wasn't acting cocky at all and he even asked me if I thought he could get into Wellington. As if I had a clue. And Amy Brubaker tried to act like everything was perfectly okay but you could see in her face that her whole persona had a big crack in it now that Berkeley had turned her down. It was so obvious and scary that everyone was being extra nice to her, because she was another person who thought college was *everything*. And then people I barely knew started coming up to me and congratulating me about Wellington and even Darcy and Wendy Simpson stopped by my locker and they were being really nice and respectful and Wendy joked how she'd be lucky if she could get into Oregon State. But they didn't seem too worried about it and Darcy was still going out with her Camden boyfriend and having intense sex. That's what I had heard. And you could tell by the way she walked, how slinky and dreamy she was, that she was totally getting laid.

And then me and Beth wrote an article about how our generation didn't have any fashion ideas and how everyone picked an older generation for their look. Like people were either punk like the seventies or hippies like the sixties or nerds like the fifties and how there wasn't really a *now* look and what did it mean? We got this sophomore boy named Henry to come downtown with us to K Club to take pictures. Eric was there and he was really nice and he invited us upstairs to his office and let us take pictures down at the crowd. And Henry was so amazed by K Club and asking me if I really hung out there and I was like, yeah, sometimes.

247

So we had these great pictures to go with our retro fashion article and when it came out everybody loved it. And then
Nathan wanted us to write a fashion column but Beth thought I
should do it myself since I never wrote articles. So I said I would
and I wrote my first column about how rich kids are always hippies and wear the most trashed clothes and always pretend they
don't have any money. People liked that too and there were letters to the editor, and Jim Dietz's little sister, Mary, who was the
biggest hippie and totally rich, wrote this long letter about how
we were stereotyping people and it was this big controversy and
Nathan loved it. And then Henry came up to me and said that
Nathan had told him he was supposed to be my slave and go
with me everywhere and take pictures of anything I told him to.

But I think Cybil was my biggest fan. She cut out my articles
and hung them in her locker and we were always cracking up
how if you wrote the simplest, most obvious thing in the world
people thought you were a genius. She had a lot of good ideas and
we'd go to Taco Time or Arctic Circle and drink coffee and talk
for hours. And I even tried to change it to "Andrea and Cybil's
Fashion Corner" but she said she was already famous and I helped
her with her band image so she was paying me back.

And I thought the thing with Henry was a joke but he called
me on Thursday and wanted to know if we were going to K Club
over the weekend. I wasn't doing anything and Sins were playing in Olympia so I said sure. And then I got Beth to come so

it wouldn't be too weird. Eric was there and Party Hats were playing and it was only a medium-sized crowd. Henry took some pictures and I was sort of nervous he might bug people or embarrass us but it turned out he was totally sly and charming and people actually wanted to be in his pictures. Afterward we went for coffee at Zoso and all the trendy Metro Mall types were there and Henry took pictures of them too until the manager told him to stop.

The pictures turned out great. So that week the column was just a whole page of pictures from K Club and Zoso. Everybody loved it. So then I thought maybe it should be "Andrea and Henry's Fashion Corner" but Nathan said no because Henry was a sophomore and a slave and he wasn't allowed to have any glory.

And when I told Cybil about Henry she said she noticed him at the beginning of the year and we talked about how cute he was but what a drag he was only a sophomore. Cybil didn't think that should stop me but I was like, "What if he's a virgin?" She said maybe I could train him and I said, "Train him to do what? He's *already* my slave." And we weren't the only ones noticing Henry because the next time I saw him he was in the parking lot with Bridget Cole, who was supposedly the most popular sophomore girl. And just the way Henry acted with her made you see how confident he was and after that I was sort of afraid of him. But then on Thursday he called me again and he was like, "Where are we going this weekend?" I didn't know. I didn't really feel like going to K Club again. And then he asked if I wanted to go to a party at Bridget Cole's. I didn't know that either, because Bridget Cole was totally popular and rich and her mother was a big socialite and was always in *The Oregonian*. But I couldn't let Henry know I was afraid. And I was sort of curious. And I *was* going to Wellington. So I said okay.

Henry drove and I wore jeans and a white button-down shirt with my hair up and dark lipstick and a cool black raincoat that was Cybil's. Bridget's house was in Weston Heights a couple houses down from where Renee Hatfield used to live before she went to San Diego State. It was a total mansion. And all the time I watched Henry and I knew he must be rich too because he didn't even blink. And then the party was like all the most beautiful and rich people from Hillside and Camden and Bradley Day School. And there were people I recognized from Hillside who I never thought were that popular but I realized they just laid low at school and they were actually in with the elite crowd. And I tried to act normal but it was hard. Fortunately Henry was really nice and he got me a glass of wine and everyone was being very mature and talking and Peter Williams even played the grand piano. And then I was in the kitchen and Bridget Cole came up to me and she just launched into this thing about how she wanted to be like me, going to Wellington and writing fashion articles for *Hillsider* and also being so involved with creative people in the alternative scene and downtown and everything. And it was so weird because I didn't have a clue what to say back and I just stared at her. And then I found Henry and stayed by him for a while but pretentious sophomore girls kept flirting with him. And I started thinking of excuses to have Henry not be my slave because he was obviously ten times cooler than me. I mean, where was I when I was his age? I was a total moron. I was *still* a total moron. And it was too embarrassing having a slave anyway and probably racist and thank God Bridget didn't know about it or anyone else.

But someone else *did* know about it. I was standing by the refrigerator and this weird guy named Christof came up to me and said he heard I was somebody's master and what was that all about? I said it was just a joke and he said it sounded like an interesting joke and I tried not to be rude but he smelled like cologne and he was gross. And when I walked away he followed me and he said not many people were into that stuff. And I told him it was just a joke but then he grabbed my arm and I yanked it away and said, "I don't want to talk to you, I don't want to know you, I don't want you grabbing me, does that answer your questions?" which didn't really make sense. But it sure sounded good. And Bridget heard me and she immediately yelled at him and he tried to explain but she totally shouted him down and made him leave. And she apologized and got me some more wine and then she wanted to give me a tour of the house. So we walked around and she showed me all the bathrooms and stairs and everything but then we went in this den and sat on a couch and she looked right into my eyes and started asking me all these questions. Like what did I think about Senator So-and-So and what kind of name was "Marr" and did I think women were discriminated against in the arts? It was so strange. I mean, she was a *sophomore*. And I was like, yeah I guess so. After that we walked around some more and she saw some other people and she seemed relieved to talk to them and get away from me and I knew I had disappointed her.

But then, back in the kitchen, all these girls told me how cool it was that I had faced Christof and what a sexist jerk he was. They were all talking at once and it seemed like they wanted me to be in their crowd now. The Weston Heights crowd. And I guess I wanted to be in it too. If for no other reason than to show people like Darcy and Wendy Simpson and Amy Brubaker that I could be popular. But even while everyone was being so nice I knew it would never work. And it was so weird because no matter how much you hate popular people, the minute they like you you like them right back. It was a terrible thing to find out about yourself and a terrible situation to be in and the more I smiled and laughed with everyone the more terrible I felt.

Then Henry came and he wanted to go and I was saved. He even had my coat. We went to K Club and Eric was there and Henry checked out the band and I talked to Eric for a long time about Sins of Our Fathers. He told me he was their manager for exactly four days and then Matthew fired him because he wanted total control. And Eric made us tea and he was being so nice. And then Henry came up to change his film and when he left I asked Eric what was going on with him and Cybil. He said, "You tell me." But I said I could never tell what Cybil was thinking and he said he couldn't either and we just drank our tea and listened to the music downstairs.

36

AND GUESS WHERE HENRY LIVED? WESTON Heights. Three blocks down from Bridget and Renee Hatfield as a matter of fact. I found this out the next weekend when he invited me over to watch alternative videos on cable. His parents were upstairs and it was a difficult evening because I could tell Henry wanted to make out and I guess I did too but he wasn't going to make the first move. He was still being my slave. I was the older woman and he was the young innocent and I had to start it. But I wouldn't. I didn't like being the older woman. And then his sister came home from some junior high dance and she was totally cute and funny and she sat in front of us on the floor and kept turning around to look at me and it was so embarrassing.

Then Sins of Our Fathers got a record contract. It was Buzz Mitchell, the same guy Color Green was now suing. Matthew had arranged it and was trying to schedule the studio time to match Hillside's spring vacation. It became a big joke and Buzz Mitchell told *Rock City* magazine in Seattle how his hot new band had to get notes from their moms to skip enough school to make their first record. And Cybil was so excited but also worried if she could do it because whenever Matthew tried to record at practices she always got nervous and screwed up.

But then Matthew got it all figured out and it was really going to happen and they started practicing every night. And it was so weird because every morning Matthew and Betsy Warren were out in the parking lot doing bong hits and blasting their stereos and you'd think they were the biggest losers at Hillside except Betsy Warren got the second-highest SATs and Matthew was calling up lawyers at lunch hour to see if they would help him with the record contract.

When the *Hillsider* office heard about Sins of Our Fathers going to Seattle to make a record everyone was totally buzzing about it. And whatever attention I had been getting lately shifted back to Cybil, and now Nathan wanted to interview her and everyone criticized me because I wouldn't convince Cybil to do it. Then Matthew agreed to do an interview but only if they let him read it and change anything he didn't like but Nathan said that compromised his integrity as a journalist so he wouldn't do it.

And me and Henry went out sometimes and went to movies or to K Club. And every time I saw Eric he asked about Cybil and I told him about the record deal and he seemed happy for her. Then one night I took Henry to a practice at Matthew's house but they were doing one little drum part over and over and Matthew was yelling at Greg and Cybil was reading a magazine and Fiona was chain-smoking so much you could barely breathe. So we left.

And then on the first Saturday of spring vacation I went over to Cybil's to help her pack. We sort of talked but not that much. And she was scared because she didn't know if she'd be able to sing in a real recording studio. And then Greg's station wagon came and Fiona's smashed-up Toyota and I helped Cybil carry her stuff out. Greg jumped out to help and he was so excited he could barely contain himself. All their dreams were coming true. And Matthew yelled hi and Fiona honked and Cybil gave me a hug and got in and I waved and they all drove away.

That night there was a big party at Beth's and I went with Henry and I was telling everyone about Cybil and Color Green and how Todd had changed my life and I guess I was bragging because Amy Brubaker said, "Changed it to what?" Bridget Cole was there and I guess she wasn't kidding about wanting to be on the paper because she was schmoozing all the *Hillsider* people. Everyone except me, who she seemed to be avoiding. And she was talking about what direction she would take *Hillsider* if she were the editor and getting people to agree with her and flattering Henry endlessly because she knew how popular he was with the older people. It was really amazing to watch her work. She said she would start as fashion editor as a junior and maybe try for editor-in-chief as a senior. And nobody said a word because they knew she would probably do it.

With Cybil gone I depended on Henry for my social life during spring vacation. I went down to the beach for a couple days to stay with his family at their beach cabin. It was warm for one day and we went on the beach but then it rained and we were all stuck inside, watching cable movies with his sister and playing Ping-Pong in the garage. And it was weird too because his parents didn't think anything about their son hanging out with a senior. I guess they just assumed he was so wonderful or else they didn't care because I was going to Wellington. Parents seemed to forgive you anything if you were going to a fancy college.

And then spring vacation was over and on Monday everyone talked about their trips and stuff and they had forgotten about Sins of Our Fathers. But I hadn't. The first thing I did was check Cybil's locker. Then I went to the parking lot and looked for Matthew's car or Greg's station wagon. But there was no sign of them. And that night I called Cybil's house and her mom sounded really weird and she didn't know what Cybil's plans were and she didn't want to talk to me at all.

Back at *Hillsider* on Tuesday everybody was getting nervous because college stuff was coming back. And then Amy Brubaker complained to Nathan that I kept making my columns into photo pieces and not writing anything. Which was true. So I sat down and tried this one idea that Cybil thought of, which was: the cycles of cool. Like a look will be totally cool when it's first invented and only the coolest people will be into it. But then it will become totally uncool and the *least* cool people will be into it. Like punk rock was really cool in the eighties but now the only people into punk were skinheads and street kids. And then a look will come back into style like hippies and Deadheads even though for a while those people were the bums and street people. The only problem was I couldn't really remember the other parts of the theory without Cybil there and it seemed like it contradicted my other column about people choosing one of the retro looks.

I was getting frustrated so I walked down to the field where Henry was taking pictures of the track team, but Bridget Cole was talking to him and probably working on her plan for total Hillside domination. And I already felt faced by her because it was obvious she had studied me and found me lacking. So I went back to the *Hillsider* offices and got my stuff and walked across the street to Taco Time where I tried to remember the cycles of cool and just got more mixed up and depressed. And I realized the whole thing about fashion or writing about fashion or even thinking about fashion was *confidence*. You had to be confident and other people had to have confidence in you. Because it was all about intimidation and having the nerve to pull things off and daring to say, "This is cool and this is not." Fashion was sports for girls and that's why Cybil was so good at it because she was always confident and she always wanted to compete and she always won.

On Wednesday there was still no sign of Matthew or Cybil. And during lunch I saw Little Greg, the freshman who always dyed his hair, and for a second I thought it was real Greg and I jumped up but of course it wasn't. And at the *Hillsider* offices more letters from colleges had come. Amy Brubaker got into Smith and it was so bogus because the minute she heard, she started acting so nice to everyone but people were suspicious and said she was patronizing and it was kind of a face on her.

All day Thursday I looked for Cybil. I was really missing her. And I tried to write my column but once I got frustrated I couldn't write anything. So then Henry drove me to HOP! and some other thriftstores to try to inspire me. After that we had coffee at Zoso and I tried to write and then Carla walked in. She was with another girl who sort of sneered at us but Carla was nice and we talked about Sins of Our Fathers and why it was taking so long and she hadn't heard anything and I hadn't heard anything. And just talking to her reminded me that making a record was a pretty big deal and Sins of Our Fathers probably weren't worrying about missing a couple school days.

Then on Friday Greg showed up at school. I saw him at his locker during first period and I immediately ran over to Cybil's locker but it hadn't been touched. So I ran to the parking lot but I didn't see Matthew or Cybil's car and I asked Betsy Warren if Matthew was back and she said she hadn't seen him. So I waited around Greg's locker and the minute he saw me he looked like he was going to cry. I went up to him and I was like, "Greg, where is everybody?" He tried to ignore me and he opened his locker and I said, "Greg, where is Cybil?" Finally he shrugged and said, "How would I know? Up in Seattle. Making their big record. Making Matthew's big record."

I took Greg to Taco Time for lunch. I fed him coffee and ice cream sundaes while he cried and told me what happened. They had worked for three days and it wasn't going well and then Buzz Mitchell showed up and fired the producer and got this other guy Nick Venn who was really famous and produced Color Green and all the big new bands. And the first thing Nick Venn said was to get a drummer who could keep the beat. Matthew said okay but Cybil and Fiona defended Greg but Matthew won and Nick got another drummer. And they told Greg he was still in the band but for the record they were going to use the other guy. But then after a couple days the other guy told Matthew he wanted to be in Sins and Matthew told Greg he was out. And when Greg went to Fiona and Cybil they said there was nothing they could do.

I got scared as Greg told me this because I remembered how he thought he was going to be famous and have his own studio and everything. And you could see this terrible confusion in his face and he kept mumbling about keeping the beat and how he could keep the beat, he really could, and didn't I think he could keep the beat? I said I always thought he was a good drummer but then what did I know about drums?

37

SO THAT'S WHERE CYBIL WAS. THE LAST SURVIVOR of Bed Head, Thriftstore Apocalypse, and the original Sins of Our Fathers. I didn't know what to think. On Saturday I drove by Cybil's and then Matthew's but neither was home. Monday I had this strange feeling they would show up. They didn't. On Tuesday I saw Mrs. Katz talking to Greg in the hall and I went over to listen and they were talking about Cybil and Matthew and Mrs. Katz said that she wasn't responsible because Cybil was eighteen and Matthew was so close that by the time they dragged him back he would be. So they were free. No one was waiting for them to come back. No one except me.

And then Greg's story got to *Hillsider* and everyone talked about it and Amy Brubaker said that obviously Sins of Our Fathers was no longer Hillside news if they didn't go to school here anymore. Nathan asked me about Greg and if they should do an article about him and I said that Greg was really freaked out and they should leave him alone. But Amy just scoffed and

Nathan said it couldn't hurt to ask and then I got mad and said they didn't know what they were dealing with and this wasn't some stupid swim meet or food drive and if they were smart they'd stay as far away from Greg as they could get.

And I guess I was right because the next day word went around that Greg had fallen asleep at the wheel of his station wagon and went off the road and got a concussion and a broken leg. In a way I was relieved because maybe it would shock him out of his depression. But then after lunch a new rumor went around that he was in Intensive Care at the hospital and he had taken a bunch of his mom's tranquilizers and he hadn't fallen asleep at the wheel, he had blacked out. And it was so weird because they called *me* into Mrs. Katz's office to talk to this counselor guy because Greg didn't have any other friends. And it was so horrible because the counselor guy was creepy and it was all *secret* and like an interrogation about what I knew and they wouldn't even tell me if Greg was okay or what had really happened. So after school I got Henry and we drove to the hospital and went in and they wouldn't let us anywhere near him. And they wouldn't tell us anything. And when I finally went home my parents asked me about it and I tried to explain what happened and how he got kicked out of the band. But they couldn't believe that being a drummer in a band in high school was that big of a deal. And I got so mad and said Sins of Our Fathers have *lawyers*, they have *managers*, they're in the paper in Seattle, and it's a *huge deal*. But my mom just said she hated the name Sins of Our Fathers and how people should take responsibility for themselves and stop blaming everything on their parents.

The next day was the same. Nobody knew anything. And the teachers were all being really weird and pretending everything was okay. And then at *Hillsider* there was a big argument about if they should write about Greg's accident and if they should mention that he had been kicked out of the band. Which was a pointless argument since Mrs. Schroeder would never let them print anything about it.

Later I went with Henry to Taco Time and I just missed Cybil so much. I just wanted to see her and talk to her about everything and I was so scared she was going to vanish up into the spotlights and I would be left down in the horrible real world. And I told Henry the whole history of Greg and the band and how Greg thought everyone talked about him and how he was going to have a studio in his basement and all these other bands were going to record there. And then I remembered when he and Cybil had matching shaved heads and I started crying and Henry came and sat with me on my side and put his arm around me. And I swear he must have grown a lot because all of a sudden he was taller than me and his arm fit over me perfectly.

On Friday morning it had been almost three weeks since they left and Matthew and Cybil's cars were still not in the parking lot. And when I walked into senior hall I could tell something was wrong. People were acting weird and avoiding me and one girl almost dropped her books when I walked past. Then I saw Mrs. Schroeder. She was standing by my locker. She tried to smile as I approached and then she told me that Greg had brain damage and he was a vegetable. My knees collapsed and she tried to hold me up and then a boy helped me into a classroom where I could sit down. And I tried to focus my eyes and there were all these people standing around me and I looked up at them like, *What are you staring at?* Mrs. Schroeder shooed them away and I tried to stand up but I was too wobbly. And I was trying so hard not to cry but I couldn't help it and Mrs. Schroeder gave me tissues but something about her just made me furious and I wouldn't let her touch me.

Saturday was my eighteenth birthday. I ate some cake with my parents and then I got on the phone. I was looking for Carla. I called where she used to live but it was disconnected. I didn't know what else to do so I started calling places and asking if she was there. I called Monte Carlo. I called Zoso. I called HOP! Most people were nice but the woman at HOP! started whining about their phone being for business use only and I told her to shut up and I hung up on her. Finally the guy at Poor Boy Records knew her new roommate and gave me the number. I called it and she was there and I was so relieved to hear her voice. And I told her about Greg and then I said I wanted to call Cybil in Seattle because she probably didn't even know. Carla thought that was a good idea but she didn't know how to contact them except to try Tori or Buzz Mitchell or maybe call the studio. And I guess another reason I had called Carla was to see what she thought about Greg and see how she reacted but she didn't seem that upset. Finally I said, "Isn't it sad though, about Greg?" She was like, "Yeah, I guess." I said, "He was such a nice guy." She said, "Was he? I never really noticed him." And that seemed so cold and I wanted to say, *Yes, he was!* but I didn't. And then I called Cybil's house and got an answering machine and then I tried Matthew and got his mom, who didn't seem to know about Greg and I sure wasn't going to tell her.

That night it was still my birthday so Henry came over and we went to Scamp's but I didn't feel like frozen yogurt. So we just drove around for a while and it was Saturday night and everyone was cruising downtown and partying and blasting their car stereos. Then we went to the twenty-four-hour McDonald's on the East Side and drank coffee and watched everybody run around in the parking lot. And then in the bathroom I saw these two girls who were obviously best friends and they were doing lipstick and talking about their dates and that's when I decided to go to Seattle.

When I got home I asked my parents if I could have the car to drive to Seattle and they were immediately suspicious. Like where was I going and why and what was I going to do? I said I was going to find Cybil and my mother was immediately against it. So I said, "Fine, I'll take the train," and this University of Washington student had almost been raped on the train the week before, so I had them. So then my dad made all these conditions like what I had to do and when I had to be back and I agreed to everything and I didn't even hear what he said.

That night I had a dream my whole high school was on a train going to New York City and we got there and we ran around and it was so fun. And Greg was there and Cybil and Richard Kirn and Mrs. Schroeder and we went to the Empire State Building and rode in taxis and walked up and down the sunny streets. But then I woke up and I was back in my room in Sunset Park and it was gray and dismal outside and I tried to go back to sleep but I couldn't. So I got up and put a sweater in my old camp pack and made myself a sandwich. And my mom was already up and drinking coffee and for once she didn't bug me. She asked me if I had everything. And then she told me to be careful and kissed me and I got in her Honda Civic and I left.

I felt better once I got going. It was raining and I had the windshield wipers on and there wasn't much traffic. I drove by the Methodist church on Shelby Road and people were dressed up and running through the rain to the entrance. And on the freeway I looked around at the other people driving and it was a lot of Dads in pickups and families in Sunday clothes. And as I circled the city I could see bums sitting under the overpasses and people on top walking with their umbrellas. And then I crossed the Columbia River which was huge and still and there was a big barge of logs going beneath the bridge. And then I was in Washington State, which was just trees and highway for as far as you could see and that's when I realized I forgot to bring tapes.

When I got to Seattle the sun was just breaking through the clouds. It was quite beautiful and I swear Portland doesn't feel like it's anywhere, but Seattle really feels like it's in the top left-hand corner of the whole country. I passed Boeing and then the Kingdome and then I could see the bay and the ocean and I imagined Japan out there somewhere. But then I was in the city and things got complicated with all these weird exit ramps and expressways and stuff. I found a sign to the university and I got off and found my way to the coffee shop strip. I parked by a magazine store and got a copy of *Rock City*. I called their offices and told them I was looking for the studio where Sins of Our Fathers were making their record with Buzz Mitchell. They gave me the phone number. So I called the studio and some guy answered and he didn't know anything so he gave me Buzz Mitchell's home phone number. That was pretty scary but I called it and he was asleep and really grumpy and pretentious-sounding. I said I was Cybil's friend from Portland and I had brought her some stuff but she didn't know I was coming that day and where was she? He said, "Katrina's." I said, "Where's that?" He didn't know. And just by his voice I knew I had to be pushy so I started whining about how I was only here for the day and how pissed Cybil would be if she didn't get this stuff. And he was sort of laughing at me and then he said, "Just a second," and then someone else got on the phone and they gave me directions.

38

KATRINA'S NEIGHBORHOOD WAS CLOSER TO downtown but not nearly as nice as around the university. The streets were full of potholes and there were no curbs and the lawns were all weedy and dead. Katrina's house was at the end of the block. It was old and weather-beaten. I parked and looked around and wondered if the Honda would be safe. But of course it would. I got out. I took a deep breath and walked across the driveway to the door. There were three different locks and I knocked and I could hear a TV inside and no one answered so I knocked louder. Then the locks started coming undone and the door opened and it was dark inside and a man looked out at me. He had long jet-black hair and the whitest, palest skin I had ever seen. And at first he wasn't really paying attention but when he saw how normal I looked he got suspicious. And I realized I should have dressed cooler to visit Cybil. Even under these strange circumstances.

"Is Cybil here?" I said, "Or Katrina?" He just looked at me and then I heard a voice behind him and footsteps coming toward us and then the door opened more and it was a woman. She looked like the man. Really pale. And she had this huge rat's nest hairdo of red and brown and black hair and her face was pretty but with no makeup and really hard-looking and sort of mean. And she wore a T-shirt with no bra and her breasts were swinging around in her shirt and I was scared like maybe they were having sex or maybe it was the wrong house. And it was so dark inside. And I could hear a TV in the background. It sounded like cartoons.

"Who's looking for Katrina?" said the woman. The man nodded toward me. He was smiling now. But she wasn't. She asked me who I was and what did I want. I said I was Andrea Marr and I was looking for Cybil because I had to tell her something. She seemed unimpressed so I kept talking. I said I was from Portland and me and Cybil were friends from high school and I had to tell her about this other friend of ours and I was just visiting for the day and that *Buzz Mitchell* told me to come here. The woman looked me up and down and said, "Buzz Mitchell, that *dick*." And then I remembered who Katrina was. She was the one who fought Todd when he tried to marry Tori. She was the crazy lesbian.

But then she smiled at me. I guess because of how clueless I seemed. She said Cybil was upstairs resting and if she was asleep she wasn't going to wake her up. I didn't know what to say. Then she went upstairs to see and the man invited me in. It was dark inside and it smelled like incense or mold or maybe pot. And I could see into the kitchen and there was a cat licking something out of a frying pan. The man went into the living room where the TV was and sat down on the couch. I followed him and I got the feeling he would have been nice to me but he was afraid to because of the woman. So I just stood there and listened to Katrina's footsteps going across the ceiling. And then the man lit a cigarette and offered me one and I said no thanks but I tried to smile and not seem too prissy.

Then I heard Cybil's voice above me. It was muffled and I couldn't hear the words but it was definitely her. And then I could hear Katrina and even though her voice was deeper and more demanding, Cybil's soft voice was winning the argument or the conversation or whatever it was. And then there were more footsteps and the woman came down the stairs and yelled at the cat. And then softer footsteps came down and I could hear whispering in the kitchen. And I was so nervous I just stared at the TV and then I looked up and there was Cybil.

The first thing I thought was how dirty she was. And also her hair was dyed black and cut really short and it had bangs straight across like a French person. And she had this old sweater and ripped-up jeans and filthy tennis shoes that I'd never seen before. And all the time I was looking at her clothes she was looking at my face. She was watching my reaction. Then she said, "Jeez, Andrea, aren't you even going to say hi?" I said hi and sorry and that her hair was different. Cybil said, "Do you like it?" I said, "Yeah, yeah I do." And Katrina was listening and she scoffed all the way from the kitchen but Cybil told her to shut up. And then Cybil told me I looked nice too and I was like, yeah right.

And then she went to the coffee table and got a cigarette and lit it and I watched her and it was so weird to see her smoke. She was incredibly good at it. She looked like a movie star. And the man told her to get out of the way of the TV and then the cat in the kitchen meowed like it was getting kicked and I said, "Did you hear about Greg?" Cybil nodded. She looked at the TV for a second like she was thinking and then she said, "Do you have your car?" I said I did and she said, "Do you want to go somewhere?" I was like, *please.*

Outside the clouds were flying by so fast you could see them moving over the telephone wires. And in the distance you could see this huge gray wall of rain just beyond the Space Needle and for the first time I was afraid of Seattle, or maybe just respecting it as a big city, full of danger and creepiness and desperate people who had run away to follow their dreams. Cybil walked ahead of me and she wore a beige trench coat that made her look like a waif or a street child from London. And I guess she thought I was going to scold her because she seemed afraid to look at me and she didn't say anything. We got in my car and drove and she directed me to a coffee shop. She asked me what I was doing in Seattle and I said I just felt like driving somewhere and I thought she might want to see me. And I said I was sorry for intruding and she said, "No, it's okay, Katrina and Rick are just paranoid of new people." There was an awkward silence and then she told me about Rick and how he was a good bass player but his band was getting jerked around by their manager and he just sat around watching TV all the time.

At the coffee shop we got tea and sat outside so Cybil could smoke the cigarette she bummed from the boy behind the counter. We didn't talk for a long time and it was so weird to see her smoking. Finally I asked her how she found out about Greg and she said her mom told her. I asked her what she thought of it. She said she felt bad. Very bad. And she was nodding and she seemed like she was about to start laughing or something and it was the weirdest vibe I had ever gotten off her. And so I said how the teachers wouldn't tell us at first and how Hillside reacted and how people didn't blame her or Matthew but they did wonder what happened. Cybil just nodded. And then I got mad because she was making me do all the talking while she just sat there. So I stopped talking. And then nobody talked. And then, finally, she said she wanted to go see Greg. I said, "Well yeah, that would be nice." But it sounded really snotty and I immediately regretted it. And when she finished her cigarette she bummed another one off a girl sitting next to us.

Then she wanted to walk so I said okay and we started walking. And she said there was nothing she could do about Greg and he was always sort of crazy and I probably didn't know how bad he was but she and Matthew knew. They knew better than anyone. And then she said how the people at Hillside would never forgive them because they didn't know what the stakes were, that in Seattle nobody even blinked about something like that. People there died all the time from heroin or suicide and it was always because they wanted to be rock stars. And I tried to understand her point of view but it just sounded like excuses and she seemed so cold. So I said, "Yeah, Carla wasn't very impressed either." And Cybil turned to me and looked right in my face and said, "Don't worry, Andrea, I was plenty impressed."

Things got really quiet then. Cybil went into a store and bought cigarettes and when we got back to the car we just sat there and she smoked. And then I started to apologize but she said it was her fault and to forget it. And then she said how she always had trouble in these situations because she never seemed to have the proper feelings. Like the football player who was glad when the Camden students killed themselves. That's how she was, not *glad*, but just not sad in the *correct* way. And that I was lucky because I always had the right feelings and the right reactions. And that I should try to understand that other people weren't so sure of themselves, especially if they had spent their whole lives hiding things and disguising their feelings because they weren't normal or they were outside the group or they were, like she was, gay.

And I guess I knew Cybil was gay but I never really thought about it. I guess I didn't want to think about it. And if I ever did think about it I just thought the stuff they tell you in health class: that gay people are no different than you or me and you could be friends with them just as easy as anyone else. But what Cybil was saying now was that I could trust myself in this really deep way and she couldn't. And it seemed like she was right, or at least it made sense. And then she said that's why she was always so in love with me and looked up to me all these years, because I was like the perfect All-American girl. Not like a stupid cheerleader but interesting and smart and going off to a good college. And never having to hide anything. And not having secrets. And even when I did bad things they were the *right* bad things, the *normal* bad things, like drinking or staying out late or having sex with boys.

39

AND IF I WAS SMART I WOULDN'T HAVE SAID anything but of course I had to start blabbing about how *I* always thought *she* was the All-American girl and she always seemed to have perfect style and this inner confidence and blah blah and then I realized what an idiot I was being and she was just smoking and looking out the window. So I shut up. And it was dark now and the sky was murky green and the air was wet and smelled like the ocean. And then I started to think it was all a bluff, that it was just a bunch of drama to make me forget what they did to Greg. But she was Cybil. She was my best friend. I had to believe her. I just had to. And I started the car and Cybil said there was a Taco Time down the street and so we went there.

We got burritos and ate and then we drove to the studio because she wanted to show me where they were making the record. And she told me how they "constructed" the song and how weird and disconnected it was and how Nick Venn was such a genius. And we got there and it was locked and it was just this building but Cybil still wanted to walk around it so we did and my shoes got all wet from the grass. Then it started to rain and it was getting cold so we got back in the car and drove back to her house. And I told her all the other Hillside news and she nodded a lot but you could tell she wasn't really interested. When we got to Katrina's I turned off the car and we talked a little more, about nothing really, and it was actually pretty awkward and it was like we just wanted to sit together a little while longer. Then I asked her if she would come back and finish school. She didn't think so. Matthew had found a place to live downtown and he was already planning his investments from the money they'd make on the record. We both laughed about that and then it was quiet and then she leaned over and gave me a hug and I tried to give her a really good hug but she sort of cut it off and got out. And she walked in front of the car lights and she looked so cool with her French haircut and her trench coat. And she waved once more and then she ran up the steps and into that horrible house.

I started the car. I drove back toward the university and got on the freeway and it was raining and dark and I could barely see. I drove for an hour and then I pulled off at a rest stop and called my dad. I told him I'd be late and he said that was fine and was I okay? I said I was but his voice sounded so warm and familiar I started to cry. And then I hung up and it was pouring down rain and the huge trucks were splashing along the interstate and I just stood there in the phone booth crying my eyes out for Greg and Cybil and everybody. Because things happened so fast and everyone went flying out in the world in a million directions and everyone was going somewhere different and everyone ended up alone.

I got home late. I fell asleep for a couple hours. I got up and went to school. And on the way I thought how boring I was and how I should do something wild like dye my hair or make out with Eric K Club or take Ecstasy. But when I got to school I had the opposite feeling. With Cybil gone I felt free to be a normal Hillside student. And I worked on *Hillsider* all that week and went to a Sunday party at Beth's where her parents let us have little half-glasses of wine and we sat around having intellectual conversations.

And then Henry invited me to Sophomore Dance and at first I scoffed but he kept bugging me and saying it would be a goof so I agreed. He wore a thriftstore suit and I wore my fish dress and my hair up and afterward we went to a party at

Bridget Cole's house and got drunk. And then for Senior Prom Richard Kirn called me and he wanted to go just to "observe" and I hadn't talked to him in a while and we had such a nice conversation I decided to go. He got a real tux and I dug out that stupid dress my mom made me wear to the Wellington interview. And we went and everyone acted very mature and was nice to each other, even people they hated. Darcy was there with her Camden boyfriend and he was pretty cute. And Rebecca had Tom Petrovich following her around like a puppy. And then Wendy Simpson had a big party afterward and Richard didn't want to go but I made him. And we sat off to the side and talked for a long time and sipped champagne and I told him all about Seattle and Katrina and he listened and nodded a lot but didn't really say anything.

And the next thing I knew we were all lined up in the gym for graduation rehearsal. And Mr. Miller and Mr. Angelo blew whistles and said, "Listen up, people!" And everyone goofed on them and Nathan was behind me and he was being so obnoxious because he got into Stanford and he kept saying, "What can they do to me now? Huh?" And after school we planned the last *Hillsider*, which was the big joke issue, and we sat around after school thinking up "The person most likely to's."

And the days zoomed by and the seniors were like this big herd of sheep and they told us to come on Saturday at noon and we did and they graduated us and that was that. I was done with high school. And it was muggy and hot and we all stood around in the parking lot in our gowns and hats and people yelled back and forth and took pictures and after a while it got boring and I got in the car with my parents and went home.

And then I had to look for a job, which became very depressing very fast. There were so many people looking for jobs that every place you went already had a million applicants and they all looked so desperate you wanted to give up and let them have the job. So I mostly hung around the house and got bored and I finally got a job at Robin's Egg at Sunset Mall as a waitress. The customers were the stereo salesmen from the mall and secretaries and stuff. And the kitchen staff were all these suburban types and it was so depressing. And the only fun of the summer was going to shows at K Club with Henry but the new bands weren't that good and they were mostly boy bands and all these jock guys were showing up and slamming and you never saw Carla or anybody cool there anymore.

In July I wrote Cybil a letter in care of Buzz Records. And then I wrote Todd in care of Tori. But both letters were so boring I wasn't that surprised when they didn't write back. They both had more important things to do. But just when I gave up I got a postcard from Cybil saying they finished the record and they were going to tour and probably play at K Club at the end of the summer. And then I saw Eric and he confirmed it and showed me his schedule and it said Sins of Our Fathers in huge letters on Saturday night, August 27.

And then in the first week of August I got a letter from someone in Pasadena, California, named Marissa Hentoff. I opened it up and it was my soon-to-be roommate at Wellington. She was writing to me to introduce herself and tell me what kind of stereo she had and what kind of music she liked and how she was into the Grateful Dead and pro-choice and trying to shut down nuclear power plants.

Then I went shopping with Mom. We went to Kruger's and got some Levi's and crew-neck sweaters and other stuff my mom thought people wore back east. And I managed to get some money out of her to go to HOP! but when I went there I was too nervous because even if Marissa Hentoff was a nerd there would probably be people there from New York who were totally fashionable and I would feel like an idiot with HOP! clothes.

My mom got my plane ticket. It left on August 27. But I didn't have to be at Wellington until the twenty-ninth and I wanted to see Sins of Our Fathers and my mom got pissed and said how ungrateful I was and when was I going to quit this stupid rock band stuff? And it was weird because in a way I sort of agreed with her. And I was almost afraid to see Cybil because she would be so different and I would just remind her of Hillside and Greg and all the stuff she didn't want to think about. Even in Seattle when she was trying to be nice I could tell she wanted to be away from me. And I guess I wanted to be away from her too. And I tried not to think it was bad, it was just one of those things.

And then I quit my job a week early because the manager at Robin's Egg had been charged with sexual harassment by one of the waitresses and Robin's Egg Incorporated was sending investigators and giving us lie detector tests and it was so horrible there I couldn't stand it. And then I went to a party at Nathan's and all the people who were going to good colleges were there and talking about the deals they got on their plane tickets and what classes they were taking and what their majors were going to be. And it was so weird because Amy Brubaker was there and she was being so nice to me and wanting to exchange addresses and practically begging me to come visit her at Smith.

40 THEN I STARTED PACKING. AND GETTING in fights with my mom. And summer was ending and the days were getting shorter and there was the first feeling of fall in the air. And one day I was coming back from the store and I stopped at Hillside and walked around the buildings which already seemed really dinky and juvenile. And I walked down onto the field where we played soccer in freshman gym class and looked out into the woods

where Cybil used to kick the ball. And then I went across the street and had coffee at Taco Time and wrote Marissa Hentoff a letter telling what kind of stereo I had and how I was pro-choice and into shutting down nuclear power plants and had she ever heard of Color Green?

And the day before I flew I tried to wash all my jeans one more time and my mom was yelling at me and my dad was yelling at my mom and I felt so sick I could hardly eat. And I wore my bathrobe all day and ran around and looked at myself in the mirror and of course I was getting the hugest zit on my chin. That night I watched TV and talked to Henry on the phone and ran back and forth from the dryer to the washer and upstairs to my suitcases. And between my mom's criticisms and my own fashion insecurity I was bringing probably the most boring wardrobe ever assembled. And I complained to my mom and she said, "What do you think Wellington is? A bunch of juvenile delinquents? Do you think they'll be dressed in thriftstore rags?" And it seemed like she was probably right.

But I brought all my tapes. My Color Green tapes and tapes of Sins of Our Fathers and that one tape of Cybil singing by herself. For my personal mementos I brought Brad's bullet and Todd's guitar pick and some old posters of Thriftstore Apocalypse and K Club and Outer Limits. But besides that I had pretty ordinary stuff. Which was okay. Because since Cybil had left, I had become more mainstream and I sort of enjoyed it. Like talking to

Richard, or going to Nathan's party, or just being like a normal person and not trying to be so cool all the time or so shocking. And in a way, I had missed high school, or at least the typical high school experience. Even *Hillsider* I had come to late and I was never really accepted there. And the next day when my parents drove me to the airport, I was looking out the window and thinking that Wellington would be my second chance. It would be my chance to start over. I'd have four years to develop a normal social life and be a real person and do all the things a regular person would do.

We got to the airport. We checked my bags and walked around. Then we had coffee in the little espresso place and there was a boy at the next table who was obviously going back east to college. He had a short haircut and penny loafers and lots of zits. And I was watching him and thinking how fun college was going to be and how I should befriend Marissa and try to at least understand politics and be as intelligent as I could. And I guess my mom was reading my mind because she was looking at me with so much pride.

Then we went to the gate. And then the doors opened and people started going in. I said good-bye to my parents and gave them each a hug and my mom started to cry. And I slung my pack over my shoulder and my mom dabbed her eyes and I kissed them both again and got on the plane. And as I sat in my seat waiting for takeoff I felt so inspired I wanted to get out a book and start studying right then. And in my mind I could see myself, signing up for classes, talking to professors, getting into literature and art, and maybe working on the school paper. And then winter would come and it would snow and I would meet Marissa for hot chocolate and we would discuss *issues* and sexual politics and we'd plan rallies to shut down nuclear power plants. And I would be dressed like everybody else and learning so much and making friends and being right in the thick of college life . . . But of course that's not what happened. Not even close.

TURN THE PAGE FOR A GLIMPSE
AT ANOTHER EDGY, COMPELLING
STORY FROM BLAKE NELSON:

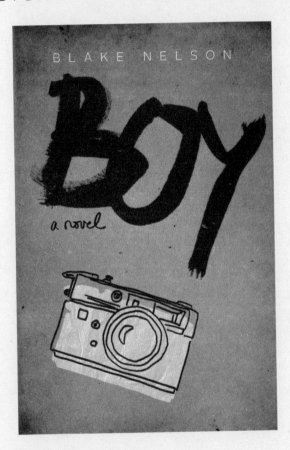

I remember the morning Antoinette became a "known" person at our school. I was in Mr. Miller's geometry class. It was first period and everyone was half asleep. Kaitlyn Becker was scribbling in her math book, her head sideways on her desk. Someone was whispering in the back row. I was sitting by the window, staring out at the courtyard. A thick fog had settled in, which made the trees look ghostly and mysterious. The benches and walkways looked like they were from another time. What made it do that? The moisture in the air? The blurriness of the light? Fog made things look *sad*, I thought. Like a *memory*. Like something that had happened a long time ago and could never be undone.

There was an announcement, which I didn't quite hear, and when I turned back toward the room, our teacher was gone.

"Hey," I said to the boy next to me. "What happened to Mr. Miller?"

"He went to the office."

"What for?"

"I dunno."

I looked around. The whole class had been left sitting at

our desks, with no one in charge. That was unusual.

Then we heard adult shoes clacking down the hall. An adult voice called out. One of the kids stuck his head out the door to see what was going on. A teacher yelled for him to go back in, sit down, and close the door.

Something was definitely up. We sat in our seats, looking at each other, wondering what had happened.

In the hallway after class, everyone was buzzing about a girl named Antoinette Renwick. She had been taken to the office by the principal. A police car had been seen in the parking lot. People weren't sure what had happened. Had she done something wrong? Was she under arrest?

I vaguely knew who Antoinette Renwick was. She was one of the new kids that year. She had black hair and thick dark eyebrows. She also wore weird clothes: old sweaters and skirts and non-Nike tennis shoes.

Like everyone else, I spent the rest of the day wondering about Antoinette. Had she brought drugs to school? Maybe she'd stolen something. I didn't know where she came from. Texas, someone said, but they weren't sure. Maybe she was poor or came from a messed-up family.

After school, the news went around that Antoinette's older brother had jumped off the Vista Bridge and died. A suicide. Everyone was stunned by that. Nobody knew this older brother, Marcus Renwick. He was nineteen, someone said.

Everyone felt bad for Antoinette, but there wasn't much they could do, since nobody really knew her. And anyway, she was long gone by now, since the cops had come and taken her that morning.

Before I left, I heard some girls mention the street she lived on. It wasn't that far from my house. When I got home, I decided to ride my bike over there and see what was going on.

I found her street. I didn't have the actual address, but it was obvious which house it was. A police car was in the driveway, and a bunch of other cars were parked around it. I rode up on the sidewalk across the street and stopped and stood there, straddling my bike.

I couldn't see anything, really. Everyone was inside. The house looked pretty normal: two stories, a small yard, a tree, a garage.

Then a taxicab came around the corner. I tried to look inconspicuous. The taxi stopped in the street. An older woman holding a wadded Kleenex got out. She was crying and trying to talk on her phone at the same time. She nearly dropped her bag as she went inside.

I felt a little weird then, like if the neighbors saw me it might seem strange that I was standing there, spying on the Renwick house.

Then the front door opened again. This time Antoinette came out. I thought about taking off, but she didn't see me. She didn't even look up. She was wearing one of those oversize arctic parkas. She sat down on the front step. She pulled her knees up into her chest, tucked her hair behind one ear, and stared straight down at her feet.

After a minute she checked behind her, and when she saw no one was watching, she pulled a cigarette from her pocket and slipped it in her mouth. She lit the end. That was pretty weird. Nobody at our school smoked. And definitely no sophomores did. Maybe kids smoked in Texas. She took a drag and blew out the smoke. She flicked the ash.

Then she suddenly looked up. Her eyes went straight to me. She must have sensed she was being watched.

I was busted. I didn't know what to do. I gripped my bike handles and swallowed.

"Hello?" she said. "Can I help you?"

I shook my head no.

She studied me for a moment. "You go to my school," she said.

I nodded.

"What? You can't talk?"

"I can talk," I said.

"What's your name?"

"Gavin."

She took another drag of her cigarette and squinted at me. "My brother died today," she said.

"I know."

Antoinette stared in my direction. But she wasn't seeing me anymore. She was seeing something else. I don't know what, the harshness of life, maybe. She took another drag from her cigarette. Her hand was shaking now. Her lower lip began to tremble. Her face seemed about to collapse.

I felt my heart nearly leap out of my chest for her.

Then the door made a noise. Someone was trying to open it. Antoinette quickly slipped the cigarette under her shoe and ground it out. She tossed the butt into the bushes. The door opened and a woman's head appeared. She said something I couldn't hear. Antoinette stood up and went inside.

It was almost dinnertime when I got back to my own house. My mother asked me where I'd been. I told her the whole story, about the cops coming to school and the new girl and how her brother had killed himself. And how I rode my bike to her house to see what was happening.

"So you know this girl?" asked my mom.

"No," I said. "I just wanted to see the house."

"What for?"

"To see what it looked like."

"What did it look like?"

"Like the house of someone who died."

My mother gave me one of her looks. Then she told me to get ready for dinner.

I also had an older brother: Russell Meeks. He was seventeen, a senior at my same school, Evergreen High. He was working on his college applications, so that's what we talked about at dinner that night. Russell was very smart and ambitious. He wanted to be a lawyer, like my dad, so there was a lot of focus on what college he would go to. The Ivy Leagues were what everyone was thinking, since they're supposedly the best.

I ate and listened. My brother had recently started talking in a new way. It was a very clear and careful way of speaking, but it also had this special nasal quality to it, like he was smarter than you, like you probably wouldn't understand what he was talking about, that's how smart he was. Nobody else in my family mentioned this new tone. Maybe they didn't notice it. Or maybe they accepted it as part of Russell's gradual changing from normal kid into Ivy League college student.

It was mostly him and my dad talking. My dad had gone to college back East. And then to New York City for law school. He always brought this up when he talked about his past. What New York was like. How different it was from

Portland, Oregon. How you didn't know how the world worked until you'd lived back there, where the important people were, where the real stuff happened.

Anyway, Russell was saying something about a friend of his who was applying to Cornell. So then my dad had to give his opinion on that. They got in a big debate about which was better, Harvard or Stanford or Cornell. That's when I realized Russell had learned his new tone of voice from my dad. It wasn't the exact same style of talking, but it conveyed the same basic message of *I'm a douche bag*.

As she cleared the table, my mother brought up the news about Antoinette. So then I had to talk. I told about the suicide in my mumbling way, which, as usual, drove my father crazy. "Speak up, Gavin!" he said. "Nobody can hear you!"

"I said," I repeated. "That a girl in my grade got taken out of class because her brother killed himself."

"Was that the jumper?" said Russell. "I heard about that. The guy who jumped off the Vista Bridge?"

I nodded that it was.

"Do you know this girl?" said my dad.

"No," I said.

"Who's she friends with?" asked my mother.

"Nobody, really. Her family just moved here."

"That's so sad," said my mother.

"Who are his parents?" asked my dad. "What do they do?"

"What difference does that make?" I mumbled into my plate.

My dad didn't bother to answer. This was the kind of thing he hated to talk about. Suicidal teenagers. People who had problems. People who weren't achieving and succeeding and going to top colleges and New York law schools. Russell, too. They would much rather go drink brandy in the den and talk about whether Cornell was better than Stanford.

After dinner I went upstairs to my room. Tennis was my thing. That was where I'd achieved and succeeded. I'd won a bunch of local tournaments in the twelve and unders, so my room was like that: a bunch of trophies lined up on a shelf and my walls covered with posters of my favorite tennis stars. Roger Federer. Andy Roddick. Rafael Nadal. There were lots of Nike swooshes everywhere. Sometimes at night I'd practice my serving motion in my room, while I listened to music. Sometimes I would bounce a tennis ball on my racquet face. I had once done that 1,217 times in a row, which was still a record at my tennis camp.

But that's not what I did that night. A couple weeks before, my mother had bought some old art books at a rummage sale. One was a book of landscape paintings from the 1700s. These showed scenes of cows and fields and little valleys. I'd brought this book up to my room and cut out one of the pictures and thumbtacked it to the wall above my desk. I did this as a joke, really. I wasn't into art.

I just felt like looking at something different for a change.

But that night, after the encounter outside Antoinette's house, I found myself looking through the art book again. And then I decided to take down my Roger Federer poster. I was bored with it. I unstuck it from the wall and went through the art book and found two more paintings that I liked, one of a road going past a farm, with a huge sky and clouds above, and another of a harbor, which also had clouds and a big sky. I cut them both out, trying to keep the cut line as straight and neat as I could. Then I thumbtacked them to the wall where the Roger Federer poster had been, one on top of the other, keeping them just the right distance apart.

Once I'd done that, I started looking at my other posters. One of my oldest ones showed the history of tennis in the United States. It was pretty lame, with all these old dudes and their old-style shorts. So I went back to the art book with my scissors and slowly turned the pages, looking for something to replace it.

I was listening to the college radio station while I did this. They were playing good electronic stuff, like they do at night. So I had this fun night of redoing my room and listening to music and cutting these pictures out of this art book. The other thing was: I kept thinking about Antoinette. Not like anything in particular, just having her in the back of my mind. As the night went on, I realized I was doing this for her. I was making my room into something she would like.

ABOUT THE AUTHOR

Blake Nelson is the author of many young adult novels, including *Recovery Road* (now a TV series), the coming-of-age classic *Girl*, and *Paranoid Park*, which was made into a film by Gus Van Sant. He lives in Portland, Oregon.